The Dorset Boy book10 - Silverthorn

CW01498077

This is a work of Fiction. All characte
although based in historical settings. If y
the story, it is a coincidence, or maybe I a

Acknowledgements

Thanks to Dawn Spears the brilliant artist who created the cover artwork and my editor Debz Hobbs-Wyatt without whom the books wouldn't be as good as they are.

My wife who is so supportive and believes in me. Last my dogs Blaez and Zeeva and cats Vaskr and Rosa who watch me act out the fight scenes and must wonder what the hell has gotten into their boss. And a special thank you to Troy who was the Grandfather of Blaez in real life. He was a magnificent beast just like his grandson!

THANK YOU FOR READING!

I hope you enjoy reading this book as much as I enjoyed writing it. Reviews are so helpful to authors. I really appreciate all reviews, both positive and negative. If you want to leave one, you can do so on Amazon, through my website, or on Twitter.

About the Author

Christopher C Tubbs is a dog-loving descendent of a long line of Dorset clay miners and has chased his family tree back to the 16th century in the Isle of Purbeck. He left school at sixteen to train as an Avionics Craftsman, has been a public speaker at conferences for most of his career and was one of the founders of a successful games company back in the 1990s. Now in his sixties, he finally writes the stories he had been dreaming about for years. Thanks to inspiration from great authors like Alexander Kent, Dewey Lambdin, Patrick O'Brian, Raymond E Feist, and Dudley Pope, he was finally able to put digit to keyboard. He lives in the Netherlands with his wife, two Dutch Shepherds, and two Norwegian Forest cats.

You can visit him on his website

www.thedorsetboy.com

The Dorset Boy, Facebook page.

Or tweet him @ChristopherCTu3

The Dorset Boy Series Timeline

1792 – 1795   Book 1: **A Talent for Trouble**

Marty joins the Navy as an Assistant Steward and ends up a midshipman.

1795 – 1798   Book 2: **The Special Operations Flotilla**

Marty is a founder member of the Special Operations Flotilla, learns to be a spy and passes as lieutenant.

1799 – 1802   Book 3: **Agent Provocateur**

Marty teams up with Linette to infiltrate Paris, marries Caroline, becomes a father and fights pirates in Madagascar.

1802 – 1804   Book 4: **In Dangerous Company**

Marty and Caroline are in India helping out Arthur Wellesley, combating French efforts to disrupt the East India Company and French sponsored pirates on Reunion. James Stockley is born.

1804 – 1805   Book 5: **The Tempest**

Piracy in the Caribbean, French interference, Spanish gold and the death of Nelson. Marty makes Captain.

1806 – 1807   Book 6: **Vendetta**

A favour carried out for a prince, a new ship, the S.O.F. move to Gibraltar, the battle of Maida, counter espionage in Malta and a Vendetta declared and closed.

1807 – 1809   Book 7: The Trojan Horse

Rescue of the Portuguese royal family, Battle of the Basque Roads with Thomas Cochrane, and back to the Indian Ocean and another conflict with the French Intelligence Service.

1809 – 1811   Book 8: La Licorne

Marty takes on the role of Viscount Wellington's Head of Intelligence. Battle of The Lines of Torres Vedras, siege of Cadiz, skulduggery, espionage and blowing stuff up to confound the French.

1812   Book 9: Raider

A busy year. Marty gets involved with the prelude to the war of 1812 with America, the murder of the British Prime Minister, the run up to the battle of Salamanca, a cruise in the Ionian Sea, and a private mission to the Caribbean to rescue his children from slavers.

1813 – 1814   Book 10: Silverthorn

The prince finally gets his way and Marty is made a viscount and promoted to Commodore but there is a price as he is back to the Caribbean as Governor of Aruba. That of course is a front as his real mission is to ferment rebellion in South America. Then back to Europe and the abdication of Napoleon and his exile to Elba.

1815-1816   Book 11: Exile

After 100 days in exile Napoleon returns to France and Marty tries to hunt him down. After the battle of Waterloo Marty again escorts him into Exile on St Helena. His help is requested by the Governor of Ceylon against the rebels in Kandy.

Contents

Chapter 1: Elevation

Chapter 2: Preparation

Chapter 3: Passage

Chapter 4: Aruba

Chapter 5: Patrol

Chapter 6: Colombia

Chapter 7: Venezuela

Chapter 8: Advisors and Betrayers

Chapter 9: A Privateer Affair

Chapter 10: Silverthorn

Chapter 11: Tortuga

Chapter 12: To Plug A Leak

Chapter 13: Recovery

Chapter 14: Toro Toro

Chapter 15: Hammer and Anvil

Chapter 16: Victory

Chapter 17: Exile

Chapter 18: The Warning

Epilogue

Author's Notes

An excerpt from - The Pharaohs Mask – A Charlamagne Griffon Chronical

Chapter 1: Elevation

Cheshire in the Spring of 1813 was beautiful. Fruit trees were blooming pink and white, hazel catkins dangled yellow and full from the branches, hawthorn and blackthorn were like huge snowballs of blossom. Along the banks of the roads, primroses shone, and in the woods, bluebells carpeted the floor.

Martin and Ryan walked the hedgerows with bird guns made by a new and highly talented young gunsmith called James Purdey in London, who Marty had discovered working as an apprentice. He had been so impressed with his workmanship and the quality of his guns he had ordered two brace and offered to set the young man up in his own business once his apprenticeship was finished in a year's time. He had gifted Ryan with one set, keeping the other for himself and would pass them on to his son, James, when he was old enough.

Troy ranged ahead looking for rabbits and James's spaniel, Fudge, who rooted around in the hedgerow to flush out birds. A pheasant broke cover with a raucous squawk,

"My bird!" Ryan said as it was to his right. He shot true and the bird tumbled out of the air for Fudge to pick up and return to his master.

"Nice shot," Marty said.

Sam, following on behind, took the gun from Ryan and passed him its fully loaded brother,

"Captain, can I ask you something?" Sam said.

Marty stopped and gave him his full attention,

"I thought there was something when you asked to come with us."

Sam shuffled his feet and put the gun butt down to load it as he talked.

"It's me and Hanna."

Marty suppressed a smile; he knew what was coming next.

"We wants to get married and I want to ask you if that's alright."

"Are you sure that's what you both want?" he teased with a straight face.

"Oh yes, Captain! We loves each other and it's all we wants!"

Marty grinned and stepped forward to slap him on the back,

"You don't need my permission and you have my blessing. When do you want to tie the knot?"

"Matai and Tabetha, says we should get wedded at the same time as them, then we can have one big party."

"We can make it a three way," Ryan laughed.

Marty looked at him, eyebrows raised in question.

"Louise and I want to marry as well."

"Oh! I wondered what you were meaning there." Marty laughed, "Caroline will have a field day organising this."

They took three more birds that morning, giving two nice brace for the cook to prepare in a week or so once they had been hung properly. They returned home in high spirits, the dogs yapping and chasing each other in play.

"Three at once?" Caroline said and immediately started planning in her mind what would be needed to celebrate three loyal friends' marriages. The celebration would have to be carefully planned and she would employ all the resources of the estate.

Marty had a special marriage gift for Ryan who had decided he didn't want to go back to sea and had resigned his commission. Both he and Louise had sufficient money to live their lives comfortably, but Marty knew that they both needed a challenge to be fulfilled. Caroline had taken Louise under her wing and the two of them were busy running her various businesses, but Ryan needed something as well.

Marty presented Ryan with his offer as they drank a brandy together after dinner, two days before the big day,

"Ryan, you know that Farrell Mountjoy is retiring."

"Your estate manager? It's about time; he must be sixty years old,"

"Sixty-eight actually." Marty sipped his brandy and gazed into the fire. "You have been showing an interest in how the estates were run and I wondered if you would be interested in taking over from him?"

Ryan looked thoughtful, he had found the whole management exercise of running an estate fascinating and had been following Mountjoy around to learn what he could.

"I don't need the money," he said.

"But you do need something to stimulate you. Sitting around being a man of leisure doesn't suit you at all."

"I'm finding that out, Louise is busy getting used to her peg leg and working with Caroline, which leaves me at a loose end."

The 'peg leg' was as a result of a battle in the Mediterranean where Marty was attempting to rescue Louise from the French, after she had been caught spying for the British in the guise of Linette. The Toolshed had come up with the design for the articulated replacement after her leg had to be amputated below the knee by Shelby their surgeon. Now she moved so smoothly on it that you wouldn't know she had it.

"Can I talk to Louise before I answer?"

"Of course."

The weddings were scheduled for the end of May and the invitations were sent out by fast courier to Admiral Turner, the officers of the flotilla and Ryan's family. None of the others had family in England other than the Shadows and other members of the Stockley household.

All the attendees gathered in the week running up to the big event and the house was full of children. Marty's son, James, came home from Charterhouse, Admiral Turner had two children now and Ryan's sister brought four more.

Marty thought Turner had a sly look about him as if he knew something which the rest of them didn't but no matter how he tried he couldn't get him to make a slip and reveal it. In any case, he soon found himself too busy distracting the grooms who were getting increasingly nervous as the preparation inexorably progressed.

Banns were read and the vicar of the estate church rehearsed the men until they could say the required responses automatically. The wedding day came; the service was scheduled for eleven. All three men were dressed by Adam, Marty's valet/steward, who made sure that faces were closely shaved, hair trimmed, cravats were tied just right, shoes and buckles shone.

Marty was relaxing in the library reading the latest newspaper when there was a knock on the door and their butler entered with a letter on a silver tray.

"This has just been delivered by royal courier, Sir," he said and offered the tray to Marty who took the letter.

Marty saw immediately that it had the king's seal on the envelope which was of the finest quality paper.

"What on earth is this about?" he said as he took up a paperknife and carefully opened it by slipping the knife under the seal. He unfolded the letter inside that had another seal on a ribbon at the bottom and read.

Dear Sir Martin,

It is with the utmost pleasure that the king has asked me to inform you that you have been granted the title of Viscount of Purbeck for the duration of your life and that of your heirs.

It went on to tell him he had to attend St James Palace on the fifteenth to be invested and was signed by the king's secretary.

"Well, I'm damned" was all he could say.

"Good news, Sir?"

"Yes, Jenson, but we will keep it to ourselves until after the weddings."

"Very good, Sir."

Georgie finally got his way; I wonder what they have in store for me in return? he thought as he carefully folded the letter back into its envelope.

The triple wedding went as planned and the celebration took the rest of the day. He said nothing about his news to anyone, even Caroline, the day belonged to the couples, but he did mutter to Turner at one point that he had heard from the palace. Turner smiled joyfully, Marty guessed he knew this was coming and if Marty knew him, that wasn't all he knew.

He told Caroline as they lay in bed that night. She was delighted and they celebrated in the time-honoured fashion. As they lay sated Caroline said, "So that's what's had James Turner looking so smug."

"You noticed as well."

"He has been as smug as the cat that got the canary since he got here."

"I think he knows something else as well, maybe we will find out in the morning. I can't imagine this comes without some strings."

At breakfast Marty announced his news to his officers in attendance and as soon as he did Turner stood and tapped the table for attention.

"Let me say on behalf of everyone here, congratulations Lord Purbeck, the title is well deserved."

The table was banged, and hands clapped as they celebrated his elevation to Viscount, but Turner hadn't finished,

"I also have some news for him and many of the rest of you from the Admiralty." He took a paper from his pocket and continued.

"Captain Martin Stockley is promoted to Commodore and given the position of Military Governor of Aruba." Cheers from around the table. He held up his hands for silence after a minute.

"Wolfgang Ackermann is promoted to Captain of the Unicorn, the flagship of the squadron." More cheers and not a few teasing catcalls.

"Now for some not so good news, The Hornfleur and Alouette are being taken out of service." Groans from James Campbell and Angus Frasier, he let them wait for a long moment.

"However! I can also announce the addition of HMS Leonidas, a thirty-eight-gun frigate, to the squadron which will be commanded by," he paused dramatically, "Captain James Campbell with First Lieutenant Angus Frasier."

When the cheers subsided, he concluded by saying, "The Nymphe, Endellion and Eagle make up the rest of the squadron. You will leave for the Caribbean after Lord Martin has visited the palace and been invested. All ships are ready for sea I believe?

James you and Angus need to get to Southampton to take over the Leonidas by Wednesday."

After breakfast Turner and Marty had a private meeting.

"There's more to this posting than just being Military Governor isn't there. You could send any of a dozen rear admirals or commodores to do that."

"Officially you are there to run the territory and to use the squadron to help protect our Caribbean possessions against the American privateers that are ranging out of Charleston and other ports. Unofficially, you are there to help the South American rebels in the Spanish countries against their royalist rulers."

"Aren't the Spanish our allies?"

"In Europe yes, but we want to weaken their hold on their possessions in South America. Rebellions are brewing in Argentine, Chile and Venezuela, if they can be coordinated then the Spanish could lose all three, weakening them as a competitor to British trade."

"I see. Our 'involvement' will be totally unattributable then."

"Naturally, that's why we are sending you. You are to make it look like they are being supported by the Americans or French if possible."

"If it is a diplomatic posting, should I take the family with me?"

"Yes, that would be the norm."

"It's going to be strange not being Captain."

"Yes, but you will get used to it, you need to think of the bigger picture now."

"You know Caroline is going to empty the shops of London before we leave."

"Yes, and Juliet will help her."

They left for London in time to make their appointment at St James Palace. Captain James Campbell and his first lieutenant had left several days before to take command of their new ship. Marty was very happy that the crew for the Leonidas was being made up of the crews put ashore from the Hornfleur and Allouette. James only needed to recruit a few sailors to get him up to complement.

In the months since they returned from the Caribbean in the Bethany, the flotilla had been recalled from its duties in the Mediterranean and the ships refitted. Marty had half expected them to be reallocated back into the Navy proper and was delighted to keep his old team together. The loss of the Alouette was hard but she was old when they had gotten her and was becoming increasingly hard to maintain.

The house in London was as they had left it and the house four down from it that had been owned by the dead slaver, Graves, had new occupants. The appointment at St James called for full-dress uniform with all his honours. That meant a very quick visit to his tailors who had to create a new uniform from scratch. Now he had to go through the indignity of a fitting, which he hated. This one was made worse in that he had to stay there until it was done.

He also needed a new hat as Caroline judged that his captain's dress hat just wouldn't do. A new Bicorn hat with gold braid was created and delivered while he was at the tailors.

"They had your hat size already and had a suitable hat nearing completion that would serve, all they had to do was add the appropriate gold braid," Caroline said as she placed it on his head to see the full affect. Marty just harrumphed making her laugh.

At St James Palace there were only two awards being made on the day and Marty was second. He was ushered into the room and, as he expected, was greeted by a beaming Prince Regent.

"Martin! Martin welcome and congratulations," the prince enthused completely against protocol. "They finally let me have my way and reward you as I wanted."

Marty, wary that there was an audience, bowed and replied quietly, "My thanks, your highness,"

The prince, however, wasn't to be suppressed.

"Oh, not all my credit, you deserve it. Taking a seventy-four with a frigate!"

That was still one of the things Marty had done he wasn't proud of, but he hid it and bowed again.

"There is a ball tonight. You and Caroline will be guests of honour."

Marty groaned inwardly and comforted himself that it would all add to his cover story for Aruba. The ball would be the typically lavish affair that the prince was famous for and he would be in the company of the good and the great. Caroline would thrive on it and he wouldn't deprive her of her moment of glory.

On his way out he was intercepted by the Chamberlain, Francis Ingram. "My Lord Purbeck."

Martin smiled at him, "Hello, Francis, I suppose you want to know how young Brazier is doing?"

"I must admit to being curious if the stories he has told me are true."

"Probably, he is not prone to exaggeration. Your son is a brave, skilled young man who has the potential to be a great captain one day."

"Thank you for that, but he told us of his, aah, lapse."

"That was just the reaction of a normal young man, thrown into one of the worst hand-to-hand fights I have seen. Most only get to experience killing another man face to face once or twice in their entire career, he killed two with his pistols and at least one more with his blades in one combat."

"Thank you for that, he tells me that you will keep him on?"

"Why on earth wouldn't I? He is a valued member of my crew, please do not worry on his account."

Ingram sighed and looked relieved; the stress lines around his eyes relaxing. He looked at Marty with a slight smile. "He may be my bastard son, but I truly care for him and his mother."

"Marty patted him on the shoulder and replied, "I know, and I know he will also make you proud."

"I will see you at the ball tonight?"

"I do not seem to have a choice and my wife would have me assassinated if we missed it."

Ingram laughed, he knew Lady Caroline and knew Marty was only half joking. They shook hands and parted; Marty hoped he wouldn't be proved a liar.

The ball was everything he expected and more. Prince George had gone to town to celebrate the elevation of one of his favourites. His entrance was loudly announced, and he had to shake, or bow over, the hands of everyone in the room. His victory over the French seventy-four and his elimination of the white slaver, Graves, had assumed mythical proportions and he and Caroline had achieved some kind of hero status.

He was wary though as not everyone thought that. There was still a strong pro-slavery faction who while condemning Graves for dabbling in white slavery, would not condemn him for trafficking blacks. The second thing was that Prince George was not universally popular, especially with the commons, because of his excesses. He was grateful that his latest mission would take him out of the limelight for a while.

Caroline shone like a jewel gliding from person to person with an effortless grace that made Marty feel like he was being towed in her wake. She wore her honours with pride including the golden, ruby-eyed tiger that Marty had been awarded in India. Its eyes glittered a warning that she may be beautiful and graceful, but she was also dangerous.

The evening passed in a flurry of dancing and eating, both he and Caroline drank sparingly so when Marty was accosted by a woman who was drunk enough to proposition him, despite Caroline's reputation, he was able to defuse the situation without causing a scene.

Admiral Turner and his wife, Juliet, arrived later in the evening and they brought along Admiral Hood. The old warrior was showing his age and needed a cane to help him walk but his mind was as sharp as ever.

"Congratulations, Martin, well deserved. How are young Thompson and that beautiful French spy getting along?"

"Thank you, Sir. Ryan and Louise were married a week ago."

"Were they bedamned. I heard about her accident; will she take to keeping house now she is inactive?"

"She will be running some of Caroline's business interests while we are in Aruba and as for her keeping house, she has Cheshire to run."

Hood nodded. "God forsaken place Aruba, you will have your work cut out, it's still full of Dutch."

"I'm sure we will manage."

"Taking the family?"

"Yes of course."

"Be cramped in the Unicorn."

Caroline joined them and chipped in. "We will be going in the Bethany."

That was news to Marty, but he wasn't surprised, Caroline was planning on taking the entire London household except the cook and an elderly retainer who would stay on as housekeepers. She had also taking on a pair of tutors for the children. The Bethany was much better suited for that than a frigate and it would reduce any strain caused by having Caroline and her maids onboard a ship full of randy sailors.

"Damn good idea," Hood agreed.

Chapter 2: Preparation

Shelby, the Unicorn's surgeon, presented Captain Wolfgang Ackermann with a request for funds to stock up the squadron with citronella, Jesuit Bark and other remedies for tropical climes. His passion and main interest was tropical medicine and the main reason he had joined Marty in the first place. Marty had anticipated this and given Wolfgang a substantial purse to cover the preparation of the ships.

"Mr Fletcher will assist you, Doctor, I have provided him with the required funds, Commodore Stockley also asked that you get enough for his household."

"I wish we could take the infirmary in Gibraltar with us. Those nurses are well trained now," Shelby said.

"We will be stopping there on the way; you could ask them if you like. I understand that they were stepping out with a couple of our marines."

Even though their marine contingent was being reduced due to the loss of the Hornfleur, many of them were being transferred to the Leonidas and Nymphe. Marty wanted as many of his old team with him as possible.

"Talking of marine officers, do we have a replacement for Paul la Pierre?"

"Yes, he will arrive tomorrow, Captain Declan O'Driscoll, an Irish renegade, by all accounts, who has a reputation for solving problems in creative ways."

"He will fit right in then."

"Captain, Sir," Midshipman Brazier said as he joined them on the quarterdeck.

"Yes, Mr Brazier?"

"Mr Howards' compliments, this message just delivered from the commodore and two new midshipmen just came onboard."

Wolfgang opened the message.

"We will be joined by the Bethany which will carry the commodore, his household and family on the way out."

"That will make life more comfortable." Shelby grinned knowing that Wolfgang had been worrying how he would accommodate everyone. "Who are the new mids?"

"Mr Brazier?" Wolfgang asked.

"Stephen Donaldson, fourteen years old with four years' sea time, two of which was on the Leopard. His father is a post captain and asked specifically that he join the Unicorn."

"Yes, I know Captain Donaldson. I served with him at the beginning of my career. The other?"

"Quinton Stirling, twelve years old, one year at sea, on paper."

Wolfgang groaned inwardly as he guessed that the boy had been put on the books of a ship at age eleven and hadn't actually set foot anywhere near a real ship. He was the youngest son of a merchant whose daughter Wolfgang had a fancy for, and he had reluctantly agreed to take him on. Now he was here.

"Have them report to me in my cabin at six bells. Kindly ask Mr Farrell to join as well."

Farrell was his new fourth lieutenant.

Shelby smiled to himself. Wolfgang had been avoiding a command of his own for years, preferring to stay as second to God. Now he couldn't avoid it any longer with Martin being made Commodore.

"If you excuse me, I will let Mr Fletcher have my list of requirements."

Wolfgang nodded and turned his attention to the mainmast where a new extended top mast was being hoisted up. He meant to experiment with skyscraper sails this trip to see if he could get another knot out of her. He would need it to keep up with the Bethany.

At six bells precisely, there was a knock at the door to his cabin and the marine sentry announced, "Lieutenant Farrell and midshipmen Stirling and Donaldson, Sah!"

Wolfgang, like Marty before him, encouraged his marine guards not to shout when they announced visitors.

"Enter."

The three lined up in front of his desk.

"Welcome aboard, you are the newest and youngest of my gentlemen in waiting," he said to the two boys. "As such, you are expected to obey without question the orders of your superiors, including Mr Brazier and Mr Shepherd who know infinitely more than you do about everything."

The boys, wide eyed and terrified by his severe look and German accent nodded. Stirling sniffed as snot threatened to drip from his nose.

"Mr Farrell as Fourth is responsible for the midshipmen and will take care that you are educated in all things you are expected to know." He turned his attention to Farrell, "It was not so long ago that you were a mid, assess these boys' knowledge and arrange with the gunner's wife and the master for their lessons. They should both be allocated sea daddies. I suggest Bill Warwick and Edmund Farmer, both solid hands who know everything that needs to be taught. If they need tutoring, Mr Brazier is ahead of where he needs to be and can spare the time."

He looked back to the boys. "Were you given any money to come aboard with?"

They both nodded.

"Give it to me and I will hold it for you, if you need some come and see me and we will discuss what you want to buy and whether I will allow you to buy it." They handed over their purses which if allowed to keep would be depleted in days by the more ruthless members of the crew.

"That is all. Dismissed."

Farrell shepherded them out and Wolfgang smiled as he heard their piping voices asking questions as soon as the door was shut.

Fletcher was happy, he had a full purse of Martin's money an extensive shopping list and four men to help him. Well, they were actually his guards as the sum of money he was carrying was substantial. Much of the list was the regular stuff you would expect for a long voyage across the Atlantic, but some items were special.

His first stop was a Chinese pharmacy where he bought their entire stock of citronella. It wasn't enough so he got the name and address of another that could supply the rest of what he needed. He did get all the Jesuit bark that he needed and opium in liquid form.

A small diversion found them outside a non-descript warehouse where he had a short talk with an evil-looking man with a long scar down his face. Money changed hands and a deal was sealed with spit on hands that were firmly shaken.

He met another man with cold dead eyes in a tea house; a paper was passed over and money changed hands as a deal was struck. The man left his tea un-drunk and pulled his collar up to hide his face. The marines were sat at a table outside a pub across the road and recognised a professional when they saw one.

Fletcher finished his tea and collected the men. Their next stop was the second Chinese pharmacy where he found the rest of the citronella he needed. Next was a regular British pharmacy where he handed over a list of things that Shelby had asked for. He haggled and got a good reduction on the street price due to the quantity and variety of things he needed. The goods would be delivered to the dock the next day.

His next stop was a metal merchant where he secured a range of brass, copper and steel stock, then a coal merchants that stocked good quality coal for the squadron's galleys and charcoal for the

Toolshed boys. Fresh fruit and veg, lemon and lime cordials by the gallon (they kept better than pure juice), steers, pigs, rabbits and chickens, spices and dried herbs for the lower deck, Wardroom, Cockpit and Captain's private stores. Wine by the case, cheese and butter winged its way to the squadron.

"You get much better prices when you order in bulk for so many ships," he said to his escorts as the purse dwindled in size and the number of parcels they had to carry increased.

"Really?" the marine, Hardy, said.

"Oh yes buying in bulk is the—" Fletcher finally realised the marine was being sarcastic.

Caroline didn't disappoint. She and Juliet went on a shopping spree of epic proportions. Marty, sensibly, stayed well out of the way and went out on his own. He only had one thing he needed to buy other than clothes suitable for a military governor and that was found at Wilkinson's the swordsmiths.

"Lord Purbeck, good morning." Geoffrey Wilkinson greeted him in person. "You are here to collect your order?"

"Indeed, I am, I trust it's ready?"

"Of course. Stanley bring his Lordship's order please."

The shop clerk reached under the counter and produced a pair of beautifully-crafted naval officer's swords. Twenty-six-and-three-quarter-inch, straight, fullered blades, blued and engraved with navy insignia highlighted in gilt. Cast gilt-brass hilts with knucklebow guards bearing crowned Anchors in langets, and chequered wire-bound ivory grips. The sheaths were beautifully made and set up to hang the sword at an angle that wouldn't tangle in the wearer's legs.

"Very nicely done, I will pay cash."

Wilkinson had to suppress his surprise; the aristocracy never paid cash. Marty sensed it and explained, "I will be leaving soon for South America; I don't want to leave unsettled bills behind me."

"Very good, my Lord, the invoice, Stanley, if you please."

Stanley had to search through a file to find it but finally passed it over. Marty took out a heavy pouch and counted out one hundred golden guineas.

The Leonidas joined the squadron at Chatham and Marty called an all-captains meeting on the Unicorn.

"Gentlemen, we will soon be leaving on an extended posting to Aruba where, as you know, I have been appointed Military Governor." There was a round of applause. "But right now, we are here to congratulate Wolfgang and James for their promotion to Captain." More applause and cheers. "To mark the occasion, I would like to present both of them with swords."

Midshipman Brazier stepped forwards, the swords across his arms.

"Wolfgang, you have ever been a rock for me to lean on and run our ships in the most exemplary manner, take this and wear it with honour and pride." He unclipped the plain functional sword that he wore and clipped on the presentation blade.

"James, since you joined me you have shown initiative and resilience beyond measure. Your loyalty and leadership are without question and a captaincy is well overdue. The Leonidas has gained a fine captain."

When the cheering and applause died down, Marty announced, "And now Roland has prepared a celebration feast so we should retire to the dining room."

What a feast it was served. A delicate French Onion soup flavoured with Anis, a turbot swimming in beur blanc sauce, a five rib of roast beef and two brace of pheasants served with a rich red wine gravy and vegetables, a selection of possets and puddings with custard and finally a cheese board, nuts and thin toasts. This was all washed down with a selection of wines chosen to go with the food by Roland.

Marty, Wolfgang and James stood together after the meal on the quarterdeck smoking cigars.

"There's more to this mission than you being Governor isn't there," James said.

"Yes, but we will talk of it once we are at sea."

"One of those missions then," Wolfgang said.

"We will also help the Jamaica Squadron against privateers."

"That will be a long sail North, you won't be needing the ships for the other part then."

Marty didn't answer and they let the subject drop.

"Ryan has agreed to be my estate manager and Louise will take over the day-to-day running of Caroline's businesses," he said to fill the silence.

"That's good, he was still thinking about it when I left," James said.

"The more he talked to Mountjoy, the more he realised that running the estate was at least as challenging as a ship."

"But less paperwork I'll warrant," Wolfgang said causing them all to laugh.

"But the way, you will be receiving a shipment that needs to be distributed amongst the squadron tomorrow. Let's just classify it as trade goods for now. Once it's loaded, move the squadron to the Roads, the Bethany will join you there."

The Bethany was in India dock and her captain, Phillip Tarrant, was scratching his head as he saw the line of wagons queuing up on the dockside waiting to be unloaded. What he could see would fill at least one of the Bethany's holds and he had a suspicion there was more to come.

Frederic Cooper, Marty's senior footman, was checking off every item as it was transferred against lists he had preprepared. He was an ex-military man and very thorough. He worked quickly but efficiently, and a steady stream of furniture, baggage and other goods came aboard that were either sent to a cabin or down into the hold. Tarrant worrying about the trim of his ship, gave orders to his first mate, Mark Sinfield, to shift some to the after hold.

"Do you think there is more to come?" Sinfield said.

"Lady Caroline is moving house, what do you think?"

The goods kept coming until around four o'clock in the afternoon when Fred climbed the gangplank and approached Tarrant.

"All present and correct, nothing damaged. Her Ladyship and the household will join you tomorrow morning."

"Aye I expected that as I had a message from the commodore that I should be ready to sail on the afternoon tide and make for the Roads to join the other ships."

Fred looked along the deck and noticed that the guns were thirty-six-pound carronades rather than the expected six or nine pounders normally found on a commercial trader.

"Lord Martin likes to know his ships can look after themselves if anybody can catch them," Tarrant said. "Did he say if he would sail with us or on the Unicorn?"

"I believe he will sail on the Bethany; his sea chests were brought aboard from the last wagon, he is on the Unicorn now and will meet us there."

"Does that make us the flagship?"

"I do not know, I was in the army I know nothing of navy protocols."

Caroline and the household, escorted by the Shadows, arrived the next morning as expected. There were just a few bags to bring on board and they were soon shown to their cabins.

Tarrant was overseeing the warping out from the dock when he became aware that there were a pair of small children on his quarterdeck watching the manoeuvre. They held hands and when he approached them from behind, he could hear them talking in some kind of foreign language. They were so fascinated by what was going on, they didn't seem to be aware of him at all.

A movement from the corner of his eye alerted him that someone else was approaching.

"There they are, those two are always getting away and into trouble," Mary said.

"They're no trouble mam, but are they foreign?"

"No, they are Lady Caroline's youngest, twins. I expect you heard them speak their private language."

Tarrant turned his attention back to the warping out as it was getting to the point where the lightermen would take over and tow them out into the river.

"Get that messenger away, boys!" he shouted and a hand threw the light cable expertly to the boat waiting to take them in tow. The boat pulled it in until they had the cable which was looped over the stern post.

The twins thought that was wonderful and jumped up and down cheering, causing Tarrant to give a rare smile. Mary knelt behind them and wrapped them with her arms.

"Mawy, did you see, the man thwew a wope and that man caught it and now they are pulling the ship," Edwin said in his piping falsetto, eyes wide.

"Yes, dear, those men are very strong."

"I want to tow a ship when I gwow up."

"I'm sure you will, dear."

Tarrant had to smile again at the innocent pleasure the children got from what was a mundane task for him.

They sailed to the Roads and joined the squadron. The ships were anchored in a group and they were directed to moor near the Unicorn. Marty came aboard. "I will sail on the Unicorn until we are ready to pick up the trades because of the risk of encountering French privateers. We are a powerful enough group that they should avoid us, but some are daring enough to try for one of the smaller ships or the Bethany in spite of that. If we are attacked you are to make all speed and get away. The safety of my family is your first concern," he said to Tarrant as he was about to leave with Adam and a small sea chest.

"Of course, Milord,"

"And do not let my wife tell you anything different."

"Will you transfer your flag here at that time?"

"No, the flag will stay with the Unicorn, I will move back to her once we get to the Caribbean."

Chapter 3: Passage

Marty had Wolfgang divide the captain's cabin in two rather than he take over the whole thing. That way they both had room to sleep and work. Troy was confused as to why his domain had suddenly been halved in size and took to wondering between both parts.

Marty found his new commodore's uniform uncomfortable and opted to dress in his old captain's uniform which Adam had added his rank insignia to. He stood on the quarterdeck next to Wolfgang and gave the order,. "Signal, prepare to sail."

The signal, already prepared, shot up the lanyards and was almost immediately acknowledged by all ships.

"Execute."

The signal was lowered, and Wolfgang nodded to Howarth who had the anchor cable up and down.

"Set the foresail, ready the topsails and mains."

The wind filled the foresail with a boom.

"Raise anchor."

As soon as the anchor broke free, the ship's head fell away under the pressure from the foresail.

"Set topsails and mains! Haul handsomely now."

The Unicorn caught the wind and picked up speed as she carved a graceful arc to turn Southwest, the Bethany matched her and fell in a cable behind, the Nymphe was next followed by the Leonidas. The Eagle and Endellion ranged out to either side.

The formation effectively surrounded the Bethany with armed ships. God help the French privateer or country ship that tried to take her.

"By God they look magnificent," Marty said as he looked astern at the line of ships.

"I think we can set all plain sail; they should have no problem keeping up," Wolfgang said.

"Tarrant must be having to hold the Bethany back; it will make life easier for him."

Minutes later, the Unicorn had everything up to her royals set and Marty noticed the extra length of mast stick up on the Main and Fore.

"Planning on trying skyscrapers?"

"At some time, I want to see if we can get an extra knot using them."

"Or lose one as they push the bow down."

"Indeed, but we won't know until I try."

The discussion continued until Marty went below to his cabin, broken only by Wolfgang giving the odd order for a course correction.

Dinner was good but not up to the standard that Roland provided, Wolfgang had his own cook who was a Bavarian from somewhere called Regensburg. He went in for hearty food: potato dumplings, sauerkraut, and pork were on the menu that evening followed by a delightful apple tart called a strudel. Wolfgang, Marty and Howarth dined together. It was congenial and the conversation casual.

They made as much Westing as they could before turning Southeast to clear Ushant. That would enable them to make Southwest again past the dreaded Bay of Biscay, weather permitting. If they were to see any French ships it would probably be in that region.

The weather was blustery but clear and the Endellion and Eagle stayed out on the horizon during daylight, closing up at night. All ships burnt lights at night to keep formation and it was around midnight as they approached Ushant that Marty woke to a lookout's cry. The Eagle on the landward side of the formation had fired a rocket.

Marty quickly pulled on a coat and went on deck where Wolfgang was already on duty fully dressed. He looked at Marty in his nightshirt and overcoat. "Lucky it's not breezier."

"Quite. What's the problem?"

"The Eagle seems to have spotted something between us and them. The clouds are covering the moon, so I imagine he saw our lights being covered."

Marty grabbed a night glass and scanned their port quarter. He saw nothing.

"May I?" Wolfgang said and when he got it, scanned from the quarter forward. "There he is."

"What do you see?"

"Looks like a sloop or a schooner from the brief glimpse I had."

"I wonder if he thinks we are a merchant convoy?"

"He will get a surprise if he does."

Wolfgang scanned again then moved to the seaward side, the moon emerged from behind the cloud.

"He is taking the wind gauge and slowing."

He tracked whatever he could see.

"I don't think he knows the Endellion is out there, Trenchard has doused his lights."

"He always was a crafty one. Let's keep their attention on us. Fire a rocket."

Wolfgang gave the order and a blue rocket shot into the air. They waited a few minutes and fired another.

Suddenly the sky to starboard lit up as the Endellion fired her guns, silhouetting the strange ship.

"Light them up!" Wolfgang ordered and white rockets flew up that burst into bright white flares that floated slowly to earth. The squadron was bathed in light and so was the intruder.

"The Leonidas is moving into the attack as well, it's definitely a French privateer."

The Nymphe and Unicorn continued firing illumination rockets which lit up the scene like daylight. The Frenchman found himself bracketed and under the guns of the frigate. They did the only sensible thing they could and struck, the Endellion had shot away rigging and she was disabled enough that she couldn't get away.

"All over and they hardly got a shot off!" Marty crowed.

First light saw them tack to the South-Southwest the French Schooner following the Leonidas like a puppy.

They made Gibraltar and the schooner was handed over to the prize court. Pellew who was still in command of the Mediterranean fleet, invited Marty and Caroline to dine with him.

"Congratulations on your promotions," he smiled as he greeted them. He had put on more weight and had gout in his left foot.

Caroline kissed him on both cheeks and chided him,

"You have not been looking after your health."

"My dear, when you have been at sea for as long as I have, the chance to spoil oneself is irresistible. I have served for a long time and deserve my little luxuries."

The dinner, all seven courses, showed which luxuries he liked to indulge in. It was accompanied by a different wine for every course and finished with the largest decanter of port that they had ever seen.

After dinner, Marty was handed a thick packet with the admiralty's seal on it and told not to open it until he was at sea at thirty degrees latitude. He was intrigued, the package had obviously been sent before they left and was more than a letter. His guess was it contained intelligence that he could use in his mission.

On their return to their former headquarters, they found Shelby with two young women with bags waiting on the dock.

"Antonia and Manita have agreed to accompany us, they are both trained nurses. Can you find room for them on the Bethany?"

"If they share a cabin, I think we can make room," Marty said.

Shelby looked relieved. "Antonia has been walking out with Lieutenant Beaumont and Manita with Sergeant Bright."

That explained their willingness to leave their home.

Caroline took them under her wing and took them to the ship where she rearranged the berths for her staff to make room for them.

Marty had one last thing to do, he wrote a letter to Juliana, the leader of the Spanish resistance group telling her where the gold in Valencia was hidden. He gave the letter to Frances Ridgley who ran the British Intelligence operation and asked him to ensure that it was delivered as soon as the French were ousted from Valencia. His hope was it would help those who suffered under French rule get their lives back on track.

They set sail; the ships even heavier as they had taken everything that could be reused from the old base leaving an almost empty shell. Marty sat in his cabin and looked at the package sitting on his desk; it must contain sensitive information if he couldn't open it right away. He shrugged to himself, it wouldn't be long before they reached thirty degrees, so he put it in a drawer and locked it.

They sailed South towards the Canaries where Marty would change over to the Bethany for the crossing. He gave orders that unless they were attacked, they would leave even the fattest most attractive French ships alone, but as it turned out they only saw one sail on the horizon and couldn't tell what it was.

They crossed thirty degrees and Marty opened the packet. It contained what he expected: the names of contacts and their locations in Venezuela, Chili and Argentina. Colombia had declared independence in 1810 when Simón Bolívar led a rebellion. Now there was intelligence that as soon as Spain was back under Spanish control King Ferdinand planned to reclaim his lost territories. That wasn't in British interests.

Marty read the papers then spent a day encoding the information into a notebook using his unique personal code. There was no code book as it was all in his head so if anything happened to him the information would be safe.

Once it was encoded, he destroyed the original papers by tearing them into strips and burning them in a metal bucket. The ashes were dumped into the sea from the stern gallery. He didn't want to be the one to put the lives of the rebels at risk.

They reached the Canaries and stopped at Santa Cruz to re-water and replenish their fresh provisions. The squadron caused quite a stir as the locals normally saw single ships and to have six at once was a spectacle. A crowd built up on the dock cheering the British ships and they basked in the reflected glory of Wellington's successes on the peninsula.

Marty moved his gear to the Bethany and left Wolfgang to enjoy the full freedom of his cabin. Caroline was pleased to have him back and the children were delighted. Beth, who was now twelve, her imagination fired by being on the ship, had taken to wearing her sword and watching the Shadows when they trained. She wanted Marty to give her lessons.

The twins were in full-exploration mode and had to be watched constantly or they would disappear only to be brought back in the arms of any sailors who found them. Once they got as far as starting to climb the ratlines before being gathered up by Antton. Mary and Hanna took to watching them together so that there was at least one pair of eyes on them at all times. They were spelled by the nurses to give them some time off.

Marty indulged his daughter and treated her desire to learn the sword seriously. Caroline had gifted her a shorter version of her own sword and Marty was soon with her on deck going through the forms.

"My dress and all these petticoats get in the way," she said after their first session.

"Let's have a word with your mother," Marty suggested.

Caroline tapped her chin in thought as Beth explained the problem.

"I think I know the solution," she said.

The next time Beth came on deck she was dressed in what looked like a satin dress but when she moved, it was in fact a pair of voluminous trousers that stopped mid-calf based on a ladies riding skirt. She wore button-up calf-length boots and a white cotton blouse that was buttoned to her neck. Marty was surprised at how mature she looked and had to swallow a lump in his throat; his little girl was growing up.

Beth in fact was tall for her age, taking after her mother, she was coltish at twelve years old with long legs and long slender arms. She shared the same auburn hair and hazel eyes and was developing the same beauty. However, Marty didn't have to worry about sailors getting the wrong idea as Troy followed her around everywhere.

The new outfit worked, and the new freedom of movement it gave her saw her advancing to the point where she could spar with Marty with live blades without him fearing for his fingers.

All of this, and the fact he was sleeping with Caroline every night, made the crossing pass quickly and before he knew it, he was transferring back to the Unicorn.

Chapter 4: Aruba

They anchored at Barcadera, it being a deep-water port with a dock where they could offload the Bethany. Marty had no intention of offloading the 'special cargo' the warships carried on Aruba where it could be seen.

After they had been there a couple of hours several carriages pulled up from which a flustered-looking delegation of worthies debarked and made their way up the dock to the ship.

"Milord Purbeck?" one called up.

Marty looked down and took in the chains of office and their well-dressed and groomed appearance.

"Caroline, I think the reception committee has arrived, we better go down and present ourselves."

Caroline had been waiting for this and had forbidden anyone apart from the crew from going ashore until they had been greeted properly.

"About time too."

"They probably expected us at Oranjestad."

"Why didn't we stop there then?"

"Because this is a better port to offload the Bethany."

Caroline let it drop, if Marty didn't want to tell her the real reason, she wouldn't push for it. Marty knew she thought he had some sinister or clever reason for mooring here but it was just the nature of the port, nothing else.

They walked down the gangplank side by side, him in his full-dress uniform, glittering with honours and her in a beautiful blue silk dress trimmed with lace that showed off her auburn hair. Caroline carried a parasol to protect her from the tropical sun.

The man with the biggest chain stepped forward and made a bow, "Milord, welcome to Aruba. I am William de Coq the Burgermeister of the Island and these are the council of elders. May I say how happy we are to see you, as we heard you were coming several weeks ago".

That was news, he only knew not long before they left so someone in England must have known long before he was told.

"Mister de Coq, gentlemen, a pleasure to meet you I am sure. May I introduce my wife, Lady Caroline."

De Coq presented them to the gentlemen of the council, Marty noted their names and the fact that they were all Dutch. One of them was a farmer, the island grew a lot of beef as the land wasn't suitable for plantation crops, another a mine owner, gold was mined on the island along with phosphate. The other represented the merchants and ship owners. When the introductions were over, le Coq invited them to travel with them to Oranjestad, where their official residence was located.

"Can we organise carts to carry our belongings?" Caroline said.

"I can take care of that, you can use my carriage and I will follow on by horse," Bart van Gerwen, the farmer, said.

Le Coq rearranged the carriages so they and the children were in his with him, and his previous passengers were in van Gerwen's.

"I understand the necessity of a military governor with the situation in America, but you have more ships than we expected."

"The Bethany is one of our private fleet, the other ships are my squadron. The Unicorn is my flagship. The Bethany will go back to the India trade after she has been unloaded, and the rest will go on patrol looking for American and French privateers."

"Daddy, will the Shadows stay with us on the island?" Edwin said.

"Yes, they will come with the carts."

"The Shadows?" de Coq said.

"Our personal guards and my followers."

"Uncle Antton is teaching me to fight!" Edwin piped.

Le Coq looked surprised at that, but Caroline explained.

"All the children try and emulate their father, so it is safer to teach them how to handle weapons and themselves properly."

"I have heard of your reputation and some of your, let us say, exploits in the Caribbean. The Burgermeister of Bonaire is particularly vocal about you."

"Yes, we did have a somewhat fractious meeting last time I was in Bonaire. Is it the same man in charge?"

"Yes, he is sixty-four now."

"And he is still angry at me?"

"You wounded his pride; he finds that hard to forgive."

Marty shook his head; he would probably have to deal with that at some time. He looked out of the window and when Edwin climbed on his lap started pointing things out to him.

Caroline took up the conversation. "So, what do you produce on the island?"

"We have several gold mines and phosphate has been found which is a useful export as its used in agriculture."

"And in weaponry. Phosphorous burns really well," Marty added.

"Indeed, the other main product on the island is beef which we export to many islands in the near vicinity."

"That explains the ramp pulled up at the end of that dock," Marty said.

"Yes, we have special ships to transport live cattle that are loaded using the ramp."

After an hour or so they pulled into the driveway of a substantial colonial house. The drive was long and lined with trees. The house built at the top of a small hill to catch the breeze and was surrounded by gardens. The other carriages left them to go into the town which was spread out below in a very neat grid. The house was, as they had been warned, sparsely furnished. The previous resident having taken most of it back to England with him.

The children and Troy, who had followed the carriage and enjoyed the exercise, went exploring while Marty and Caroline finished talking to de Coq who seemed reluctant to leave them. When he finally left Caroline rolled her eyes and said, "I thought he would never leave, the rest of them will be here soon and I have no idea where we will house them."

"Well let's have a good look around and see what we have."

They started in the servant's quarters and worked their way up through the house to the bedrooms on the first and second floor.

"Those rooms in the roof are warm but at least they have screens on the windows so they can get some air at night," Caroline said as they completed their tour.

"This place was built for the comfort of the owners not the servants, who were probably slaves. You sort out where you are going to put who, and I will go for a look around outside," Marty said. He shed his coat and hat and went outside.

He was examining an outbuilding that once could have been a slave shed when a voice barked, "You there, I'm told the new governor chap is here. Do you know where he is?"

Marty looked up and stopped himself from reaching for his knife when he saw a man in the uniform of a major of infantry.

"That would be me I believe, Commodore Martin Stockley at your service."

The man, red faced with the heat, looked surprised as he took in the young-looking man with his hair pulled back in a sailor's ponytail. He recovered himself and sketched a bow. "Major Richard Goodman, Suffolk Regiment of Infantry. Heard you had arrived and thought I would introduce myself."

"Pleased to meet you," Marty shook his hand, "just looking to see what we have in the way of housing for my men."

"Marines?"

"Some as formal guards, they would never forgive me if I let the army guard my residence."

Goodman laughed. "The pride of the service, what."

"Exactly and I have my own followers to house as well."

"Followers?"

"A navy tradition, people who follow me from posting to posting. Provides some continuity although I have been lucky in my career to lead a consistent set of men."

"That's the difference between the services, in the army we stay with the same regiment for our entire career. Must be difficult changing from boat to boat."

"Ship to ship," Marty corrected him, "but you are right, it's a very lucky officer who stays with a single ship his entire career."

"How many followers do you have?"

"A cook who is French, a steward who on land is my valet and six specialist crewmen who act as my guards and help with special missions, and my cox."

"Sounds intriguing, the most exciting thing that happens around here is when they bring a gold shipment down from West Point."

"I will do my best not to disturb your peace." Marty smiled.

"Good God! Feel free! We are desperate for some kind of action."

The sound of carts coming up the drive had them walk to the front of the house. The first cart was pulling up and they could see that there was a line reaching back beyond the entrance to the driveway.

Caroline appeared and Goodman bowed deeply, obviously taken with her beauty. She greeted him politely then excused herself as she instructed the men where to take the items from the cart.

Marty turned to him and said, "We are going to be a while sorting this lot out even with the extra men from the crew they have brought, will you join us for dinner on Saturday evening? Say six o'clock for drinks."

"Would be delighted, may I bring my adjutant?"

"Absolutely and your ladies if you have them."

Everything was in the house by nightfall, not necessarily in the right place but inside. Roland took over the kitchen and prepared a surprisingly good meal. Caroline had prioritised the kitchen and bedrooms and had made sure the beds and kitchen goods had been the last loaded on the ship so the first off.

Marty knew that until his household was in order, he couldn't think of starting his mission in South America, but he could get the squadron organised for its counter privateer activities. He dispatched a message to Wolfgang to move it up to Oranjestad then report to him at the house. Tarrant was to go to Jamaica, find a cargo and return to England.

Wolfgang arrived the next day to find Marty trying to organise his study.

"Hello, Wolfgang, give me a hand with this desk please, I want it nearer the window for more light."

The desk satisfactorily placed, they moved the club chairs Marty favoured into place and sat. Marty tugged on a bell pull and when Tabetha arrived, ordered coffee for them both.

"We need to offload the special goods somewhere we will not be seen and where they can be stored securely until we need them. Have you any ideas?"

"Well, we thought about those islands sixty odd miles to the West. They form part of an archipelago from the Venezuelan mainland and, as far as I can tell, are uninhabited. I was talking to an old man at the dock, and he got to telling me tales of the pirates that used to operate out of the island."

"The Dutch used to encourage them, cheap goods."

"Quite, he spun a yarn about some caves near the North coast that they used to store their loot which the locals stay away from because they are haunted."

"Something the pirates encouraged I expect. I think I prefer the island. It would only take one curious local to find the cave."

"It wouldn't hurt to take a look, the nearest is only an hour's horse ride away."

Marty brightened; this would get him away from the chaos for the rest of the day.

"Let's go and have a look, do you know where they are?"

"One is due West of here in some limestone cliffs."

Horses were organised, Matai and Antton decided they would tag along and the four left after lunch. The ride was warm, and Marty soon stripped down to his shirt. He wore a broad-brimmed hat as the sun was fiercely strong. The land was arid, and he could see why it wasn't suitable for plantations.

"Now I know why that groom insisted we take these oversized waterbags. There is no sign of any surface water."

The groom was a local, he and the horses came with the property, and when he found that they were going for a ride across the island in the afternoon he filled large waterbags and hung them from each of the saddles. He also made it clear from his attitude he thought they were silly to even try.

Aruba is largely flat, the highest hill being only around six hundred feet, so the horses had an easy time of it, and it made it easy to spot the limestone cliffs. They soon spotted the caves which were five hundred yards inland from the North coast of the island.

They ducked under the low entrance and, lighting small lamps, made their way inside. The roof rose allowing them to stand upright, and they could see that the cave went back quite a way with natural pillars holding the ceiling up. As they moved deeper, Marty shone his lamp along the ceiling. "Look at this, it must have been done by the original inhabitants of the island."

He pointed out a shield-shaped drawing in what looked like red ochre with a central boss and lines radiating out from it.

"Looks like these caves have been known about for a long time," Wolfgang said and pointed out more recent marks made by someone called Rafael in 1797. It was very interesting but not a suitable hiding place for their goods.

They rode back to the house and considered their options,

"Have a look at those islands and if they are suitable, find somewhere to offload the cargo. You will need all your speed to catch any privateers. Send the Eagle back here, I want her for my own use, take the rest of the squadron North. Capture or sink any French or American ships you come across."

"Do you want us to stop over in Jamaica and give our regards to the admiral?" Wolfgang said.

"Yes, that would be the proper thing to do but make sure you have your orders to hand as he is bound to try and second you."

Saturday came around and he remembered he had invited the major and his adjutant to dinner. They arrived at six o'clock sharp, the men in full uniform with nicely-dressed ladies on their arms.

"Milord and Lady may I introduce Femke van Drenth, Captain Reginald Southerland, my adjutant, with his lady wife, Melinda."

"Please, for this evening call us Caroline and Martin," Caroline said.

Adam served a light Rhenish wine he had chilled by wrapping in moist cloths.

"That is delicious," Melinda said as she took a first sip, "it is so fresh."

"Caroline is somewhat of an expert on wine," Marty said with a fond look, "she made sure we brought a decent cellar with us."

"I heard you came on your own ship?" Goodman said.

"Yes, we have a fleet of fast traders that normally operate on the India run, we used the flagship to come out. It was easier to transport the household than on warships."

Femke laughed, a barking sort of sound not unlike a seal, "The number of carts to bring your belongings to the house is already being talked about all over the island."

"The packet arrived just after you did, you know, it brought the latest papers. They talked about your affair with that fellow Graves, it must have been horrendous to have your children kidnapped." Melinda said.

"It was truly horrible but some good came of it," Marty said.

"Oh? What was that?"

"Graves died, his plantation burnt, and his slaves were freed."

"How did he die?" Goodman asked.

Marty gave him his wolf smile. "Shot in three limbs, a knife through the fourth and burnt to death."

"Now dear, do not spoil people's appetites, suffice to say he died as he had lived." Caroline smiled sweetly.

"Dinner is served, milady," Adam announced from the door.

"Perfect! You will love our cook; he's French you know."

"They are everything we have read and heard about," Goodman said to Sutherland the next morning as they nursed their hangovers, "He was Wellington's head of intelligence when Peters was in Portugal last year, he says our new boss has a reputation of ruthless, cold bloodedness."

"Utterly charming couple though,"

"She is as ruthless as him by all accounts. She fought a duel against that fellow in London. Carved him up."

"Well for whatever reason they sent him here I have the feeling that life is about to get more interesting."

"Here's to that!"

Chapter 5: Patrol

Wolfgang took the squadron sixty miles West of Aruba and found the small, uninhabited islands that formed the Archipelago Monjes.

"Calling this an archipelago is pushing it a bit," Howarth commented. "It's no more than two or three islands in the mouth of the Gulf of Venezuela."

"But could be perfect for what we want. All the ships are too heavily loaded as they are to chase down privateers," Wolfgang said. "Get Mr Brazier into the tops, I want an accurate report on what is there and two men with deep-water leads in the bow. If it is an archipelago there may well be rocks not far under the surface."

The island they were approaching was the biggest of the three that could be seen, but even so was only seven-hundred yards long East to West and one hundred and fifty wide. It had a wide white beach on the Eastern point that extended around the Southern side and evidence that a reef extended out to the North. The centre was raised in a slight hill above the gently-sloping beach.

"There are a couple of depressions that look big enough we could stow some of the goods, and it looks like it would stay dry," Howarth said.

Dry was important, sea water sloshing around on the stores would not do them good at all even carefully packed.

"Get the men to prepare some of the old sails we use for patching. I think their colour will about match that of the scrub and sand," Wolfgang ordered.

They hove to and Wolfgang took a boat to the island with Wolverton the gunner and the master at arms. They walked up the beach and made their way to the centre.

"Rock and sand, let's have a look at the hollows we saw from the ship," Wolfgang said. "This is a lot deeper than it looks, if we dig out the sand, we can pile a lot in here." Wolverton said, push a stick down into the centre of the dip.

"Get a team ashore and clean it out."

The North coast of Venezuela was out of sight twenty-one miles to the Southwest but if they could have seen the islands, they would have seen lights burning deep into the night. When morning dawned the Unicorn and Linonidas rode higher in the water and the island had a somewhat more rounded appearance.

Now it was the Nymph, Eagle and Endellion's turn. They took the next biggest island to the North and unloaded and concealed their cargos under canvas and sand.

The Eagle turned back to fight the current West and return to Aruba, the rest of the squadron turned Northwest towards Jamaica. They had the trade wind on their quarters and the current on their sterns.

Port Royal was a shadow of what it had been before the earthquake of 1692, but the royal navy still claimed what was left of the peninsula and had a hospital and yard there. The Jamaica squadron used it as their headquarters and the flagship was moored in its shelter. They caught them by surprise as they glided in and dropped anchor.

A signal was eventually sent up requesting Wolfgang to go aboard. He was already in his best uniform and had a boat waiting.

"Captain Wolfgang Ackermann, permission to come aboard," he requested formally.

A flag captain greeted him,

"Horatio Turnbull, welcome. Aah, I expected the commodore or a post captain."

"The commodore is attending to his duties as Military Governor on Aruba, I command his squadron in his stead."

"When were you made?"

"Three months ago."

Turnbull nearly choked.

"I think we had better go to my cabin,"

"Is the admiral aboard?" Wolfgang said as they went below.

"Rear Admiral Cochrane is ashore. I will send him a message when I have established what to tell him."

They sat in a spacious cabin. *The life in a second rate,* Wolfgang thought.

"May I see your commission and orders?"

Wolfgang passed over the neatly-folded package and Turnbull took his time reading them. When he had finished, he called his clerk, "Copy these and return them as soon as you are finished."

He turned back to Wolfgang, "For the admiral, you understand. From what I read you are to support us in combating the American and French privateers, but you are not under our orders."

"We are to cooperate and bolster your force, but we stay under the ultimate orders of our commodore."

Turnbull frowned, this was most irregular, he didn't like not being able to exert control over a newly-promoted captain, who wasn't even English to boot, and then there was his commodore.

"We do not want to overlap with your ships, so the commodore asks that we coordinate."

"That's easy we are stretched just covering the convoys, and the Northern islands. As much as the admiral wants to, we are unable to take the fight to the Americans at this time." He went to a chart. "We think many of them are coming from New Orleans as well as Carolina. The Bermuda squadron has the passage covered but many get past and are creating a nuisance further South which would be good hunting for you. We will have to wait for the admiral of course, as you are effectively under Admiralty orders, we will have to see how he reacts."

Wolfgang knew what he meant; the admiral wouldn't get a share of any prizes the squadron took. Well, it would give him the measure of the man.

Turnbull composed his message and included the copy of Wolfgang's orders and commission. All they could do now was wait but Turnbull was a gracious host and it wasn't long before they were told the admiral's barge was approaching.

Sir Alexander Inglis Cochrane was known as a fighting admiral. He had been involved in most of the navy's more successful operations against the Americans and had been in the Caribbean since 1805.

"Stockley has the leeward squadron and is under the orders of that pirate Turner," Cochrane stated as he entered his cabin and closed the door. "I received a confidential communique two weeks ago."

He held out his hand to Wolfgang, "Congratulations on your well overdue promotion, sit down and we can talk."

Turnbull looked surprised then cross.

"Pull your horns in, Horatio I was not at liberty to tell you and I still cannot tell you everything."

"According to what I was told you had a Baltimore clipper in the squadron as well, didn't see it moored with the rest."

"The commodore is using it for his own use."

"Hmmph, up to no good for someone no doubt. Well, you are here and are welcome, we need the help. What have you discussed already?"

"We are asked to patrol the Southern Islands from Dominica onwards; the Jamaica and Bermuda Squadrons will take care of the ones to the North. That fills in the gap they cannot cover at the moment," Wolfgang said when he got back on board the Unicorn.

"That makes sense, the currents dictate that they would take the passage out past Cuba to the North past Bermuda," Arnold Grey said.

"We have a month or so to get us some prizes before the hurricane season forces us back to the Lesser Antilles."

"I thought that Cochrane was a fighter. I would expect him to take the fight to the American ports," Howarth said.

"There is a plan to take the fight to the Americans in the winter, but for now we patrol and try and keep the Americans from raiding and taking prizes. Interestingly, he doesn't share everything with his flag captain."

"Not like our commodore then."

"Quite, get us underway we have a patrol to do."

They rounded Cuba and headed East, a cutter from the Bermuda squadron saw them and exchanged signals but apart from that they only saw coastal craft and a Spanish trader. They reached Haiti and spread out line abreast, seven miles apart, to cover the maximum amount of sea. The Endellion was closest in shore, then the Unicorn, the Nymphe and last the Leonidas.

"Santo Domingo is in Spanish hands, Guadeloupe has been gifted to the Swedish and the rest is British until we get to Bonaire and Curaçao, which are Dutch," Arnold explained having taken the time to get up to date on the local political situation while they were in Jamaica.

"So, we don't need to worry about French privateers then?" Gordon McGivern, the second, said.

"There are a few that hide away but in general the Americans are the biggest threat. I was told that there are several hundred on the loose down here."

"Even if that is an exaggeration, we still have plenty of targets, if you were them at this time of year what would you be doing?" Wolfgang said.

"With the hurricane season approaching in a month or so, I would make my way as far down as I could and either work my way up the islands with the current or be ready to head over towards the Lesser Antilles and out of the hurricane belt."

"Would they come up the Atlantic side or Caribbean side?"

"If I was them, I would stay on the inside to get the best of the current."

Wolfgang considered this to come up with a strategy. "We will go between Domingo and Puerto Rico to the Caribbean side and cast a net. The ships will spread out with the frigates in the centre, the Edellion to the North and Nymphe to the South. We will follow the islands down and see what we catch."

With the frigates in the centre, hull down on the horizon they could be twenty miles apart, the two smaller ships would add another twelve miles on either end of the line. This meant that they were an hour apart so would have to engage and hold on to any targets they found until help could arrive if they needed it.

Days passed with no sign of anything until the Nymphe signalled a sighting. The Leonidas changed course to close with her and almost immediately got a signal to stand off. Andrew Stamp, Master and Commander of the Nymphe, had spotted the strange sail ahead coming up on the horizon and had his own ideas of how to capture it.

"Raise a red ensign."

"Sir?" Midshipman Jonathan Williams said.

"We will appear to be a trader, Mr Williams."

"Aye, aye, Sir."

The sails resolved into a schooner layout typical of the type preferred by the Americans.

"They are closing fast," Lieutenant Stanley Hart said, observing the ship approach.

"We need to get out of these uniforms, take your jackets, waistcoats and hats off. You too, Mr Williams. I want us brought to action and all guns loaded but not run out. The gun crews to remain hidden behind the sides. Only the minimum crew is to be visible for sail handling."

This was a trick Marty had pulled a number of times in the past, it relied on fooling your opponent into thinking you were harmless and getting them in close where the carronades could do their work. Andrew hoped it would work for them.

The ships closed, the schooner eased to the North to get the wind gauge and as they got to a mile,

"Wear ship, slovenly now make it look like we are panicked."

The Nymphe came around in a most un-navy-like fashion, sails flapping and finally settling on the reciprocal course, running for her life.

"Slacken the main; we want them to catch us."

He could sense the excitement amongst the men they were ready for a fight and hungry for prize money.

The schooner soon caught them and started to close; her American flag streaming from her stern. She ran out her guns; six pounders but enough to cripple rigging.

Andrew waited until she was half a cable away and they had fired a shot across their bows. Her deck was full of men showing they were getting ready to board.

"Bring down the ensign and run up our colours, run out the guns and give her a broadside."

Jon Williams hauled down the civilian pennant and the Americans cheered but that was cut short as the British flag went up and the gun ports flew open, revealing the gaping maws of the fourteen thirty-two-pound carronades on that side.

The guns barked with their usual chuff-boom and their loads of small ball flew the one hundred yards to the thin sides of the schooner.

"Nymphe has engaged, Sir," Second Lieutenant Robert Plowright report to Captain James Campbell. Standing orders demanded they support the Nymph.

"Very good, wear ship and steer for her. It will probably be all over before we get there but they may need help."

They had begun the turn when the lookout called down,

"Sails to the East, two ships, schooner rigged heading for the Nymph."

James immediately realised what had happened. The Americans had employed similar tactics to them, and the other two ships were closing in for the kill.

"Make all sail, we need to intercept them, the Nymphe will have a hard time against three."

Andrew got the call from his own lookouts before the smoke from their broadside had cleared.

"Sails on both quarters five miles distant closing fast."

"Damn, it's going to be warm work. Stanley, we need to disable that schooner as quick as we can, load with cannister over small ball and take down their rigging."

The gun crews worked fast; they could reload their carronades in a minute flat when they trained but no one was shooting at them then. The schooner let fly their own broadside despite the damage the Nymphe's guns had done, the eight six pounders sent chain into their rigging, bringing down blocks and rigging onto the nets.

The Nymphe's second broadside fired, and the combined load swept the schooner at deck height and above. It was like a hailstorm of lead, the one-inch balls of the cannister spread out and merged into a wall of destruction by the time they reached the other ship shredding their rigging, sails and any poor souls unlucky enough to be caught. The four-inch small balls followed, gauging whole sections out of the rail and upending one of the guns.

Desperate, the schooner's captain tried to close but he was losing way rapidly and the Nymphe pulled ahead.

Andrew put the stricken ship out of his mind, it would be an hour before they could make enough repairs to get underway again and the Lionidas would be there by then. His concern were the other two ships that were closing to within three miles. He suddenly remembered an action a few years before with Captain Stockley.

"Wear ship; run out both sides. Bring her around to go head on with them."

The helmsman noticed that when he was focussed like this, his Captain's Sussex accent came out making the 'th' in with sound more like a 'v'. He spun the wheel as Stanley called the orders for the sail handlers.

"Put us between them but be ready to turn when I give the order, Stanley we will tack to port on my order."

Stanley gave the order for the crew to prepare.

I hope this bloody works.

He could see the crews on the other ships, just a mile away, without his telescope. He looked North and could see the Lionidas under full sail but still over forty minutes away. He had to give the Americans their due, they were game, or they hadn't seen the frigate bearing down.

He brought his attention back to the approaching ships. Three quarters of a mile, they were reducing sail, clearing their guns, staying a cable or so apart. They were bigger than the first one, three masted where it was only two. That meant bigger guns as well probably.

Half a mile and his helmsman was allowing them to drift to starboard a little,

"Hold her steady, damn you, right down the middle."

"Aye, Sir." The crewman was sweating.

A quarter mile.

"Ready the helm."

Two cables.

One cable—

"Hard to port, fire as you bear!"

The Nymphe spun on her heel and crossed the bow of the left-hand schooner. Her guns lit up.

The schooner's captain, taken by surprise, swung to port to avoid the sudden turn and took the full force of the Nymphe's broadside on his starboard bow. His foremast was cut off and fell to the side, shot scythed down the deck, ripping men to pieces.

Andrew watched the ship swing and realised it wasn't swinging fast enough. The current had reduced their own speed and they were barely making way as the bow swung through the wind, threatening to send them into irons. He watched in horror as the bowsprit of the schooner swung over the rail and the shattered port bow slammed into his starboard quarter.

It was a glancing blow, but it was enough to put them into irons. The schooner scraped past their stern, ripping the Nymphe's rudder off.

"Get that bowsprit set and pull the bow around," he ordered

"Rudders gone, Sir."

"Use the foresails to haul her round we need to get her with the wind."

He looked aft, the schooner was stopped in the water her; crew frantically trying to cut away the foremast and get a sail over the hole in her bow. The second schooner had gone to the smaller one's aid and was taking men off. The Lionidas was getting closer and twin puffs of smoke showed she had fired her fore chasers.

Back at Aruba, Andrew and James faced Marty in the study of his residence. Marty read their reports without comment as the two young captains waited nervously.

"You made two mistakes," he said to Andrew, "first, you didn't assume the American were part of a larger group, the second was you failed to take account of the effect of the current on your speed."

Andrew didn't say anything; he knew that Marty wasn't finished.

"But we all learn from our mistakes and in this case, you came away with two prizes and the damage could be repaired. I trust you will remember this next time."

"Aye, Sir, it was a hard lesson, and my fellows will not let me forget it in a hurry."

"I'm sure they won't."

"James, you were happy with the way the Leonidas handled?"

"She needs to be a little more to the rear now she isn't so heavily laden, has a tendency to gripe. We are shifting the trim now."

"Good. There is an all-captain's dinner here tonight; make sure you are on time."

The dinner went well, Caroline played the hostess to perfection as always and then left the men to talk.

"Now the hurricane season is upon us, the Americans will either retreat to their home ports or carry on their activities along the Western reaches out of the corridor," Marty said.

"We should patrol from Trinidad up?" Wolfgang said.

"It will take too long to beat down to Trinidad. I suspect that our friends – the Dutch on Bonaire and Curaçao – are still operating a 'no questions asked' trading policy which we should examine. What I want you to do is go down to Bonaire and take a look. If there are any American or French ships in Kralendijk Bay, cut them out or burn them. It will be harder or impossible to do that in Curaçao as their defences are much stronger."

"What do you want to do with the two American schooners?" Wolfgang said.

"I will keep them here; I have an idea that I can use them for my other mission."

Chapter 6: Colombia

Marty, Garai and their guide, Rodrigo, made their way through the streets of Turbo, the port on the Colombian coast where the Eagle had dropped them off. It was a normal day, the street vendors were selling Almojábana the local cheese bread buns, churros, arepas and more. Having missed their morning meal, Marty stopped and bought Almojábana for all of them. It was approaching midday and soon the town would start siesta.

The relaxed feel of the town was due to the lack of any occupying Spanish troops. Colombia had achieved independence from Spain in 1810 led by Simón Bolívar when they followed the example of Haiti. It could all change now the war on the peninsula was approaching its end. Once Napoleon was kicked out of Spain, the Spanish would turn their attention back to their former possessions.

They made their way across town to a livery stable and kicked the door until a sleepy owner came to see them.

"Don't you know its siesta?" he said grumpily.

"You would rather sleep than make some money?" Rodrigo said. "We can buy horses somewhere else if you'd prefer."

"Alright, alright, keep your shirt on. What do you need?"

"Three riding horses and mules. We also need tack."

The livery man's eyes grew sly as he looked them over, Marty was dressed well, and it looked like the others were his man servants.

"I have a fine stallion for the gentleman if he is interested." He led the way to a corral where a fine sixteen-hand black Andalusian strutted around. "He is magnificent, no?" He turned to look at Marty and realised he had stopped by another corral.

"Señor the stallion is here."

Marty was looking at a solid-looking gelding. It had a good head, steady eye, deep chest and strong hind quarters. He clucked at it and it walked towards him. He climbed over the rail and approached it murmuring as he came. He reached up gently and stroked its nose, then ran his hand down its neck, over its shoulder and down its leg. He picked up the hoof and examined it, then gently moved around the horse and checked each hoof in turn finishing back at the head where he checked the teeth. Happy, he moved on to another gelding and a bay mare that were watching curiously from across the corral and repeated the procedure.

"I will take the geldings and this mare."

"Señor knows his horses; those are my best."

Marty gave him a straight look,

"Whatever I chose would be your best, what do you want for them including tack and three mules of my choice."

"I could not do that for less than eighty reals, Señor."

"Pah! The going rate is forty."

There followed a spirited and entertaining bargaining session which ended with Marty paying fifty-two reals for the animals, tack and a large bag of oats. The trip to Medellin and his contact would take six days so their next stop was to a general store for travel rations.

Fully stocked, they set out at dawn the next day. Marty rode relaxed in the saddle but fully alert. He was armed, of course, with his Durs Egg carbine, pistols and a variety of edged weapons. Rodrigo had got him a broad sombrero hat to shield him from the sun. They made good time during the cool of the morning, slowing as the heat built up until they stopped for a midday meal. The next stop was at Apartadó for the night, where they slept in a hay barn, as the tavern had more fleas than a farmyard cat.

The second day passed without event and they overnighted at El Vanadó where a farmer gave them beds in his bunkhouse for a peso each. The third day dawned bright and clear and they set off for Bejuquillo which was their longest leg yet. The road skirted the edge of a range of hills to the West and Garai noticed a rider pacing them.

They camped early that night, one of the mules had picked up a stone in its hoof so they had to take it slower while it recovered. Marty had an itch between his shoulders as he and Garai made a show of settling down on their bedrolls either side of the fire.

Two men slipped into the camp an hour after midnight, pistols in hand. One stood over Marty and the other moved to Garai. They raised their pistols. Suddenly, there was a flare of bright light from the fire embers that startled and blinded them.

"Are you going to kill them?" Rodrigo asked as he tied the hands of one of the bandits.

"Should I?"

"They probably belong to a bigger band up in the hills, if you kill them we will probably end up with the rest chasing us. What was it that made the bright light?"

"Just something some friends of ours made."

They left the bandits tied up, found their horses and let them loose, they would probably make their way back to the rest of their band, eventually. They made as much distance as they could the next day and saw no more trouble.

They rode into Medellin; it was small considering that it was the second city in Colombia and the home of Simón Bolívar. It was late in the day, so they found a good quality taverna that had rooms and enquired where they could find the great man.

The next morning Garai took a note to the house and waited patiently for an answer. Marty had written a month before, introducing himself and telling him he would visit in preparation. He knocked on the door and handed the note to the girl who answered it. She took it inside giving him a coy look over her shoulder.

"Señor Bolívar will see your master at two o'clock this afternoon," she said on her return, fluttering her eyelids.

"See you then." He gave her his best smouldering look and she giggled as she took a last peek before closing the door.

Precisely at two, Marty and Garai presented themselves at the door and were shown to a courtyard garden. Bolívar sat by a fountain surrounded by a circular bench. He stood as Marty approached.

"Señor Bolívar," Marty said.

"Mister Stockbridge, your letter said you had some important information for me."

"I will get to the point; the French are about to be kicked out of Spain by the British. In fact, I will predict that Napoleon is defeated by the end of the year."

Bolívar considered that. "That will free them to return their attention to the Americas."

"Yes, they aren't happy that they have lost control of what they see as their possessions."

"How do you know this?"

"I was in Portugal when the British and Spanish started their offensive, they took Salamanca, and Madrid. The British General Wellesley will not be stopped now."

"Please sit and tell me what you know."

Marty told him all the news he had up to the time they left Gibraltar and that King Ferdinand was preparing to return.

"I would like to see the people of South America free and not under the Spanish thumb," he concluded.

"Why does the fate of my people concern you?"

That was a very good question.

"America needs good neighbours, and the wealth needs to stay here, not go to Europe."

"Is that your real reason? You speak Spanish very well but there is a hint of another accent there. French perhaps?"

"I will admit to having sympathies with the French revolution, as well a strong royalist, Spain is not in the interests of the French people either."

"You would not want to see the Bourbons back in power?"

"A republic or royalty is a choice for the people, I would not want to see another terror."

Bolívar looked at him steadily for a moment assessing him, this was a crucial moment.

"I think there is more to you than you are saying but your actions will speak louder than your words. How can you help us?"

"I can supply weapons."

"Aah now we get to the chase, you are an arms dealer."

"No, I said I can supply weapons. There will be no charge."

Bolívar sat back and steepled his fingers under his chin, he had a sharp-featured face and dark well-groomed hair.

"You are backed by a government then."

It was a statement not a question and Marty didn't reply.

"I will not ask questions if the weapons are serviceable and not junk you are dumping on us."

"All the weapons are in good order, I have muskets, pistols and cannon."

"Enough to outfit an army no doubt."

Marty inclined his head.

"All I have to do is deliver them to where they will be of most use."

"Who trains the soldiers?"

"You need instructors?"

"The only professional soldiers in New Granada are the Spanish and I hardly think they will train the men who will throw them out. The army in Colombia is made up of militia."

"I can provide instructors who can provide weapons training."

"All this for free?"

"The weapons are donated by friends; the instructors are mercenaries and have to be paid. Their captain is an Irishman."

"How many?"

"We can supply twenty, plus the captain."

They negotiated and settled on a daily rate. Bolívar was a sharp negotiator and made Marty work to get the rate he wanted. He said he would consult with the other Juntas and let Marty know.

"I will have a ship call at Turbo in a month's time. Leave a message with the harbourmaster."

The trip back to Turbo was edgy, the bandits would have freed themselves and Marty and Garai were on high alert.

"On the hill at two o'clock," Garai said.

"Got him."

The man disappeared leaving a cloud of dust.

"Señor, what will you do? They will not come with only two men this time," Rodrigo said.

"What do you think, Garai? Take the fight to them?"

"Probably only six to ten of them, we've practically got them outnumbered."

"What?" Rodrigo squawked.

It was obvious the bandits must have a camp in the hills, so they left the trail and headed up the steepest hill in the area. They dismounted below the top and left the horses with Rodrigo.

"There is smoke over there," Garai said from where he lay to scan the area.

Marty swung his telescope in that direction, a camp sprung into focus.

"It's in a dip, more of a dry gully. Would be well concealed from anywhere but up here because of the scrub around it. There are seven I can see." He swung the telescope slightly.

"Hold on, what's this?"

A woman was dragged from a shelter and pushed towards the fire, the man pointed to the cooking pot and said something, she answered, and he slapped her across the face.

"They have a captive, no make that two, there is a child as well."

Rodrigo watched as the two men he had been riding with for the last two weeks transformed. Señor Stockbridge had two double-barrelled pistols hung under his arms from a harness and two short-barrelled pistols on his belt. He wore a short sword and a large fighting knife. He watched him slip two more knives in his boots and another two in sheaths on his forearms.

Garai wore four pistols in a similar way and had a short-barrelled blunderbuss. He was also festooned with knives.

"You wait here, we shouldn't be long and don't be alarmed when the shooting starts. Come when you hear it stop."

Rodrigo crossed himself and muttered a pair of Hail Marys, he held a rosary and prayed for them.

Marty and Garai split up and moved quietly on foot through the brush towards the camp. The plan was to approach it from opposite sides and Marty was taking the longer trip around to the far side.

There was a sentry on a rise near the entrance to the gully and he was Marty's responsibility. Garai used the terrain and brush to conceal his movement and just happened to glance through a bush at the sentry when he suddenly disappeared. He reappeared a few moments later and settled down as he had before.

He reached a point he figured was about right and gave a warbling bird call. One of the bandits about four yards away picked up his musket and turned in his direction. He took a step forward, peering to see what had made the call then fell to the ground, clawing at the hilt of a throwing knife. Garai moved forward; the sentry on the rise came up on one knee his gun ready. He fired and another bandit fell.

Marty dropped his rifle in favour of his double-barrelled Mantons and moved swiftly down the rise to the camp. The man stood by the woman, was the next to go down – shot in the head from twenty feet away. The roar of the blunderbuss told of the dispatch of another two.

The remaining two broke and ran for their horses. Marty sighted carefully and dropped one with the second barrel of his righthand pistol. The last made it to his horse and spun it around to ride out of the gully.

"Skipper!" Garai called and tossed Marty a musket he had picked up.

Marty caught it and brought it straight to his shoulder. The bandit was almost at the top of the bank. He fired and the rider tumbled backwards off his horse.

"That's all of them."

"Amateurs."

The woman was stood, mouth open, staring at the dead bandits lying around the camp, when she became aware that a man was talking to her.

"Señora, are you alright? You are safe now."

She looked at him, he was dark haired and had brown eyes that were concerned. It struck her he was quite handsome.

"My son!" she said as her senses returned.

"He is safe, look he is with Garai."

She turned; her son was walking towards her, hand in hand with a second man.

"Phillippe!" she cried and dropped to her knees; arms outstretched. The little boy, who was around six years old, ran to her and she gathered him in her arms. Tears ran down her face leaving streaks in the dirt.

She looked up at the two strangers who had freed her. "Thank you."

"Our pleasure, what is your name?"

"Consuela Martina de la Plenta, these pigs were holding us for ransom."

"Was your husband going to pay?"

She tossed her head. "He was arguing about the amount. They were going to cut off one of Phillippe's fingers and send it to him with their next reply."

"We will take you home, do you have any belongings to gather up?"

She collected together the few things the bandits had let her keep and when she stepped out of the lean-to a third man had joined.

"This is Rodrigo, I am Martin and that is Garai."

Garai nodded to her as he saddled one of the bandit's horses. The rest were in a string being led by Rodrego.

"Can you ride?"

"Yes, although not normally on a man's saddle."

"Where do you live?"

"We have a ranch outside of Carepa."

They mounted up and moved out. Garai had Phillippe on his lap.

"Aren't you going to bury them?" she said.

"Why? The jackals and buzzards need to live too."

She left it at that. If this strange man didn't want to, then she would send men from the ranch to bury what was left of them.

They rode the fifteen miles or so to the ranch and while they rode Marty thought about the kidnapping, something didn't sound right about the whole thing.

"Do bandits normally kidnap people around here?"

"No, but it is not unknown."

They passed through a gate in a rail fence that denoted the perimeter of the homestead. A mounted hand saw them and rode at speed to the house, so by the time they reached the yard in front of it, Senior de la Plenta was coming out of the door. Marty noticed he had a shocked look on his face which he quickly changed to one of surprise and smiles.

"Consuela, you are home!"

"No thanks to you, you miserly ass!" she shouted as she dismounted, "you thought to negotiate with my and your son's life?"

She was advancing on him now, angry.

"My dove—"

"Don't you my dove me, you pitiful excuse for a—" she stopped mid tirade as a woman came out of the house.

"What is she doing here?"

de la Plenta looked horrified.

Consuela advanced on the other woman; hands clawed.

"It's not what you think," he said lamely.

"Should we intervene?" Garai said to Marty.

"Who is that woman?" Marty asked Phillippe.

"Seniora Maria, she lives in the town, daddy visits her."

"Aah so that's how it is,"

Marty dismounted and went to de la Plenta, took him by the arm and led him away from the cat fight that was in full flow on the porch. He spoke quietly to him, then took him back to his wife.

Consuela had won the fight and was dragging Maria by the hair down the steps and towards the gate. She literally kicked her off the property and the defeated woman ran back towards town followed by a few well thrown clods of dirt.

"What did you say to her husband?" Garai said as they rode back towards town.

"I asked him why Maria was there. He told me that she had turned up two days after Consuela had been kidnapped."

"Bit of a coincidence."

"Yes, I pointed that out, then he told me it was her who told him to offer less."

"Really? Are we going to talk to her?"

"No, he worked out on his own that the only way she could have known that Consuela had been kidnapped was if she had something to do with it but with all the bandits dead it will be impossible to prove."

"You don't think he had anything to do with it?"

"No, he was torn between two women, but now he has found out that a mistress is far more expensive than a wife and ten times as vindictive."

Chapter 7: Venezuela

Safely back at the residence, Marty turned his attention to his duties. The fact he had disappeared for over two weeks hadn't gone unnoticed and he explained it away as a diplomatic mission. The Eagle would visit Turbo every week after a month to check if there was a communication from Bolívar with instructions where to send the guns and the men.

Marty paid a long overdue visit to the garrison and inspected the troops. He met Lieutenant Peters who turned out to be a friend of Lord Sebastian Ashley-Cooper, the lieutenant who had joined his marine force in Spain.

"Sebastian had nothing but good things to say about you when he returned to the regiment. He was a changed man somehow, more confident and less rakish."

"What is he doing now?" Marty said.

"Wellington made him a captain and he has a rifle brigade. Skirmishers, suits him to a tee."

"I must write to him; he is a very capable officer."

"The men are ready for inspection," Goodman said after a sergeant reported to him.

"New territory for me, inspecting sailors is not the same as inspecting soldiers," Marty said.

"You have marines. It's much the same with them."

"I suppose it is. Spit, polish and pipeclay."

He walked down the front rank of men, stopping every so often to ask a question or pass a comment. He turned around the end of the rank and started along the second rank when he came upon a familiar face.

"Edgar isn't it?"

"Yes, Sir."

"You were one of Wellington's stewards."

"Yes, Sir, I was,"

"How come you are here?"

Edgar blushed and the man next to him sniggered.

"I was 'avin a liaison with a lady in Lisbon and her 'usband found out. He was not best 'appy and demanded satisfaction. His Lordship decided it were best if I were posted somewhere far away to avoid a situation."

"Very wise of him," Marty said, supressing a smile.

The inspection over, he was entertained by the officers.

"Not much happens here, the Dutch are more interested in getting on with their lives than causing trouble," Goodman said.

"What about Bonaire and Curaçao?" Marty said.

"They keep themselves to themselves in the main, but they do visit relations here and the councils stay in touch."

"So, I gathered. It seems that the Burgermeister of Bonaire has a long memory."

"That was you? I thought it was a coincidence."

The junior officers hadn't heard about Marty's previous exploits in the Lesser Antilles and pressed him to tell them the story. He gave them the version that he had given to the Admiralty with no flourishes but with a slight exaggeration of the funnier parts.

"You knocked the Burgermeister flat? No wonder he holds a grudge," Peters said as they all laughed at his description.

"Well, I wanted to impress on him we were serious," Marty said blushing.

They treated him to a very good lunch, and he was glad to have a carriage to take him home in the afternoon. Apart from settling the odd dispute he had discovered there was not much for the governor to do, which suited him fine as he wanted to get on with his mission.

"We expect the squadron to return in a couple of weeks and I want those schooners ready to sail, are there shipwrights on the island?" Marty asked de Coq over a coffee.

"Werner van den Berg runs the local shipyard down in Barcadera, I'm sure we can find some hands to move the ships down there."

"My men will skipper them, so we only need a dozen sail handlers between the two of them."

"They will be easy to find, there are always hands looking for work. I will ask around."

"Thank you, is there anything I can do for you?"

"There is actually, I need a message sent to my family in Rotterdam."

"Can't it be sent via Caraçao?"

"Only if we want the French authorities to read it. They open everything that is sent from Aruba."

"I see. Give me the letter and I will make sure it gets to them."

"You do not want to know what it says?"

"Will it say anything detrimental to the British or allies?"

"No, it's to do with business."

"Then I don't want to see it."

"You are very trusting."

"Not really. If this comes back on me, it will come back on you."

Marty didn't say but he would have John open it and copy it before it was sent. Just to be sure and nobody would ever know.

De Coq gave him a sideways look,

"How will you get it to them?"

"That, my friend, is a secret. If I told you I would have to kill you."

Even though Marty was smiling, de Coq wasn't at all sure he was joking.

Crews were found and Wilson and John Smith skippered the schooners down the coast to the shipyard. The master shipwright came onboard to look them over.

"What do you want done?"

"Repair the damage and convert them to carry cargo," John said.

"That's a first, normally people want these converted to warships."

"Aye well we may want them converted back later but for now we needs 'em to carry cargo."

They walked through the schooners. The smaller one, the Robin, had patched up rigging and a chunk out of its mainmast. Her hull had also been damaged

"Do you want to keep the guns?"

"Aye, got to be able to protect ourselves."

Van der Berg knew better than to ask any more questions.

The larger ship, the Mayfly, needed her bow rebuilt and a new foremast.

Marty had a couple of special additions he wanted made to the ships and when John specified them van de Berg said, "It will cost four hundred guineas to get the two ships ready and take a month."

"Is that the fastest you can do it?"

"Yes, the price includes moving you to the top of the list."

"And keeping the extra modifications secret?"

"We have dealt with smugglers before, we know what not to talk about."

John let him think what he would, as long as they got the work done and it was kept quiet then they would be happy.

Marty was keeping the Eagle busy; he had a contact in Venezuela, and he sent Matai to find him in Caracas. Matai returned after two weeks,

"Caracas is full of troops who are loyal to José Tomás Boves. They are lawless and are killing and stealing whatever and whoever they want. They are particularly aggressive towards the middle class and landowners. Boves seems to be working with a Spanish regular officer called Francisco Morales. Your contact, Francisco de Miranda, is in a Spanish prison. He led the last war of independence which Boves and Morales overturned.

The hopes of the majority of the people lie with Bolívar and New Granada, which is what he calls the combination of Colombia, Venezuela, and the other Spanish countries."

Marty considered this. "Is there anybody there who is working with Bolívar?"

"Nobody in the North but there are rumoured to be a couple of rebel leaders in the South."

"Do they work together?"

"Not as far as I can tell, they seem to be independent and have separate agendas."

Typical, Marty thought.

"Do you want me to go back and see what I can find out?"

Marty looked at a chart of Venezuela that Matai had bought in Caracas.

"Angostura looks like a good place to visit, you can sail right to it up the Orinoco River. Take Garai and Antton and see if you can contact either of those two rebel leaders. Find out who they are and what the difference is between them."

"Aye, aye, Commodore."

Marty grimaced at the honorific.

"That doesn't have the same ring as Cap'ain."

Matai grinned.

"Maybe we should just call you 'C' it would be a good code name as well."

"Or M for Martin," Marty joked looking back at the chart.

"No that wouldn't be proper. I'll tell the boys from now on you are C."

Marty looked up from the chart to object, but Matai was already closing the door behind him.

The three Basques wasted no time in boarding the Eagle and Trevor Archer set sail immediately. He needed no new orders from Marty as his current ones gave him all the freedom he needed. The clipper had been resupplied and watered and was ready for sea.

They left Aruba and made a leg a few points North of East towards St Vincent. At the three hundred-mile point they wore to the Southeast to pass between Trinidad and Tobago after which they swung South to find the mouth of the Orinoco.

The estuary came into view on the fourth day.

"Reduce sail to topsails and royals," Archer ordered. "Have you ever sailed up the Orinoco Charlie?" he said to his sailing master.

"No, can't say that I have," he said looking at the gaping maw of the ten-mile-wide estuary, "but there looks to be plenty of room. The chart shows that the river is up to a mile wide all the way up to Angostura."

"All the same, I want two men on leads all the time and we will only sail in the light. Put a lookout on the foremast yard to look ahead for snags and sandbars as well."

They entered the estuary and after thirty miles the river narrowed to a couple of miles wide and started to get shallower. The leadsmen called the depth continuously and were changed every hour. The current was sluggish, and they could make four knots against it which allowed them to cover fifty land miles a day.

"How far up this damn, insect ridden, muddy stream do we have to go?" Archer said as he slapped at yet another insect gnawing on his neck.

"About two hundred miles, as the crow flies, but everything in South America is twice as far away than you expected."

"Captain," Midshipman Sykes said, "may I remind you of the oil Mr Shelby gave us?"

"What? Oh, the citronella! I forgot about that. Break it out, have all hands apply it and refill all lamps with the oil. Now you have reminded me I believe he said that it needs to be reapplied every three hours."

Soon the ship had taken on a light citrus fragrance and the sound of mosquitoes being swatted decreased dramatically.

"That stuff actually works," Archer said.

"Shelby introduced it when we were here on the Tempest," Antton told him.

"Was that when the commodore captured the Spanish treasure ship?"

"Aye, that was a hell of an adventure."

"Why don't you join me for dinner and tell me about it."

They anchored for the night well away from the shore as soon as the sun dipped towards the horizon. Every lamp was filled with citronella oil and would burn all night.

It rained, that is to say they had a downpour that lasted three hours and deposited several inches of freshwater on the deck. The water ran out the scuppers, down the hatchways when they were opened and leaked through any gaps in the deck caulking, making the below decks area horribly damp. They woke up to a dawn with steam rising from every part of the ship and the surface of the water as soon as the sun touched it.

"We will have to wait." Charlie said, "we can't see fifty feet ahead of us."

The sun rose as fast as it set that close to the equator and the mist burnt off rapidly allowing them to set sail with a light breeze behind them that gradually got stronger as the land warmed up.

"Set the royals and topsails, I want the spanker and foresail set as well," Archer said. They had two fathoms of water under the keel and the current had picked up a bit so he wanted the extra thrust those sails would provide.

"According to the log we are making eight knots," Midshipman Sykes said on his return from the bow. Archer looked at the shore and watched a particular tree pass. "We are only making half that, there must be four knots of current running."

"Aye that's because of all that rain last night, the water has to go somewhere," Charlie said.

As the day passed the current slackened and they had to reduce sail to maintain five knots of progress. The land passed by at walking pace and at the end of their third day they stopped at the town of San Félix.

Their American flag was accepted as friendly, and they were offered trade goods as cargo. Tempting as it was, Archer didn't want to load the Eagle up on the upstream part of the trip, so he made a couple of promises to stop on their return trip. He also got a request from a pair of local merchants to transport them up to Angostura.

"What do you think, Matai? Would it be useful to have a couple of locals to milk for information?" Archer said.

"Certainly. It's amazing what they will let slip if you can get them relaxed. Leave them to me."

They stocked up with fruit and veg and bought a couple of small pigs. Fresh meat would be welcome. The merchants came aboard and were provided with cabins that were hastily erected by the carpenter.

The river upstream of San Félix was much the same as before and they would make Angostura by the end of the day.

"What is the political situation like down here? Up North its chaotic with counter revolutionaries burning everything."

"That swine Boves and his half breeds, the Spanish's dogs. He is a traitor to his people. He has ambitions to be the lord of all

Venezuela, his masters need to be careful he doesn't turn on them." Raimondo, the older of the two merchants fairly spat.

"I didn't know that. We were warned off visiting Caracas so decided to try our luck down here."

"You were wise my friend," the younger, Carlos, said, "we are still free of Spanish rule here, Bolívar will free the rest of New Granada in time."

"He cannot be everywhere, there must be a local head of the revolution?"

The two men looked at each other conspiratorially then put their heads together and whispered.

"What interest do the Americans have in the revolution?"

"We support it, we have prospered since we threw off the yoke of the British and we want to see our neighbours prosper without the Spanish stealing all of the wealth."

"But you are Spanish, no?"

Matai laughed, "Me? No! I am a Basque. We hate the Spanish and the French for stealing our country and oppressing our people."

"When did you leave your home and go to America?"

"When Napoleon started conscripting my people into his army and navy. If you didn't join, he would take your family hostage to force you. I escaped with my family on an American ship and made a home in Portland. I was fishing until I joined the Eagle."

This seemed to convince them he was a friend at least.

"I have met Bolívar you know."

"You have? Where?"

"The owner of this ship is very rich and has decided to support the revolution, we went to Medellin, to his home and agreed to supply him weapons."

"He has money to buy them. We are poor down here."

"Oh, he doesn't have to buy them, my boss represents a group of rich men who want to help the South become independent."

That got their attention and they whispered again.

"When we get to Angostura will you be staying long?" Raimondo said.

"I will be trying to make contact with the leader of the revolutionaries so we will stay as long as that takes."

"Wait on the ship. We will contact you, we will contact General Piar and ask him to meet you."

"You took a bit of a risk there didn't you?" Antton said.

"Not really I heard them talking in one of their cabins and they were assuming that none of the crew spoke Spanish. They were discussing how they would tell Piar that the people of San Félix would support him," Matai shrugged.

"I think we need to be careful in any case, Garai and me will stay away from them, let them think you are the only one on the ship who can speak for C."

Garai laughed. "If that sticks, he is going to be really angry with you."

"We need a code name for him that people will not link back to him, so that is as good as any," Matai said.

The ship made dock and the two merchants went ashore, Antton and Garai followed them. All of the Shadows were experts in their craft and could follow someone at a distance, from behind, in front and even the side without being seen. Raimondo and Carlos had no idea they were being tracked and went straight to a taverna where they met an obviously military man of around twenty-five years of age. He took them to a house and was much more careful to check whether they were being followed.

The door to the house was answered by a very pretty woman and the three entered.

"No way to see inside from here," Antton said as they met up at a roadside food vendor's stall.

"The place is not overlooked by any other buildings; someone chose it carefully." Garai squinted into the evening sun that was going down over the roof of the house. It was the highest roof in the street and the windows on that side were secured with ornate wrought iron cages.

They hung around to see if anybody else turned up but all that happened was the merchants left after a couple of hours. They followed them to their lodgings then returned to the ship.

The next morning Carlos came to the ship and asked to see Garai and said, *"We had a meeting with General Piar and told him about you, he would like to meet you this afternoon."*

"That was very fast, I would be pleased to meet him. Are there any conditions?"

"Conditions? What do you mean?"

"Well, I assume he has security. Do I need to provide proof of who I am?"

Carlos looked surprised and said, "No, he will take our word for that. I will come back at two o'clock to take you to him."

Once Carlos had left, Matai met the other two in the wardroom,

"Something smells off about this, it's far too easy," Antton said.

"What did you think of the man they met? Was he what you would expect from a revolutionary?"

"Looked like a soldier, well dressed and very upright. Wore a sword."

"What kind of sword?"

"Brass hilt, ornate knuckle guard, cross guard, knotted cord on the cross guard, curved thirty-inch blade."

"Hmm, that sounds like a Spanish infantry officer's sword. Do we know anything about General Piar's history?"

"All we found out is he is a mestizo, that's someone who's a mix of European and Indian blood. He has been part of the independence movement since he was old enough to fight and fought on Curaçao against the British."

A crewman knocked on the door. "Captain's compliments, but he says that the ship is being watched."

Matai went up on deck and made a show of walking along the shoreward side and casually watching the activities of the various stevedores, vendors and merchants. He exercised for ten minutes or so then went back below.

"Three men, all cut throats by the look of them. One is about fifty yards behind the stern leaning against the entrance to an alley. The second is right across from the ship sat on a bail of something and the third is thirty yards beyond the bow cleaning his fingernails with a stiletto."

"Someone is taking precautions at least," Antton said.

"So, we go ahead with the meeting then?" Matai said.

"Yes, but we take our own precautions. Let's be sure this is all what it's supposed to be before we get C here."

Carlos arrived precisely at two o'clock and collected Garai, he retraced the route he had taken the day before but went straight to the house. Matai and Antton had left the ship individually an hour before and taken up positions where they could watch the house unobserved.

Garai and Carlos were allowed into the house by the same pretty girl that Antton had seen.

"Good afternoon, Sir, who should I say is calling?"

"Garai Mendoza."

"I am Catalina," she said giving him an appraising look.

He returned it, it wouldn't hurt to have a contact on the inside and he was a single, red-blooded man. She led them through to the back of the house and through a door into a library. The sun shone through the single window illuminating dust motes that swirled along with smoke from a cheroot.

The young military gentleman from the taverna was stood in the shadows to one side the sunlight from the window illuminated his sword and left leg. Another elegant-looking man with black hair that was neatly combed, a high forehead over a long straight nose bounded by deep-set brown eyes and a strong chin, sat in a high-backed winged chair. He was jacketless and wore a white linen shirt and black cravat held in place by a silver pin. He was twirling a long-bladed knife between his fingers.

"Mr Mendoza, so nice of you to visit," he said in perfect English.

"Thank you, I'm afraid we haven't been introduced."

"Oh, my apologies, that is very remiss of me, General Manuel Piar Gómez at your service."

"I am a little troubled, I do not have any way to confirm you are who you say. This could be a trap by the Spanish."

The soldier in the shadows, as Garai thought of him, made a move for his sword. Garai reacted immediately and a knife thudded into the wooden panel an inch in front of his nose, he froze.

"Let's not be hasty," Matai said calmly.

"Relax, Stefano, if he meant us harm you would be dead already." Piar said. Stefano pulled the knife from the wall and examined it.

"Your security is hopeless. I could have killed you no end of times already," Matai said.

"Point taken," Piar said putting the knife on his desk then stood hands carefully held out to the side. He walked over to a painting on the wall and invited Matai to look at it. "This was painted in Curaçao in 1804 when I took command of the 'Revolution' a war ship at the liberation of Haiti."

The painting had a plaque screwed in the middle at the bottom, 'Capitán Manuel Carlos Maria Francesco Piar Gómez, El Revolución 1804' and the picture was indisputably the man stood in front of him. Matai ran his finger over the plaque and noted the dust that came off it.

He bowed to Piar, "General, please forgive my caution. Your security still needs looking at."

Piar laughed and walked back to his chair indicating that Matai should sit as well. Matai held out his hand to Stefano for his knife,

"That is no blade for a gentleman," he said as he handed it back.

"I never said I was a gentleman," Matai replied.

"I am told you are a Basque," Piar said.

"Yes, I escaped with my family to America when the French started forcing us into their navy and army."

"Along with many others. Now tell me about these generous Americans."

"It is simple, they see that it is in their interest to help South America throw off the yoke of Spanish rule. It is especially important now that the British, Portuguese and Spanish are throwing Napoleon out of the peninsula and it looks like they will finally defeat him."

"You really think they will?"

"Yes, the French are being assaulted from all sides and once they lose Spain, the British will be able to push up through the Pyrenees in force."

"You are remarkably well informed about what is going on in Europe for someone who lives in America."

Matai laughed, "I am a sailor, my ship travels across the ocean to trade. We were there three months ago. In France they talk of nothing else, some are afraid, others are looking forward to the return of a king. One thing is certain, Napoleon is not invincible. Once the Spanish are free of him, they will turn their attention back to their 'possessions' and that will happen soon."

"I see, and how are you offering to help?"

"My patron has offered Bolívar weapons and men to train his troops, we would extend the same offer to you."

"All for free?"

"The weapons are for free, but the training is done by mercenaries and they need to be paid."

"I think I need to meet your patron before I agree to anything."

"That can be arranged but it will delay things a month or so."

"That is of no consequence, the Spanish are not coming that soon."

"Alright I will tell my patron, Mr Stockbridge, that there is to be a meeting in, say, five weeks."

The Eagle made a rapid run downstream aided by the current and their recent knowledge of the river. Once out in the Atlantic they swung West towards Trinidad and Tobago. Again, aided by the current and the favourable East-Northeast wind they made a rapid passage to Aruba.

"Piar, I have read something about him," Marty said after Matai had reported. He went to a cabinet and extracted an intelligence report from Jamaica.

"Yes, here it is. He was born in Curaçao, father Spanish, mother a Dutch mulato. Self-educated, speaks several languages and joined the revolution when he was twenty-three. Fought the British when they kicked us out of Curaçao in 1804, in 1807 was active in Haiti as a captain of a warship. In 1813 he led the defence of Maturin as a colonel."

"He comes over as supremely confident, not arrogant just sure of himself."

"We could do with some eyes on the inside."

"I may have an opening there, but I will need to be in Angostura to work it."

Marty looked at him suspiciously. "That 'opening' wouldn't happen to be pretty, shapely and decidedly female?"

Matai just grinned.

"You said that we should aim to get there in three weeks or so."

Marty thought for a while.

"Well, it's lucky I got those schooners ready; the Eagle is overdue for a visit to Turbo so I will send her there immediately. Call Antton in please."

Antton was nearby.

"I want you to take command of one of the schooners. John will be your first mate," Marty said as soon as he arrived. "The squadron is in port, form a crew from our men and include a squad of ten marines under Sergeant Bright. Go up to the weapons store islands and load up two hundred muskets, ball and cartridge and ten artillery pieces, powder and shot; then return here. Send Garai and Wilson in on your way out."

They had been dismissed and left to do their master's bidding.

Wilson and Garai reported to his office.

"Wilson, I want you to take command of the second schooner with Garai as First Mate. Form a crew from men from the squadron. I am expecting to hear from Bolívar soon, so go and load her up with guns and cannon from the store island. Then wait for the Eagle."

The men left and Caroline came in.

"Did I hear you say you were going to visit Angostura?"

"Only if you were listening at the keyhole," Marty laughed and grabbed her in a hug.

"You know me too well," she said and put her arms around his neck. They kissed.

"Do we have time—" Marty said hopefully.

"No, the officers' ladies are arriving in fifteen minutes and that's not long enough."

"Mummy!" Constance said from the door.

"Yes, dear," Caroline said without letting her husband go.

"Edwin has got his head stuck in a pan."

"How did he do that?"

"It wasn't me! We was playing soldiers and he wanted a hat."

Caroline sighed and kissed Marty on the nose before disengaging his arms, "I better go and find Mary or Hanna."

"I'll go, you see to the ladies," Marty said and patted her backside as he left.

His son had his head well and truly jammed into a copper pan which showed signs of being beat upon by something. He looked around and saw a pair of wooden swords beside a tree, one of which had several large nicks in its edge.

"You were testing it to make sure it worked as a helmet?" he asked his daughter.

She shuffled her feet and looked coy, "I won the battle."

"Did not!" shouted Edwin.

"Enough of that, let me see if I can get this off without having to cut off your head."

Hanna arrived having been warned by Caroline.

"Oh, my lord!" she cried.

"Hanna, please go to cook and get some fat or butter please." Marty said.

Fifteen minutes later after a lot of howling and the liberal application of butter Edwin was free of the pot. His face red from crying and a scratch or two were the worst of the effects. Marty picked him up gave him a hug and talked to him. "There now, it's all done. Are you going to put your head in a pot again?"

Edwin shook his head.

"Sailors don't wear helmets, only soldiers do. Do you want to be a soldier?"

"Want to be a mawine like Arfur." He was referring to one of the permanent guards on the mansion who got on well with the children.

"Marines don't wear helmets either. I will see if we can get you a hat."

Just then his Captain of Marines Declan O'Driscoll stepped into the courtyard.

"Aah, there you are, Lady Caroline said you were attending to a family crisis and all I had to do was follow the howling." He ruffled Edwin's hair. "Are you alright now, young man."

Edwin sucked his thumb and looked at him with big eyes.

"Edwin wants to be a marine when he grows up," Marty said, "maybe we could find a hat for him."

"I think we could, I will talk to our man who maintains the uniforms. Now I heard you have a job for us?"

"Indeed." Marty put down his son and passed him into the care of Hanna. "Walk with me,"

They left the courtyard and went out into the ornamental garden where Marty could be absolutely sure they wouldn't be overheard.

"I want you and Sergeant Bright to lead separate teams of advisors and train the revolutionaries in Colombia and Venezuela. You will be acting as mercenaries, paid for directly by the revolutions leaders."

O'Driscoll hadn't done this before and asked, "What are we to train them in?"

"Guerrilla tactics, how to shoot, close combat, the usual. I will give you men that have done this before so they can guide you. I want you to act as advisors on tactics but not actively take part if you can avoid it. You also need to be aware that if you get killed, your death will be put down as lost at sea."

"Unattributable, I see."

"The squadron will ensure any dependants are taken care of but as far as the British Government and the navy is concerned you were never there."

"They said when they asked me to join you that you were a special unit. Up to now I didn't realise fully what I was getting into."

"You can refuse to do this with all honour."

"Oh, do not misunderstand me, I will do this and any other job you hand me with relish. This is just what I have been looking for. I just hadn't experienced it until now. This gives me the opportunity to do things the way I think they should be done, not the way the navy says I should."

They shook hands.

"Then I will endeavour to find interesting things for you to do."

Chapter 8: Advisors and Betrayers

The Eagle found the Robin anchored off the biggest island in the Archipelago Monjes, fully laden and ready to go.

"As your men are all done can they help load the Eagle as well?" Archer said to Wilson.

"Surely. Are we in a hurry?"

"Yes, Bolívar is ready for the guns. O'Driscoll and his men are already ashore and raring to go."

They started loading, ferrying boatloads of crates from the island and storing them down in the Eagle's hold.

Archer and Wilson stood on the Robin's quarterdeck and watched the progress.

"What is C going to do in Angostura?" Archer asked.

"From what Antton told me he will visit the general who runs the rebels down there and make him a gift of some guns and cannon. They were here loading them last week."

"I hope nothing goes wrong he will be a long way from help."

"The squadron is in port. If he is even a few days late, Lady Caroline will have Wolfgang searching the Caribbean from Aruba to Trinidad and all the way up the Orinoco."

Marty boarded the Mayfly, the second schooner, with Sam and Chin. Matai, Sergeant Bright and ten marines were already aboard.

"Gather around, gentlemen," he said to the team that would be dealing with the rebels directly. "From now on my name is Martin

Stockbridge, I am a rich plantation owner from Carolina, and I represent a consortium of likeminded planters who want to see an independent South America. To keep things simple none of you marines know me. You are a mercenary band of ex British soldiers, were recruited independently and joined this ship in Charleston.

Sam and Chin are my personal servants. Matai is the go between who will stay in Angostura and act as liaison between the mercenaries and revolutionaries. All clear so far?"

A round of "Aye, aye, Mr Stockbridge" followed. Marty addressed the marines.

"Use your real names, that way you will not make mistakes. The job is the same as in Spain, so you all know what to do. Try not to get into any disputes with the revolutionaries, they are less touchy than the Spanish Dons but be advisors not commanders. If there is a problem, refer it to Matai and let him deal with it. If you are asked about your past, remember mercenaries are notoriously close mouthed about that. You do not have to tell them anything, they are paying for your skills and expertise – not your story."

He left the briefing at that. The men all had weapons that they had drawn from the squadron's extensive store. None of which were navy issue, most preferred some kind of sabre-style sword or the heavier cutlass, pistols of various styles and calibres and of course muskets. All carried concealed knives emulating their revered boss.

Sergeant Bright prepared his personal armoury: A 1796 pattern Heavy Cavalry Sabre, thirty-three-inch-long straight spear point blade, ridged wood hilt wrapped in leather and a simple iron knuckle guard with cross guard. The scabbard was equally brutal, being made of wood-lined steel that could also be used as a club. A brutal weapon for a big man. Two pairs of brass knuckles, one of which had a built-in spring-loaded blade. Boot and belt knives and a pair of throwing knives. A pair of fifty calibre short-barrelled barkers and a French infantry musket with bayonet finished of the selection.

Marty looked it over. "You seem to be prepared for any contingency."

"Almost, nearly forgot this." Bright held up a garrotte which he coiled and slipped into a pocket.

Marty laughed and went to prepare his own weapons.

His Durs Egg carbine was a constant companion as were his double-barrelled Manton pistols. He added a pair of pocket pistols not unlike Bright's barkers only these were rifled, and breech loaded being the latest innovation of the London gunsmiths. The selection of knives included a pair of stilettoes with forearm sheaths, a pair of throwing knives with boot sheaths, his infamous fighting knife with its nine-inch blade and clip point, a punch knife and a medium-sized folding knife.

He wore a pair of knee-length lace-up boots similar to the old calf-length boots he wore in earlier years. These provided protection when he was riding but more importantly had several hidden compartments built into the uppers where a set of lockpicks, cutthroat razor blade, slim jim and other burglar tools were secreted. The laces were extra strong and could double as garottes.

He had adopted a modern shorter hairstyle for this mission, foregoing his traditional ponytail so he couldn't secret anything in that. Caroline had given him a long evaluating look before pronouncing that she preferred his hair long. He assured her that when they returned to cooler climes, he would grow it again.

Sam and Chin were similarly well armed. Sam carried pistols and a blunderbuss, he was a notoriously bad shot with a rifle, a broad-bladed twenty-two-inch machete with a clip point and brass knuckle guard, several knives and a pair of deceptively good quality pistols. The pistols were deceptive because although they were plain and looked well used, they were in fact almost new and were very well made. He had gone to Durs Egg's establishment to get them made and had to get Marty's help to persuade the gunsmith to 'dirty' them up.

Chin had his butterfly swords which looked to be a single sword in a scabbard until he pulled them. Secreted around his person he had shurikens he had made himself, a blow pipe, and throwing darts. He carried a single pistol. "If they get close enough for that they will be dead already." And a short yet powerful bow in a bamboo tube with a selection of unusual arrows.

Marty felt that they were as well prepared as they could be, with Antton and Trevor Archer taking care of the delivery of the guns to Bolívar he was free to work the Venezuelan opportunity himself. They set sail and followed the same route the Eagle had five weeks before.

"We should have brought Charlie from the Eagle," Wilson complained as they felt their way up the Orinoco.

"These rivers change all the time; Matai knows as much about it as Charlie," Marty said. Matai did have a good memory of the route they took last time and took his turn on the foremast yard watching out for snags and sandbars.

The schooner was mainly gaff-rigged with a small square sail on the foremast and sailed well in the confines of the river. They also had sweeps which they only deployed if they lost the wind as the heat and humidity made working them torture.

They got to San Félix and stopped overnight, Marty, Garai, Chin and Sam went ashore.

"Troy would like this place," Marty said looking at the number of dogs wandering the streets.

"He would just want to fight all the males and fuck all the females," Sam said, "he's better off with the children."

"But he would be having a good time," Marty smiled.

"Boss, something's wrong," Garai said suddenly stopping and looking around.

Marty started paying attention to his surroundings and immediately noticed that they were the only ones in the street. All of the locals had made themselves scarce. Hands went to weapons and they stood shoulder to shoulder in a circle facing outwards so they could watch all the approaches. A group of men appeared from an alley ahead of them and another from an adjoining road behind them, cutting them off.

"Eight this side," Marty murmured, "they look like Llanos,"

"Another six here," Chin replied.

"Muskets?"

"Yes."

"Same here."

The men ahead of them spread out across the road and levelled their muskets, the men behind split and levelled their muskets from either side of the road to avoid the line of fire from the forward group.

"They seem to know what they are doing," Marty said.

A man stepped out from the alley, he was tall dressed in knee breeches and silk stockings, wore a red high-collared tailcoat in the Spanish fashion.

"Señor Stanwell," he said in accented English.

"You have the advantage of me, Sir," Marty replied.

"Forgive me, I am Capitán Rodriges Miguel Caranello of his Majesty King Ferdinand's Army."

"Nice to meet you, why all the guns?"

"You are known to us señor, a gun runner and supporter of the rebel forces here and in Colombia."

"Am I really and who told you that?"

"I have my sources. Now if you would be so kind as to divest yourselves of your weapons, we will place you under arrest."

Neither Marty or his men made any move to drop their weapons, they just waited.

"We can just shoot you if you like it really makes no difference to me," the captain said, moving to the side to clear his guns.

"That means you will shoot us anyway?" Marty asked.

"You will be tried before we do."

"Oh, I see, so you are assuming we are guilty before we have our day in court."

"Of course, I wouldn't be wasting my time arresting you otherwise."

Marty waited, still making no move to remove his sword belt.

"Really this is too much," the captain huffed, "have it your way. Men! Take aim."

The grinning men adjusted their aim.

A bird gave a warbling whistle. Marty smiled and bowed deeply to the captain. When he came up from the bow, he had a pistol in each hand and had thumbed the hammers to full cock. Sam left his pistols on his belt and two throwing knives appeared in his hands. As Marty fired, they flashed through the air. Chin's hands flashed forward and shurikens hissed through the air taking down one of the six at his end of the street. Matai pulled his pistols and fired in one movement.

Before he knew what was happening seven of his men were down and the American and his men were moving like acrobats diving and rolling to come up and fire again. On top of that a body of men had appeared at the other end of the street and were firing muskets at the men at that end.

Marty fired and moved, not giving the men who he faced the chance to hit a stationary target. Bullets buzzed past him and smacked into the wooden walls of the buildings. He rolled to a kneeling position and fired the second barrels of his Mantons, dropped them and pulled his barkers.

It was over as fast as it started. The captain turned and ran and the remnants of his men followed. Marty had killed or wounded four, Sam's knives had done for two more. They were still both armed with loaded pistols ready to take on any that wanted some more.

At the other end of the street, the six Llanos were even less lucky as they took the full force of not just Chin and Garai but the marines led by Sergeant Bright who had come up behind them. Suffice to say none walked away.

"The captain, he had a bad day," Sam said his white teeth gleaming in the sun.

"Yes, looks like he lost a good dozen men."

Doors opened and people started to come out onto the street. A woman walked over to one of the Llanos that was lying in the dirt with one of Sam's knives in his gut. She gently pulled the knife out, placing a rag around the wound as she did to stop the bleeding. The man, his dark skin reflecting his ancestry of mixed African and Indian parentage, looked at her with pleading eyes.

"Cerdo español!" she spat and slashed the knife across his throat. The razor-sharp blade did its work and the man died, gurgling on his own blood. That set off the rest of the locals who laid into the wounded and dead.

"I don't think they like them," Garai observed as he watched four men kick another wounded man to death.

"No, it appears not." Marty put his pistols away before retrieving his Mantons.

"It was lucky that some anonymous friend sent a message that you were going to be ambushed. It gave Bright a chance to exercise his marines," Wilson said as soon as they got back to the ship.

"Someone has betrayed us," Marty said, his look boded ill for whoever that turned out to be.

"How did they know we would stop here?" Wilson said.

"It's a fair assumption we would overnight here as it is a day from Angostura. All they had to do was get men here and wait," Marty said, "but that's not the point. Someone must have informed on us and the only people who knew about us and our connection to Bolívar were the general and his aide."

"Unless they told others in the resistance and one of them is the traitor," Garai said.

"True, but we won't find out until we get there. Double the guard tonight, we will leave first thing in the morning. You will all dine with me tonight."

When he got into his cabin Marty found Adam, his steward, holding up his coat.

"Something wrong?"

"This was close," Adam said and turned so the coat was in front of the window. The sunset shone through a neat hole through one side panel.

"Wasn't aware of it at the time. We will be six for dinner tonight."

The dawn light over the misty river saw the Mayfly pull out into the mainstream of the river under sweeps. Sails were set to carry them upstream to Angostura and they steadily increased their speed to around six knots. They knew they were being watched but as the cat was out of the bag, they left the watchers alone.

One man, however, stood blatantly on the bank just outside of town and made a throat-cutting gesture to them. Chin took exception to that; it was one thing to be watched but that was just insulting in his mind. He strung his bow and selected an arrow, one with wicked barbs, stood by the rail and in one flowing motion brought the bow up, drew and loosed. The arrow whistled as it flew and embedded itself in the man's stomach just above his navel. The man sank to his knees his hands holding the shaft.

"Nice shot. Have you got another one of those?" Garai asked.

Chin handed him an arrow and he examined the point; the bullet-shaped tip was sharp to penetrate cloth or even leather and tapered back about an inch before spreading out into four barbs that faced backwards.

"Damn, once one of these goes in the only way it's coming out is by being pushed all the way through. Nice weapon."

For the rest of the trip, they had extra men on lookout and the ship was cleared for action. Marty expected that the Spanish or their Llanos allies would try an attack on the ship by boat, but it stayed quiet with most boats keeping their distance.

Their arrival at Angostura was low key. The American flag attracted no attention at all as before. They waited in vain for someone to arrive and take them to the general.

"Garai, you know where he lives, if they won't come to us, we will go to them," Marty said.

In light of what happened at San Félix Sam, Garai, Chin, Wilson, Sergeant Bright and two marines, all visibly heavily armed, accompanied Marty to General Piar's home. The rest of the marines disappeared into the town in pairs.

"Quiet, isn't it?" Wilson said as they left the dock area.

"Yes, just like San Félix," Marty replied.

There were only a few street vendors who watched them nervously like deer ready to bolt at the first sign of danger. The group spread, so not to provide an easy target, with Marty in the middle. They all kept up a constant scan of the buildings, roofs and windows as well as the street ahead.

They approached a junction; marines appeared from the side streets and casually nodded them through. The casual demeanour was a sham, they were on high alert and ready for anything.

They approached the house; security had been improved to the point where it looked more like a fort. There were men on the roof, the lower floor windows were shuttered, four men stood outside the door and others walking a patrol around the perimeter. The shutters had gun loops in them and as they approached musket barrels appeared and tracked them.

"Do you think that what happened to us was part of something bigger?" Garai said.

"We will find out in a minute."

They stopped three yards short of the door as the four guards lined up to block it, muskets at the ready.

"I am Martin Stanwell, and I am here to see the general."

One guard stepped back to the door and knocked. A small panel opened, and he said something to whoever was inside. The panel closed and he resumed his position.

They waited.

Several long minutes later the door opened, and Stefano stepped out. *"If Senior Stanwell and Senior Mendoza would care to step inside the general will see you now."*

"I would like to bring Mr Bright with us as he will command the advisors and the general should meet him."

Stefano looked Bright up, further up then down.

"If he leaves his musket here, he may enter."

Bright handed his musket to Wilson then stepped up beside Marty. Marty and Garai handed theirs to the marines then all three stepped through the door where they found themselves covered by three men with pistols.

"Please leave the rest of your weapons on this table," Stefan said.

Marty nodded to the other two and took off his sword belt and laid it on the table.

"And any concealed weapons if you please."

Marty smiled and placed his pistols, stilettoes and throwing knives on the table. Bright and Matai followed suit.

"Forgive us for being cautious," Stefano said and beckoned one of his men forward who patted the three down.

Satisfied, he bowed and said, *"Follow me."*

He led them through to the drawing room which was lit by lanterns. The general was sat at a desk reading some papers. He stood as they entered and greeted them,

"Gentlemen, welcome, I am sorry for the welcome, but we have seen an incursion of Spanish-backed Llanos since your last visit and there have been attempts on my life."

Garia introduced the others. *"Martin Stanwell and Benjamin Bright."*

"We were ambushed in San Félix," Marty said as he sat down.

"You were? Yet you survived as you are here to tell the tale," Piar said.

"Yes and an interesting tale we have to tell as well."

Piar nodded for him to continue.

"We were ambushed by Llanos as we walked through the town. We were forewarned by the absence of local people going about

their normal business and fought them off with no casualties to us apart from a couple of flesh wounds."

"I am glad to hear it," Piar said, *"the odds must have been fairly even."*

"No, they had sixteen to our four plus their commander."

Piar's eyebrows rose in surprise.

"And how many walked away?"

"Just three."

"Did you take any prisoner?"

"No, the locals finished off any wounded once they saw we had won."

Stefano snorted from where he stood behind the general,

"You expect us to believe four of you took on sixteen men and walked away having decimated their ranks?"

"Hard to believe isn't it?" Marty replied. *"Well, it's the truth as you will hear soon enough from your people in San Félix, but what is more interesting is who the leader was and what he had to say."*

"You spoke to him?" Stefano said and Marty thought he detected an odd note to his voice.

"Yes, he announced he was placing me under arrest, he knew my name, why I was in Venezuela and that I had dealings with Bolívar."

"How on earth did he know that?" Piar exclaimed.

"Well now that is the question isn't it. How indeed did he know all of that?" Marty stood and seemed to wander around the room aimlessly.

"He could have been told by someone in Bolívar's command, but Colombia has been independent for a while now and Bolívar's security is good. Then there is the fact that the Llanos operate only in Venezuela and the distance involved. No, I doubt the leak was from there."

"If the leak was not from Bolívar, and I agree with your reasoning there, the where do you think it came from?"

"Please forgive me for asking this, but how many people in your organisation knew about your conversation with Garai?"

Stefano stepped forward. *"Are you accusing the general of informing to the Spanish?"*

"No, I am trying to establish some facts to draw a conclusion from, do you object to that?"

"Forgive Stefano, he is very protective of me," Piar said, *"please continue."*

"The question stands. How many people knew about the meeting with Garai?"

"Only Stefano and I, I didn't tell anyone else." He turned to his aid, *"Stefano?"*

Stefano looked shocked and took a step back.

"I only told – Oh my god!"

"Who did you tell Stefano," Piar asked gently.

"Antonio, I told Antonio."

"Who is Antonio?" Marty asked.

Stefano had blushed to a bright red and stuttered.

"Antonio is Stefano's lover," Piar said.

Stefano looked aghast. *"You knew?"*

Piar smiled sadly, *"My dear boy, did you think that I would not?"* He rang a bell, and a man came in,

"Send a squad to Stefano's house and bring Antonio here." He turned to Marty. *"If you don't mind, we will clear this up before we progress to other business. What was the name of the leader of the Llanos in San Félix?"*

"He introduced himself as Capitán Rodriges Miguel Caranello of the Spanish army."

"Aah, now things start to come together." Piar then rang the bell again. *"Please bring coffee for us all."*

While they waited Piar chatted to Marty about general things. The coffee was good, and Marty was content to wait.

The front door banged and the door to the drawing room opened with a thud as two men manhandled a third into the room. Antonio didn't seem to have come quietly. Stefano looked anguished and took a step forward.

"Stefano please leave us," Piar said.

Stefano left the room his head bowed not looking at Antonio.

Marty stood. *"May I?"*

Piar nodded, he looked intrigued as to what Marty would do.

"Let him go," Marty said.

"I believe you know Captain Rodrigues Caranello."

Antonio stood straight and looked defiant.

"Oh, come now he was most complimentary about you, how you were such a good lover,"

Antonio looked shocked then concerned.

"Oh yes he told us everything when we had him stretched out on a door and were about to cut his balls off with a set of castration irons."

He let that sink in.

"Stefano was distraught when we told him, poor boy was totally unaware he had been betrayed."

"What happened to Rodrigues?"

"Oh, we hung him. The standard punishment for trying to kill me you know."

What Piar found absolutely chilling was that this was all delivered in a perfectly calm conversational manner. Marty didn't shout or accuse or threaten.

Antonio looked like his world had just caved in but Marty was relentless.

"Did you know that there are different ways to hang someone? There is the long rope method which is quick because it breaks the victim's neck or rips their head off. Then there is the short rope method where the victim strangles to death. We used that one on him, he took over five minutes to die and piss and shit himself in the process." He looked at Antonio, picked up a bucket used to hold wood for the fire, emptied it into the grate and held it under his face so he could puke into it.

"Better? Well now we have to decide which method to use on you."

"What?"

"Well, you have been damned by his confession so there's no point in a trial we will just take you out and hang you."

Antonio looked at Marty in horror then at Piar pleadingly.

"General, please, let me tell you how it was, you cannot let this man hang me. Please!"

Marty turned his back on Antonio and winked at Piar.

"Antonio if you have anything to say that could give me a reason not to let them hang you now is the time."

Antonio told them how he had met Rodrigues in the market and had immediately seen that he preferred boys. Antonio told how he and Stefano had argued over how much time he spent with the general and he agreed to see Rodrigues to spite him. He had slept with Rodrigues once when Stefano and the general had gone away for two weeks but he had immediately regretted it. He loved Stefano and didn't really want to hurt him, but Rodrigues wouldn't let him off so easily and had threatened to tell Stefano everything unless he passed on everything Stefano told him.

After he finished the general had him removed from the room.

"I thought this might be the case once you told us it was Rodrigues in charge of the Llanos. He predilection for men is known and he is particularly dedicated to the Spanish cause. That was a very interesting interrogation technique by the way, I assume it was a total fabrication?"

Marty took it as a compliment. *"Thank you, yes it was. Rodrigues got away unfortunately."*

"No matter, we will catch him in time."

Marty looked thoughtful and said, *"I have a suggestion that might speed that up."*

Stefano was not happy, he felt betrayed and hurt that Antonio had strayed and even angrier that he had given away secrets even if he had done it to protect their relationship. One of the reasons he had left the Spanish army was the absolute intolerance towards homosexuality even though it went on undercover all the time. He thought he had found his partner for life in Antonio. Now the American wanted to use him to capture the Spanish bastard who Antonio had been with. For the sake of the general he had agreed but had his own idea of what would happen after it was done.

Antonio had told all. Marty used that information to send Rodrigues a message telling him that the American arms dealer was in Angostura and he had information on what his movements would be after he had finished with the general. Marty was a fair forger of handwriting, not the artist that John Smith was but adequate and he had tried to make the message intriguing enough to hook Rodrigues. It had taken a week, but a message came back that Rodrigues would meet Antonio at the usual place.

Marty was of similar build to Antonio, broader in the shoulder but the same height. He observed the way he moved and his mannerisms, he needed to get close enough to Rodrigues to spring their trap. The morning of the meeting Marty dressed in Antonio's clothes that had been adjusted to fit him, and assumed his persona, much to Chin's amusement.

"What's so funny?" he asked the grinning Chinaman.

"You look like what Wilson call a fancy boy."

"Well, that's the idea, isn't it?"

"Yes, it suit you."

Marty's reply was short, obscene and to the point.

The rendezvous was in a taverna on the edge of town and Marty wore a broad-brimmed hat from Antonio's extensive collection which served to hide his face and hair. The approach to the tavern was across a wide-open square that was lit at intervals around the outside with torches. The flickering light also helped to conceal his identity.

Chin, Garai, Wilson and the marines were making their own, more circuitous ways to the taverna. The general had been persuaded to leave his men in their barracks. The Spaniard was no fool and any hint that there were more soldiers than usual wandering the streets would send him running like a hare.

Marty reached the doors to the taverna without incident. There were two men lounging on the porch, trying to look inconspicuous. As he passed them, he could see they were Llanos and armed. Inside it was simply lit with candles, stank of stale food and alcohol and had a fug of smoke from men smoking tobacco.

Marty looked around and spotted Rodrigues immediately at the table Antonio said they always met at. He got to within six feet before Rodrigues realised, he wasn't who he expected but he took that in his stride.

"Mr Stanwell, how nice of you to visit, from your dress I assume that poor Antonio has met his end."

"No, he is alive and well. I thought it was a good opportunity for us to meet and I didn't want you to run away again."

"That is very nice, but you do realise you have walked into a tavern that is full of my men."

"Your Llanos, yes I saw them on my way in, the four in the corner over there and the other three sat at the table by the window."

"And that doesn't worry you?"

"Not at all. I came here to remove you from the game. You have been a nuisance but no more than that."

Rodrigues smiled but his eyes darted around the room checking his men were all paying attention.

"Oh, come now, I must be a bit more than a nuisance for you to risk your life to capture me."

"Capture? Who said anything about capture? I believe I said 'remove' that is a much simpler thing to achieve." Marty pulled what looked like a short stick from his sleeve, raised it to his lips and blew into the end of it. Rodrigues stiffened,

"That dart is coated in tree frog poison and you will be dead in about two minutes. Now you understand what I meant by remove."

The poison worked fast and as the dart had hit him in the face, paralysed his facial muscles first. It would travel through his body and as it reached his vital organs stop them from working. It was efficient and very painful for the victim.

But the time anyone looked around the blowpipe was safely hidden again, and it looked like the two men were still talking. Marty kept up the sham until Rodrigues slumped in his chair a ribbon of drool running from his mouth.

"Now the fun starts," he said out loud in English and tossed his hat onto the nearest table of Llanos. The men looked up in time to see the flash of his pistols as he fired at the table in the corner. All hell broke loose as men were hit and screamed and the others lurched to their feet, reaching for their weapons.

The window and door burst inwards, and more shots rang out. The three men by the window jerked like rag dolls as bullets hit home. Marty dropped his pistols as the surviving men charged him and met them with his knife in one hand and a stiletto in the other. The fight was short and dirty. He slashed one across the guts with the fighting knife as he ducked a club wielded by the other. Distracted he didn't see the wounded man's slash which cut him across the hip. The stiletto found a home in the other man's throat.

Then Chin was there and finished the gutted man with a slash across his throat with his butterfly sword.

"You're getting careless or slow." He bent to examine the cut.

"I need more practice; I've gotten lazy."

"With rank comes sloth,"

"Where did you learn that?"

"Ancient Chinese proverb."

Marty gave him a disbelieving look. "Really."

Marty limped into Piar's study and sat, gingerly, on a chair.

"You are hurt?"

"An inconvenient scratch, I was a little careless."

"Rodrigues is dead?"

"Cold and stiff. His body along with his men is being buried in the cemetery. Unmarked of course."

Piar looked at Marty for a long moment. *"There is much more to you than a simple plantation owner, Mr Stanwell."*

Marty ignored the comment and said, *"We allowed one of the Llanos to escape. He is wounded but not severely and two of the mercenaries are following him. I expect he will lead them to the Llanos encampment."*

"Stefano, please tell Captain Fernandez to have his men ready to move out in force," Piar said to the waiting aid.

Marty waited until he had closed the door behind him, *"What will you do with Antonio?"*

"I should have him shot, but that would have a very bad effect on Stefano. They have reconciled and I would rather have Stefano as my aid than weeping over his lover and trying to get himself killed with the front-line troops."

Marty nodded. *"Talking of front-line troops have you talked to Mr Bright?"*

"Yes, we have agreed a fee for his men's services, and they will start the training next week. He also tells me his men are experts in guerrilla tactics."

"Doesn't surprise me, I get the impression they have done most things in their time."

"Indeed. The muskets and cannon have been offloaded from your ship. I am surprised at the quality of the weapons and the fact that they are all French made."

"I am pleased you approve. We went to quite some lengths to source them. My time here is done, Garai will stay and act as interpreter and go between."

"You will leave?"

"Yes, we leave tomorrow. I have business to attend to back home."

Chapter 9: A Privateer Affair

Marty settled back into his life as Governor after writing a report for Admiral Turner on what they had done so far. He was satisfied he had done as much as he could for now with respect to the revolution. He also wrote to Arthur Wellesley who was, by all accounts, giving the French a right royal hiding and crossing the Pyrenees into France.

Now it was time to turn his attention to the American privateer problem and get into action. Which is to say he had extremely itchy feet and wanted to get back to sea. He contemplated his excuses and came up with the most likely to satisfy Caroline.

"I really ought to pay my respects to the admiral in Jamaica and the governor there," he said as an opener.

Caroline knew her husband well, and interpreted the remark for what it was. "I suppose you must, we have been here plenty long enough for you to have done it already, it could be interpreted as rude or even negligent if you were to delay any longer."

That was easy! Marty thought in triumph and basked in his own cleverness. Caroline was silent for a minute or two as she ate her meal. Then popped his bubble with, "I suppose I will have to pack my gowns; the governor is bound to throw a ball in your honour."

Marty choked on the mouthful of food he was chewing and concealed it by covering his mouth with a napkin. Caroline was well aware of his confusion and went in for the kill without looking up from her plate.

"Of course, we will have to leave the children here, there is absolutely no point in exposing them to the vapours in Jamaica and while we are there, I can look in on the family plantations. I wouldn't mind looking in to investing in some myself and Tabetha can visit her family. Does Sam have family there?"

Marty knew when he was beaten. Furthermore, she was right; a governor was expected to turn up with his wife. Socialising was six or even eight tenths of the job.

"I should act the commodore as well. The men expect it," he said trying to win back some ground.

"Of course, you must, dear; you have always led from the front, but you have been getting careless lately. How is your thigh?"

"Healed, as well you know. We will be taking the squadron; they have a job to do."

"And you will command them. I will not get in the way."

They finished the meal chatting about inconsequential things happening on Aruba then Marty excused himself to go to his study, Caroline smiled as she helped Mary put the children to bed, she was looking forward to this trip.

"How did that happen?" Marty said to himself as he looked over the charts of the region. "It's as if she knew I would be taking the squadron out." He gave up trying to fathom that particular problem and, taking up his sword, went to find Chin.

He soon realised he wasn't as fit as he once was as Chin easily wore him down and decided to correct that as soon as possible. The next morning saw him, Sam and Chin set off for a run down through the town, past the military barracks and back up to the house.

"Good lord! Is that the governor?" Major Goodman said to his adjutant.

"I believe it is! What the devil is the fella doin'?

"Good morning, my lord, are you well?" Goodman called.

Marty ran up to them and stopped, he was panting a little and sweating a lot. "Morning, Goodman, fine morning, isn't it?"

"Yes. Are you doing some kind of route march?"

"Just a short run to warm the muscles up before we do some weapons training. I need to keep my fitness up."

"Quite, quite. I heard that you picked up a wound while you were away."

"Only a scratch, damn careless of me actually. You can join us for weapons practice if you want."

Goodman was intrigued as to what kind of weapons practice a governor thought necessary,

"Be up at the house in an hour, must finish my inspection first."

"Excellent, see you there!" Marty turned and resumed his run.

Goodman followed the sound of swords clashing and made his way to the enclosed courtyard of the governor's mansion. To his surprise there were a number of men, Lady Caroline and her daughter, Bethany, all engaged in sword practice.

Lady Caroline was obviously a competent swordswoman, and her daughter was holding her own against one of Lord Martin's Basque followers.

That's a damn rum thing, Goodman thought as he realised that everyone was using live blades including the young girl.

"Goodman, welcome!" Marty called from across the courtyard. "Get rid of that coat and arm yourself. Phillip, would you be so kind as to spar with the major to warm him up?"

"Aye aye, Sir!" Trenchard grinned and approached Goodman sword drawn.

"You all practise with live blades?" Goodman said as he took his guard.

"Absolutely, practice should be as near to combat as it can be." Phillip said and launched an attack with a shouted, "Ha!"

It was all Goodman could do to keep the young lieutenant at bay and soon his arm was tiring. It was inevitable that he should slow as he was using a heavy infantry officer's sword and all of a sudden, he found the point of Phillip's against his chest. "Damn, well fought, sir."

They shook hands then Phillip looked around and said, "This should entertain you."

The combatants had stopped fighting and Lord Martin and the big man called Wilson were facing off with what looked to be quarterstaffs. The Chinaman officiated and had the two men toe the line before giving the command, "Fight!"

The staves whirled and cracked against each other as the two men sought to score on each other.

"That's a bit old fashioned, isn't it? Quarterstaffs haven't been used for a hundred years," Goodman said.

"You never know what you are going to have to fight with so we make a point of learning every weapon we can. Staffs are good and can be deadly if you know how to use one."

"May sound an odd question, but why do sailors need to know how to fight with anything but a boarding pike or cutlass?"

"Our squadron gets asked to do some odd missions and we sometimes have to spend time on shore to do them."

"But Lord Martin is a commodore, surely he doesn't get actively involved in them?"

"You don't know the commodore; he leads from the front and would never ask his men to do anything he couldn't do or wouldn't be prepared to do himself."

The bout ended with Marty scoring a hit on Wilson's shoulder. He walked over to Goodman with a grin on his face. "That was most enjoyable, A week more of practice and I will be able to take on Chin again. Did you bring pistols?"

Goodman hadn't.

"No matter you can use mine, let's go to the shooting range."

The range was a short walk from the house at the end of the grounds. It had been constructed with a high sand bank at the end and partway up both sides. Targets were mounted on poles at various distances.

There was a table set up with pistols, powder flasks and bowls of bullets laid out on it. There were a beautiful, matched set of French duelling pistols, a pair of curious double-barrelled pistols, a pair of Queen Anne breech loading pistols, a pair of barkers and a pair of ugly navy issue hammers.

Goodman picked up one of the French duelling pistols, nine-inch hexagonal barrel, walnut stock inlaid with silver, gold embossed action. He looked down the barrel. "Rifled!"

"Yes they are, want to try them?"

He did and Marty showed him which powder flask to use and the correct bullets. As he was loading his pistol Marty loaded his double-barrelled Mantons.

"Which target?" Marty asked.

"That one at, what, thirty feet?"

"A bit close for that gun try for the one at fifty."

Goodman shrugged then took his stance, side on, the pistol raised in front of his face, arm bent. He took a breath and extended his arm, aimed for the centre of the target and squeezed the trigger. The action was butter smooth and a hole appeared close to the heart drawn on the man-shaped board.

"Not bad!" Marty said and stepped forward a Manton in each hand. He raised the right and fired without seeming to aim then raised the left and fired again. He fired the second barrels the same way. He didn't look to see where he had hit just returned to the table to reload.

Goodman walked forward until he could see the target clearly. There was his bullet hole and next to it in the middle of the heart four bullet holes that were grouped so closely they were touching.

Marty met him at the firing mark when he returned and handed him the Manton's.

"Try them."

They were perfectly balanced and had sights at the back and in between the end of the barrels. Again, the actions were smooth and jerk free when he fired and surprised himself by getting each pair of shots within a couple of inches of each other.

"You need to practise with your left hand," Marty said and picked up a pair of barkers. "These were made by Durs Egg in London. Try your left hand with one."

After he had fired twenty shots, he felt more comfortable shooting with his weak hand.

"A marked improvement," Marty said after Goodman nosed the bullseye of a target.

"Feels more comfortable I must say."

He looked at Marty. "Not all navy commodores keep fit and practise with weapons, do they?"

"No, I can't say that they do," Marty said.

"Your lieutenant says your squadron gets asked to do odd missions. Were you on one when you got wounded?"

"My dear chap, you are full of questions aren't you."

"Part of my job is to protect the governor, of course I'm curious especially when he blatantly doesn't need my protection and keeps disappearing."

"Touché, I suppose I owe you an explanation. As long as I have your word not to tell another living soul."

"Of course. You have my word."

Marty explained to him his role in Naval Intelligence and enough to leave him satisfied that there was something important afoot without telling him what it was.

"I understand now. That is, I understand enough."

"I have a favour to ask."

"Ask away."

"I have had to detail most of my marines including their commander and senior warrant to duties that have taken them away from my ships. That leaves me rather short-handed to fulfil my mission to suppress the American privateers."

"And you want some of my men to make up the numbers."

Marty cocked his head to one side,

"Rather more than that. I want one of your officers to command them as well."

Goodman blew out his cheeks, his first instinct was to offer one of his lieutenants but then he thought that this was probably a once in a lifetime opportunity.

"How many of my men?"

"Twenty as a minimum, twenty-five if you can spare them."

"Oh, that's not a problem they have nothing to do except practise marching here, bloody sleepy posting. You can have thirty."

"Thank you they will not be bored I can assure you. What about an officer?"

"On the basis that as a leader I should not ask my officers to do anything I wouldn't do myself, I will come along on this trip and bring young Peters, as he would benefit from some of the same experience as his friend."

"Very good but you will have to remember that even a lieutenant commander outranks you on his own ship."

"The navy has always been clear on that; never fear I know what my place will be. Will I have command of your remaining marines?"

"On the Unicorn, I will move a lieutenant from the Leonidas to act as your second and Peters can replace him. There is an excellent sergeant there who can keep him out of trouble. In the meantime, before we sail, I suggest you and the men join the marines in their training to get to know them."

Marty called an all-captains meeting. Adam and Roland served coffee then Marty stood.

"Good morning gentlemen. We will soon be leaving for a tour and I wish to present the itinerary and some of my thoughts on tactics."

He took a sip of coffee, not the Blue Mountain he and Shelby the surgeon preferred but a good Colombian bean he had picked up while he was there.

"Our first port of call will be Jamaica so that I and my good lady wife can pay our respects to the admiral and governor. We will stay there for a few days as it will give the men a chance to have some shore leave somewhere with more to do than Aruba."

That went down well with the captains as they would get to have some fun too.

"Once we are finished, we will run a patrol down the Atlantic side of the windward islands paying particular attention to anywhere American privateers could hide or replenish their stores."

"Does that include San Domingo, Guadeloupe and Martinique?" asked Andrew Stamp.

"Especially the French-held islands. We are still at war with the French and if we have the chance, we will take or sink any French ships we come across."

That was greeted by a round of hurrahs.

"Settle down, don't count your prize money before you have it in your hands. Once we reach Trinidad, we will patrol up the Caribbean side of the islands again looking into everywhere the Americans could be hiding."

"Sir, there have been rumours that there are sympathisers to the Americans in the Virgin Islands, will we investigate them?" Phillip Trenchard said.

"The Endellion and Nymphe will detach and carry out a patrol of the Virgin Islands starting at the most Northern island, Anegada, and working South. The rest of the squadron will lay in wait for any birds they flush on the leeward side of the islands as that is the way they are likely to flee."

"Just like beating the bushes for pheasants!" Major Goodman said as he entered followed by Lieutenant Peters.

"Hello, Goodman, hello, Peters. Gentlemen as you know our captain of marines, his senior warrant and many of our marines are on detachment. Major Goodman and Lieutenant Peters will join us to provide some leadership and to experience a bit of navy life. They will bring thirty men to top up the ones we are missing."

"Welcome, Sir," Wolfgang said, "the difference is these birds shoot back."

"Quite," Marty said, "Wolfgang, the major will join the Unicorn. James, the lieutenant will join you and Beaumont will move to the Unicorn to aid the major."

Goodman raised his hand, Marty nodded for him to proceed,

"I notice you use first names, is this normal in the navy between ranks?"

Marty smiled. "The squadron is a much closer-knit unit than any other in the navy and in the wardroom, we tend to be less formal, which I might say, would shock some regular navy men to the core. In front of the men, we tend to be more formal but as most of them have been with us for years—" he shrugged.

"The Shadows call the commodore 'C'." Trevor Archer said archly earning him a look from Marty.

"Shadows?" Peters said.

"My followers and if I catch any of you referring to me as 'C' I will have you serving double watch at the masthead," Marty said with a scowl. The captains grinned back at him.

Marty decided to change the subject,

"Have you had a chance to train with the marines?" he asked Goodman.

"Yes, just came from there, they don't pull their punches and that is a damned effective way of fighting hand to hand."

"We tend to get a lot closer to our enemies in boarding actions than a land battle," Marty said. "That is all for now, you are all invited to dinner at the mansion tonight. Full dress. We set sail the day after tomorrow."

The dinner was a sumptuous affair and Marty had a surprise for James, his wife, Josee, had travelled out to join him. Caroline had arranged it when she had a letter from Josee telling her how lonely she was. The tall pretty Dutch girl was a surprise to many of the men who had never met her. She was taller than most of them at six feet while still having a lovely figure. She came from Aruba originally, the daughter of an innkeeper and had met and fallen in love with James when they had visited on the Tempest. Her father still lived on the island. He was retired now and lived in a cottage the other side of town. While James was on patrol, she would stay with him.

At the end of the meal, Josee and James went for a walk while the rest of the men congregated in the games room to play billiards, drink port and smoke cigars.

"James' wife is an island girl?" Goodman said as he watched Marty expertly trap the red and Philip Trenchard's white ball in a corner and repeatedly cannoned his dotted white ball off of both balls racking up a large score.

"Yes, he met her in '04 or '05 when we stopped off here to recruit some extra hands. He was just a mid then and smuggled her back to England where they married," Wolfgang told him.

"Well done, Sir!" Goodman said as Marty got the twelve points he needed to win. "What is a mid?"

"A midshipman, the rank equates to ensign in the army. We call them gentlemen in training. They have a division to command which usually covers between eight and twelve guns, depending on the ship and the number of mids it has."

"How old are they when they start?"

"I believe the commodore was twelve when he was made, isn't that so, Martin?"

"Twelve or Thirteen," Marty replied. "It was after the siege of Toulon."

"You were there?" Goodman said. "I have read about it but not met anyone who was actually present."

The men pressed Marty to tell the story of the siege, so he sat and gave an account.

"After that the Comte de Marchet sponsored me to become a midshipman. My captain then is now my superior at the admiralty."

"Incredible, only in the British navy could a mere cabin boy elevate himself to the level you have attained, and it all started with you chopping the balls of a Frenchy. Haw, Haw," Goodman said.

Wanting to change the subject Marty said, "I have had a letter from Arthur today, they are crossing the Pyrenees and expect to drive up through France in the new year."

"Oh, excellent news, all our efforts are bearing fruit," James said which got a 'here, here' from the other men.

"Who is Arthur?" Goodman asked Wolfgang in a whisper.

"Arthur Wellesley, the Duke of Wellington."

Goodman's eyes widened he would have to tread carefully around this pleasant young man, he was obviously very well connected.

"I knew he had worked for Wellington I wasn't aware that they were corresponding."

Wolfgang grinned, seeing a chance to have some bragging rights over the soldier,

"He and the Prince Regent regularly correspond as well; Lord Martin has some interesting friends. The prince is the godfather of the twins you know."

"Is he bedamned."

The squadron left on the tide as planned, Marty had the main cabin with Caroline, Wolfgang had the coach. Goodman had O'Driscoll's cabin which was about eight feet square, he was wondering what he had let himself in for as the Unicorn hit the first waves and the motion sat him on his bunk with a thump.

"How the hell do you keep your feet with the deck moving around like this?" he asked Lieutenant McGivern who had the watch.

"This? The ship's hardly moving, you will get your sea legs soon enough. By the way, you should always ask permission to come onto the quarterdeck, especially if the captain is present and never trespass on the windward side as that is his."

"A lot to learn what?"

"There is indeed."

"I notice there's not a lot of shouting to get things done like I have seen on other ships."

"The commodore ensures that his crews are all well trained and know what needs to be done without being driven. It helps that all our crews are all rated able, except the nippers that is."

"Nippers?"

"Ship's boys. Excuse me a moment. Watch the trim of the foresail, there!" Men quickly adjusted the trim to take into account the shifting wind.

"Why are they called nippers?"

"See that rope that runs around the capstan forward?"

"Yes."

"That's the messenger, when we raise the anchor the anchor cable is attached to the messenger by short lengths of rope tied on by the boys. That is called nipping the ropes together."

"And that's why the boys are called nippers!"

"Captain on deck," the helmsman said quietly.

"Good morning, gentlemen," Wolfgang said.

"Good morning, Sir. Course Northwest, twelve knots. Wind is from East-Northeast, sea calm."

"Thank you, Mr McGivern. Carry on."

McGivern went back to pacing the quarterdeck, alternatively checking their course and the set of the sails.

"Major Goodman," Wolfgang said.

"Captain Ackermann. Did he say the sea is calm?"

"Why yes he did, not a flat calm but only a slight swell."

Goodman staggered as the deck moved and grabbed a stay.

"You could have fooled me."

Just then Marty came on deck and received salutes from the officers. He was dressed in an open-neck shirt and loose sailor's trousers.

"Morning, Goodman, fancy some exercise?"

"I'll pass if you don't mind. Haven't got my sea legs yet."

Marty laughed. "Never mind they will come in time." He called Matai and the two stood by the ratlines either side of the mainmast. Midshipman Brazier stood between them and, when both were ready, shouted, "Set! GO!"

The men raced up the ratlines to the futtock shrouds, hung out at forty-five degrees as they negotiated them and then continued up to the mast head. Matai got there an arm's length before Marty. The two returned to the deck via stays laughing and joking. Marty wasn't finished and soon he was going through some close combat exercises with the rest of the Shadows who had joined them on deck.

Caroline appeared dressed in her voluminous trousers, a white silk blouse, leather bodice and soft kid gloves that extended up to her forearms. Armed with a sword and main gauche, she looked every bit the warrior queen.

"My goodness! Does Lady Caroline often appear like that in public?" Goodman said, not sure whether he was outraged or titillated.

"She practises with the men regularly," Wolfgang said, a hint of reproach that Goodman had even asked the question in his voice.

Caroline partnered up with Midshipman Brazier and they started to fence. Soon the sparks were flying as their blades clashed in a very rapid exchange.

"My goodness, she is very good isn't she," Goodman said in admiration.

Wolfgang didn't reply.

Marty kept the squadron moving at a steady twelve knots day and night. The Endellion and Eagle ranged out ahead and to either side as scouts during the day, returning at night to stay in contact. They sighted Jamaica after a day and a half and approached in formation; the two frigates and sloop in line astern with the schooner and clipper flanking the flagship. From above it would look like an arrowhead formation.

As they passed Fort Charles the Unicorn fired a salute which was answered by the fort's guns. Caroline and Marty stood on the quarterdeck well out of Wolfgang's way taking in the sights.

"You know, being a commodore has its benefits, I don't have to worry about making a bad impression on the admiral as we come into anchor," Marty said as he watched Wolfgang giving the orders.

"Is that the flagship over there?" Caroline said.

"No, that is only a third rate, Cochrane's flagship is a second rate, the Union."

"Barge leaving the Foudroyant, Sir, Captain aboard," Brazier reported.

"Man the side," Wolfgang ordered.

The captain was received with all ceremony, Spithead nightingales tooted their whistles and the marines stomped and crashed their butts.

Wolfgang escorted him to the quarterdeck. "M'Lord Purbeck, may I present Captain Hancock of the Foudroyant."

"Captain Hancock welcome, this is my wife – Lady Caroline."

"M'Lord, my Lady." Hancock bowed. "My respects, I thought I should report aboard, Sir, as you are the ranking officer in port right now."

"The admiral isn't here then?"

"No, Sir, apparently he and his squadron have moved to the new yard in Bermuda from where he is carrying out attacks on the American mainland."

"I see. Join us in the cabin and you can tell us why you are here over a glass."

As they made their way down to the cabin Marty wondered about Cochrane as it would appear that he had left the privateer problem entirely to him.

"So, we are now making our way back to England for a refit and some rest," Hancock concluded after telling them about his trip to South America.

"Could you take some letters for us?" Caroline asked.

"Certainly, just have them dropped off before we leave on Thursday. The old girl is not the fastest, but I can guarantee that your letters will reach their destination."

"I will have a mail bag delivered tomorrow lunchtime. You must dine with us before you leave," Marty said.

Hancock took that as his dismissal and stood to leave.

"It has been a pleasure meeting you, Commodore and Lady Purbeck, I have heard many stories about your lordship's exploits."

"All of which were no doubt greatly exaggerated." Marty smiled.

Marty sent a letter to William Montagu, fifth Duke of Manchester who was the sitting governor of Jamaica announcing their arrival and requesting a meeting. A note came back, by return, inviting them to stay at the mansion and to join for dinner that evening. That kicked off a frenzy of packing and preparations before their luggage was lowered into the barge followed by Caroline in a bosun's chair.

Marty clambered down the side after Adam, Sam and Chin and they set off. A coach met them at the dock, and they were whisked off to the governor's residence in Spanish Town.

"It's a bit scruffy," Caroline said as they passed several houses that were in need of repair, "and there's little in the way of shops."

"They are all in Kingston this is mainly a residential area, but it has become run down. I don't know why they don't move the capital to Kingston, that's the commercial centre."

The residence was what was known in England as a stately pile. It was at least a hundred years old and had been added to by successive governors without taking much care to match architectural styles. The result was a grand, rather striking building that traced the history of the island from a Spanish possession to the present day.

The coach rolled up the drive into the crescent-shaped receiving area where it pulled up in front of the doors. Sam and Chin jumped down from the top where they had ridden, and Adam held the door open for Marty and Caroline to alight. Servants appeared to take their luggage to their rooms then Lord Montagu and his wife, Lady Susan, greeted them.

"My dear Purbeck, how are you? Welcome to Jamaica." Montagu said.

Marty returned the greeting in kind. "Thank you, Manchester, so kind of you to invite us to stay."

Caroline decided there and then she was having none of that. "Tush, we can be less formal than that, I am Caroline, and he is Martin."

"Then I am Susan, and my husband is William," Lady Manchester replied. "Your servants can have rooms in the servants' quarters."

Marty corrected that immediately, "Sam and Chin are members of my crew and part of my security contingent."

"How... do they need to be roomed near you?" Susan said.

"No, they will be happy enough in the servants' quarters."

"I've heard of your exploits last time you were here and read the previous governor's reports. It sounds like you are up to your old tricks, what?" William said as he led them into the house.

"Not at all," Marty replied, "this assignment was a reward for my work with Wellington on the peninsula. I am here to govern Aruba and help sort out the privateer threat."

"We need to talk about that later, but for now why don't you and Caroline get settled and changed for dinner."

Marty luxuriated in a hot bath scrubbing himself thoroughly. Somehow salt got into every pore even if you weren't on deck all the time. Shipboard sponge baths got rid of some of it but couldn't match a proper bath. Caroline had bathed first and was busy working her hair into a Grecian style that flowed over one shoulder.

Marty sighed and put out the cheroot he was smoking, a habit he had picked up in Portugal. He only had one after dinner normally, but the bath was so relaxing a cheroot seemed to make sense.

"Time to get ready, love, they will be expecting us in half an hour," Caroline chided.

"Oh, all right, it's getting cool anyway," Marty said as he stood. He caught a sight of himself in a long mirror. He looked fit and his face and arms were tanned in contrast to his white body. Scars crossed his body, evidence of his fighting lifestyle. The most recent on his thigh, pink and puckered from the water.

His clothes were laid out on the bed, a formal suit in the latest fashion, silk shirt, cravat and stockings. The jacket was already adorned with his honours.

"Is this a formal dinner?"

"Susan said that it would be attended by a number of local worthies."

"How many?"

"Around thirty."

Marty groaned.

They entered the reception room to find most of the guests already there, William and Susan met them at the door and introduced them to everyone.

"I'll never remember all these names," Marty murmured to Caroline.

"Then don't try to use them," Caroline said through a smile without moving her lips.

"My Lord Purbeck," a worthy bowed as William introduced him. He was a prominent plantation owner named Carboy and Marty realised he would have no problem as the man was the same shape as the vessel. "I understand you are here to help with the privateer threat from America."

"Yes, my squadron will patrol the Windward Islands and the Lesser Antilles."

"Then who is covering Jamaica and the Caymans? Cochrane has the fleet attacking the American mainland and patrolling the passage between Cuba and the mainland. But there are no warships here."

"We will discuss that after dinner Stanley let the commodore enjoy his dinner first," William said.

Carboy huffed but stood back to allow the conversation to move to more general things.

Dinner was seven courses with seven different wines and at the end the women retired to the drawing room and the men to the games room. Marty found himself sat with William, Stanley Carboy and two other planters.

"Now tell me what the privateers have been doing in this area." Marty said as he lit a cheroot and sipped a brandy.

"I have lost two ships!" barked Carboy who was rather red in the face from the food and an excess of wine. The others immediately chipped in with inventories of their losses.

Marty let them finish and then said, "Can you tell me where the ships were attacked and by who or what type of ship?"

"The first was taken West of the Caymans and the second North of Haiti. We changed the route after we lost the first. The Americans let the men go in small boats and they made their way to British territory. But all accounts the ship that took them was a schooner named the Silverthorn." Carboy said.

"What were the cargos?" Marty said.

"Coffee, sugar and hardwoods in the first; coffee, sugar and cacao with some cotton in the second."

"I have lost one shipment, a full cargo of sugar taken near the Turks," Spencer, the second owner, said. "They never told me the name, but it was a schooner.

"And you?" Marty asked Bevers, the third man.

"I had a cargo of sugar, coral and hardwoods taken from here and an incoming cargo of leather, furniture, cloth and wine taken near the Caymans. The captains told me that the privateers were American, one was in a clipper and the other a large schooner with three masts."

"Were the ships yours or hired?"

"Independent captains all of them."

"Has anyone else lost ships?

"Wilkinson and Greenwood have lost cargos."

Marty thought for a moment.

"Have you tried convoying?"

"No point without an escort," Carboy said to grunts of agreement from the others.

In bed that night Marty lay looking at the ceiling, Caroline rolled over and asked, "What's on your mind?"

"All the planters lost ships with high value cargos in a six-month period, either near the Caymans or through the Haiti passage. The one that concerns me is Carboy's as he changed routes after getting hit the first time, but they still found his ship."

"You're thinking that someone is on the inside?"

"Or in a position to find out what cargos are worth taking."

"Wasn't one bound here from England?"

"Yes, but that's the exception."

"Sounds to me like you need to do some snooping here on the island."

"Snooping? That makes it sound sordid. I much prefer investigating."

"Snooping or investigating, either way you need to find the connection if there is one."

Marty lay thinking for a long while before he fell asleep.

The next morning Marty decided to talk to each of the plantation owners individually. They were all still in town either at the residence or in hotels. Carboy was at the residence so after breakfast he took him for a walk in the gardens.

"How do you arrange your shipments?" Marty said.

"That's done by our shipping agent, Reginald Mallory. He has an office in Kingston."

"Does he appoint the captains?"

"They bid for the cargos in a blind auction. Each captain submits his bid on paper and the best is selected."

"Is Mallory the only one who sees the bids?"

"Yes. Now here, are you accusing him of something?"

"Not at all, just trying to get a picture of the process. Is there anyone else involved with the ships before they leave?"

"Well, there is the harbourmaster who oversees the loading at the docks. But he has been in his position for years."

"And both of the ships were out of Kingston?"

"Yes, they were."

Marty's next stop was the Spanish Maiden, an up-market inn in Kingston to meet with Spencer and Bevers over lunch. He asked the same questions; Bevers used Mallory as his agent but Spencer used an agent called Trowbridge in Montego Bay. His ships were also loaded and sailed from there.

His next visit was to Mallory's office. He walked in with Sam and Chin at his back.

"Can I help you?" said the bookish looking man sat behind a clerk's desk.

Marty passed over a visiting card,

"Commodore, Viscount Purbeck. I wish to talk to Mr Mallory."

The clerk looked at him, then at the card, then back at him before standing and giving a quick bow. "I will announce you, Sir." He disappeared through a door that led to the rear of the building. He reappeared followed by a plainly dressed man with grey thinning hair and sallow complexion.

"My Lord Purbeck, Reginald Mallory at your service."

"Mr Mallory I am tasked with investigating and preventing the privateer attacks on shipping from the British possessions in the Caribbean. I am told you are the main shipping agent for Kingston is that correct?"

"Aye, that's the truth, there be two others, but I am the one that's suffered most losses."

"Can we talk in private?"

"Surely, please come through to my office."

Marty indicated to Sam and Chin to wait for him and followed Mallory through the door into a comfortable-looking office with several cabinets for storing files, a large mahogany desk and a pair of club chairs either side of a low table. The single window was dusty and illuminated the room with a faint light. Marty took one of the club chairs.

"Can I offer you some refreshment?" Mallory said before he sat.

"No thank you, I won't take much of your time."

Mallory sat, more on the edge of his seat than in it,

"How can I help you?"

"Both Carboy and Bevers' shipments that were lost were handled by you, correct?"

"That is true, I handle all their shipments."

"Can you tell me how the auction is run to select who gets the cargo?"

"We only run the auctions when we have a single owner with a full cargo. This ensures they get the best deal."

"Is it a case of lowest bid wins?"

"Essentially yes but the age and state of the ship is also taken into account. We will not accept bids from captains whose ships don't meet our minimum standard."

"Who decides that?"

"Babbage, the harbourmaster, has a surveyor who periodically checks ships for us who are on the list."

"Can you show me the list?"

"Certainly." Mallory went to a cabinet and returned with a file.

"Here you are,"

Marty took the proffered papers and scanned them. "I see there are three ships crossed out, are they the ones that were taken?"

"Yes, they are."

"Was there anything unusual about the cargos?"

Mallory got up again and returned with three files after rummaging in a cabinet.

"These are the manifests of the ships and the records of the auctions."

Each file was clearly labelled with the shipper's name, the name of the ship and its captain. Inside was a detailed manifest with the cargo itemised. Marty scanned each one in turn and then laid all three side by side on the table.

"All three have an item marked as 'sundries' what would that be?"

"That would be personal items that they want shipping back to Britain, gold maybe or cash to be banked or it could be something they are shipping for a friend."

Marty nodded and moved to the lists of bidders. There didn't seem to be anything unusual. Some names appeared in all three and he checked a random selection against the master list of approved ships.

Then he read the copies of the shipping contracts all three had a section with special instructions from the shipper to the captain.

"Who else has access to this information besides yourself?" Marty said.

"Just my clerk, Jennings, you met him in the front office."

"Can you deliver copies of these files and the list to the governor's residence please."

Mallory looked surprised but agreed to have them there by the next morning.

After they left Sam said, "That clerk fella was awful keen to hear what you was talking about to his boss. He kept going to the cupboard by the door to search for papers, but I could tell he be listening."

"Was he now," Marty said.

Marty sent Chin to assemble the Shadows and they rendezvoused on the dock.

"Antton, I want you and Matai to put Mallory's clerk under watch, I want to know where he lives and how, who he meets and anything else you might think is of interest. John and Wilson, you do the same with Mallory. "

Orders given he set off with Chin and Sam to see the harbourmaster.

Mr Babbage was an old salt. A former captain who had retired from the royal navy some eight years previously.

"I was captain of the Arundel, a thirty-four. Retired when she was condemned. I was fifty then and had enough of the sea as I had joined when I was ten years old. No real prospect of promotion and in any case I didn't want a ship of the line."

"Why here?" Marty said.

"Arthritis, the cold makes my joints ache. Are you here to stop the privateers?"

"Yes, I'm looking into the last few to try and get an idea where to deploy my squadron."

"Rum do that, the damn yanks took the three most valuable cargos to be leaving at that time."

Marty's right eyebrow rose at that. "Really? What made them the most valuable? The manifests don't stand out as unusual."

Babbage tapped his nose and winked. "It's not what's on the manifest but what's not on it if you get my meaning."

"They were smuggling?"

"Not smuggling as such but there are some things you don't want known that you are moving back home."

Marty didn't know what else to call that other than smuggling but he let it go. There were obviously accepted exceptions to the term in Jamaica.

"Small things that can be easily concealed?"

"That sort of thing."

"Who would know about that besides you?"

"The agent, the captain and the shipper."

"How do you know?"

"Because I keep my eyes open. Small boats moving around at night, men being furtive and carrying chests. All tells a story."

Marty shook his hand and thanked him. Babbage looked at him suddenly, "I know where I've seen you before. You were the captain of the Tempest; you brought those Spanish treasure ships in back in '05."

"You have me there, yes that was me."

"Were you at Trafalgar? You left with Nelson."

"No, I was sent off to do something else at the time, but I did have the pleasure to know Nelson."

Babbage nodded, that was good enough. Anyone who knew Nelson was alright in his book.

Babbage may have been ex-navy, but Marty had Chin follow him all the same. He wasn't ready to trust anybody yet. He and Sam headed back to the residence where he had to rush to dress for dinner.

"What were you up to all afternoon?" Caroline said as he pulled on his silk stockings.

"Investigating the privateer activities. Turns out all the ships from here were carrying unlisted riches which explains why our plantation owners were so upset by their loss, it was uninsured. What I need to find out is if the ship from Montego Bay was carrying the same."

"I can ask Spencer's wife if you like."

"No, that would be too obvious, if they wanted me to know they would have mentioned it."

"You think that someone told the privateers?"

"I have my suspicions, but we need more information before I can make any conclusions."

Dinner was a smaller affair than the night before but no less sumptuous. Seven courses later Marty was wondering whether he should have his trousers let out. He sat with William. "I have to take a trip up to Montego Bay. What is the quickest way, by ship or carriage?"

"Well, it depends. If you go by ship, then it takes a while to get back as you will be sailing against the current. Its slower by carriage but if you can ride you can do it by horse in a couple of days. Will Caroline be going with you?"

"No, she wants to look in on her family plantation, it's near a place called Enfield."

"The Den. I looked it up in the records. Was founded in the late 1600s by the Conways. Cacao growers."

"Makes sense her maiden name was Conway. Strange name that, The Den. Where can I get two good horses, one big enough to carry Sam?"

"I can lend you a couple, I have one that is a Cob that can carry that big black of yours."

Marty bit his tongue, starting an argument over that comment wouldn't help his cause at the moment.

They set out at dawn, it was strange not having Troy following them but he was better off with the children. Not much would get past him and he would just suffer in the heat trying to keep up with the horses. William had given them a map and told them the best route. The horses were fit and they made good time passing through small villages and past plantations. Marty was annoyed that there were still slaves working the fields. Some waved to Sam who waved back. Marty asked, "Does it bother you that there are still slaves?"

"Yes, but it won't last forever. The movement will free my brothers."

Marty knew he meant the anti-slavery movement. Sam had paid a lot of attention to what was going on when they were in England and had asked Marty to explain the politics.

They stopped for the night at St Anne's Bay. The owner of the inn didn't want a black sleeping inside, but Marty persuaded him of the error of his ways. He was out of patience with intolerance and the prospect of a real-life viscount sleeping in the hayloft soon changed the innkeeper's mind.

They left early and were in Montego Bay as the sun was going down. Marty found an inn that was a comfortable and would allow his 'servant' to stay in his room.

They asked the serving girl where they could find Trowbridge, the agent, while they ate that evening.

"He has a house on St James Street, you will probably find him there. You can't miss it."

"Why, is it remarkable in some way?"

"It's the biggest house on the street, more of a mansion really."

Marty wondered at that, Mallory in Kingston, which was a much busier port, was comfortably off but not wealthy. Maybe Trowbridge had fingers in other pies. They would find out in the morning.

They walked from the inn and the Trowbridge residence was as impressive as the serving girl had said, Palladian in style with a pillared porch with steps up to the front door. Marty pulled a bell pull and was rewarded by the sound of ringing somewhere inside. A house slave opened the door.

"Yes?"

Marty handed her a card and asked to see Trowbridge. She grunted and shut the door in his face.

"Delightful," he said.

"I don't think she know what a viscount is," Sam grinned.

Ten minutes passed and then the door was opened by a male slave dressed in a black suit.

"The master will see you now," he said then looked at Sam. "You kin wait out here, boy."

"It's alright, boss, I will be right here if you need me." Sam grinned before Marty could say anything.

"Your boy will get himsel' shot if he seen carrying those weapons," the servant said.

"What's your name?" Marty asked.

"Joshua, master,"

"Well Joshua, Sam is a free man and if anybody tries to shoot him, they will find he isn't an easy target."

That sparked a mumbling which Marty only picked up the odd word of but seemed to be about the stupidity of blacks being free and carrying guns. This made Marty wonder about a slave who was happier being a slave than free.

He was led into a well-stocked library that had a small fortune in books in it. It smelt of leather, paper and dust. He was perusing the books when a section of shelf swung open, and a man stepped through. He was tall, taller than Marty by several inches, broad shouldered and obviously well-muscled. He was dressed in a very well-cut jacket over a linen shirt that was open at the collar. He had blond hair, pale blue eyes and tanned skin.

"Viscount Purbeck?"

"Yes, or more commonly Commodore Martin Stockley."

"Commodore, you are a navy man then."

"Yes, and Governor of Aruba."

"What do you want with me?"

"I am responsible for countering the threat of the American privateers and I am told you act as agent for one of the plantation owners that lost a cargo."

"I still don't see what that has to do with me. All I do is find him a ship and arrange for it to carry his cargo."

The door opened and a very attractive blonde woman with startling blue eyes walked in, she looked surprised that they had a guest.

"Commodore Stockley may I introduce my wife Annabel. Annabel the commodore is here to sort out the privateer problem."

That was a bit pointed, Marty thought but plastered a smile on his face and bowed to her.

"The commodore is a viscount in disguise and also Governor of Aruba."

Her eyebrows raised at that and she looked at her husband as if he was teasing her,

"A viscount, I've never met one of those before," she said with a marked Georgian accent.

"An accident of marriage," Marty said, then turned back to Trowbridge. "Can you tell me what the cargo was that was taken?"

"Let me see now," he thought for a moment, "I believe it was just sugar. Spencer would know, his plantation is above the town."

"That was all? Nothing else?"

"Not that I know of. Why do you suspect something?"

"Not really it just seems strange that the privateers would go after a cargo of sugar," Marty said thoughtfully.

"Why? It has value and they would make money from the hull."

"And they wouldn't know what the cargo was before they attacked." Annabel chipped in.

Marty looked around the library,

"You have a magnificent library."

"I must thank my wife for it," he gazed at her lovingly, "and the house."

Marty looked at her with raised eyebrows his head to one side.

"I inherited my father's fortune, Papa was a successful ship owner and when he died, he left me the business. I had no interest in running it so sold it off. Then I met Sebastian, we married and moved here."

"My wife was titled when I met her and rich. She was the best thing that happened to me as well," Marty said.

That seemed to reassure them. At worst they would think he got his position and money through marriage. Whatever, he didn't want them to see him as a viable threat.

"Well, that's all I wanted to ask you." He bowed and turned to leave then stopped. "Oh, I nearly forgot, how do you select the ships you give the cargos to?"

"I ask Mallory in Kingston to find a willing owner, we don't get the number of ships they do in Kingston here, so we have often have to get them sent over. Spencer's ship was found that way."

Marty and Sam rode up to the Spencer plantation, Adelphi. The plantation house was large, and the plantation spread across several hundred acres, planted to sugarcane. Slaves worked the fields overseen by mounted men.

They were met by a groom who took their horses and Spencer met them at the door. As usual Sam wasn't welcome in the house so Marty suggested they talk on the porch that had a couple of chairs and a table.

"There's been a plantation here for at least a couple of hundred years you know," Spencer said obviously proud of it. "Was called, Dartmoor, then Browning after the owners. It was sold off in the mid 1700s and I bought it twenty years ago."

"My wife's family had a plantation here in the 1600s. I wonder if it was theirs?" Marty pondered.

"Might have been, but you didn't ride across the island to ask me about that."

"True. I talked to Trowbridge, he told me he thought the ship was only carrying sugar. Is that true? I ask because I know that often the captains will carry a private shipment for the shipper that doesn't get declared in Britain."

Spencer bristled and Marty quickly said, "I have no interest at all in what you send back to Britain or whether it gets declared or not, we have all done that at one time or another. I am just trying to see if there is a connection between the ships that were lost."

That mollified Spencer somewhat and he said, "There was a chest of gold that was the profits from the last year."

"I see and who knew that it was on board besides the captain?"

"Mallory, it was put onboard at Kingston."

"Why there and not here?"

"Because I don't trust that American strumpet that Trowbridge calls his wife."

"You think she has a connection to the losses?"

"She comes from a sailing family and has connections back in America. That's enough for me to be careful."

"How do you let Mallory know that there is something extra to put aboard?"

"I send him a note telling him to warn the captain that there will be a special cargo that will be delivered in Kingston. The captains know what that means."

"I suppose you tell the captain who to deliver it to when you take it onboard?"

"Yes."

"You think Mallory is telling the Americans which ships to attack?" Caroline said as she watched Marty poring over the papers that Mallory had delivered.

"The list of suspects is short, and he is on it. But I'm not sure yet."

"Who else do you suspect?"

"The lovely Annabel, Trowbridge, Babbage."

"Lovely Annabel?"

"Yes, she is, a Southern belle." Marty suddenly realised the temperature in the room had dropped a degree or two. He looked up to see that Caroline had a hard look on her face and her fingers were drumming on her wrist.

"An observation that's all, put your talons away." He turned back to the diagram he had drawn. It was a spiderweb of lines and names.

"In any case the logic is pointing to Mallory, or," he suddenly smiled, "his office."

"Sam, can you find Antton or Mattai and ask one of them to report to me as soon as possible please."

Chapter 10: Silverthorn

The squadron sailed out of Kingston past Port Royal and fired a salute to the port admiral. It made a heading of Southeast and maintained it as they dropped over the horizon.

"Wear ship please, Wolfgang, set us on a course to go around the South of Jamaica to the Caymans. Signal the Eagle that they may depart."

The Eagle acknowledged the signal and sped away North by Northwest.

The two men watched as Caroline strolled the main deck a parasol held above her head as if she was the passenger on an Indiaman.

"Do you think they will take the bait?"

"Caroline had the estate manager at The Den commission Mallory to find him a ship for a load of cacao and a private shipment of bullion that they want returned to Britain. If the informant has done his job, we will find out if the ship is attacked."

"The captain is a brave man."

"Made braver with Goodman, thirty men and your gunner onboard."

The Devonian was more crowded than usual below decks as the extra men had to be kept hidden until they were out of sight of the land. The captain, Alistair Deptford, was a tough West countryman who had been at sea since he was six years old. When the commodore had approached him, he had jumped at the chance to hit back at the privateers. The extra men were a bonus and could buy them the time needed for the trap to be sprung.

"You can come up now," he called down the hatch to where Goodman was hiding.

The soldier, he was quite emphatic about not being a marine, came up with a look of relief on his face. Alistair clapped him on the shoulder as he gulped big breaths of fresh air,

"She do move more than one of them navy frigates."

"And smells worse as well!"

Goodman's colour slowly returned as his queasiness subsided.

"Sergeant," he called down, "get the men on deck and sort the swivels out."

"My carpenter will help them fit the mounts to the rails," Alistair said.

The marines brought up crates which contained the mounts for twelve swivels a side. These were to be mounted along the rail on both sides of the ship. The misshapen gunner who looked like a hunch-backed gorilla and his mate was already at work on his six six-pound cannon. The man was prodigiously strong and needed no help lifting the barrels off the carriage to be cleaned and made battle ready.

"Wouldn't want to meet him in a fight," Alistair said.

"Believe me, you wouldn't want to, he is a demon with a pair of boarding axes."

The carpenter and marines soon had the mounts fitted and the guns mounted. The marines practised firing the guns in a dumb show where they would fire, quickly replace the gun with a loaded one and fire again while their support man loaded the first swivel ready to be fired again. Alistair estimated they would get at least three rounds off before any privateer could get men over the side. The commodore had provided two barrels of grape shot for his guns as well. His ship had turned into a giant shot gun.

"Sail astern," the lookout shouted.

"That should be the Eagle," Goodman said, "we will know if it ducks back out of sight."

"She is a Baltimore clipper, isn't she?" Alistair said.

"I don't know one ship from another. Sergeant! What type of ship is the Eagle?"

"Baltimore Clipper, Sah!"

"How come you have one of those in a British squadron?"

"Captured in the Bay of Biscay, Sah."

"Useful as a fast scout, what is her armament?"

"Sixteen thirty-six-pound carronades, Sah."

"Good grief, that's some punch. Are all your ships over gunned?"

"Wouldn't say that, Sah. Sufficient for the job I would say."

"The frigates have two enormous guns mounted forward on pivots that can fire either side or forward. The commodore is a man who likes the odds stacked on his side methinks," Goodman said thoughtfully.

The squadron made good time and spread out in an arc with the frigates in the centre, the Nymphe to the North and Endellion to their South. They were West of the Cayman Islands positioned so they lay across the course the Devonian should be taking. Marty expected the American to attack just West of Grand Cayman. The Eagle would rush to the assistance of the Devonian and drive the privateer towards the net. Well, that was the plan anyway.

The Devonian came up on Grand Cayman in the early morning. She looked to be cruising along at a steady pace, maybe slightly slower than normal.

"Skipper! There be smoke comin' up from that there hill over to larboard.'

"A signal?" Goodman asked. He was dressed in civilian clothes and stood near to Alistair who was at the wheel.

"Could be, we will find out directly."

Wolverton scrambled up the ratlines and looked at the column of thick smoke rising.

"It isn't a normal campfire, get your men ready!" he shouted at Goodman who wondered at his educated voice.

"Sergeant, ready the men!"

They slipped by Old Man Bay, then they were coming up on Rum Point. Alistair checked their stern; he could just see the Eagle's topsails from the deck. At least he hoped it was the Eagle. He expected the American to be hiding behind Rum Point and would behave just as he had been told by the commodore.

"Schooner coming around Rum Point, Skipper!" yelled the lookout.

"Set the mainsails and courses!"

They looked as if they had been spooked by the unexpected sight of the schooner and were trying to make a run for it only their sail handling was bad, and they were botching the job. Sails flapped before they were tightened and drew then a halyard would be let go and the sail would flap again.

Alistair could clearly see the Eagle now, he looked forward and then spun to look astern again. The ship was flying an American flag!

"What the hell?"

"Don't worry, old boy, Lord Martin told me to expect that."

"Then why the fuck didn't he tell me! That almost gave me a heart attack."

"A ruse de guerre, they don't want to spook our American friends too early."

"Schooner is closing,"

"He's fast, are your men ready?"

"Ready and eager."

A shot rang out and a ball splashed down thirty feet ahead of their bow.

"Wait for it!" Sergeant Strong shouted to the gunners and marines who lay hidden on the deck.

The schooner approached, the American flag flying bravely from her stern. Alistair's men made a very good show of running around as if in panic.

Another shot punched a hole in their mainsail.

"Let go the sails!"

They slowed and the schooner came up alongside her deck full of men. Grapnels flew and as soon as they bit Goodman shouted.

"NOW MEN!"

Guns suddenly ran out and marines appeared at the sides and mounted pre-loaded swivels.

"FIRE!"

A sheet of grape scythed across the schooner's deck and as soon as they had fired the marines were swapping their swivels for loaded ones and firing again.

A shot echoed from astern, and they could see the Eagle just a mile away under full sail, with the Union flag flying, approaching fast. The skipper of the schooner had seen her and was yelling orders to his men to get him them out of the trap.

The ropes holding the two ships were cut with axes and the schooner's sails filled as she broke away. She had been stung but not disabled in any way.

"Now that is a sight," Goodman said as he reloaded his pistols.

The Silverthorn, he could see her name as they bore away downwind, had set all her sails and was fairly racing away. The Eagle was gaining at the moment, but it was a stern chase, and the two ships were fairly evenly matched.

Trevor Archer would have killed for a pair of fore chasers right at that moment. They could see the two ships come together a couple of miles ahead.

"Get that bloody gun shifted!" he cajoled his men as they moved the foremost carronade from the side to point forward. The carpenter was busy sawing a new port, taking little care to keep the cuts straight or square in his haste.

A carronade was not the ideal bow gun. It wasn't very accurate above a couple of cables, but it did have the advantage of throwing a bloody big ball so if it did score a hit it would do a lot of damage. Twenty minutes later after frantic sawing, hammering and straining, he had a gun that he could shoot at the enemy.

One might ask why he hadn't fitted bow chasers before. The reason was simple the Eagle was built for speed and was mainly used as a scout when in the company of the big ships. If they did get into a fight, they would use their agility to get up beside their quarry and serve them with their smashers.

They got to around half a mile before the Silverthorn got up to speed then the rate of closure dropped to mere yards per hour.

"Eight hundred yards is a long shot but keep firing so the rest of the squadron can home in on the sound," he ordered.

The gun fired every minute and a half and they could see the balls fly through the air only to splash down either side of the Silverthorn. However, it was keeping the privateer's attention on their pursuer not on the sea ahead.

"Endellion approaching off the port bow," the lookout shouted down.

"That means the frigates won't be far ahead. Get up that mast with a glass and tell me what you see," Archer said to Midshipman Gerald Sykes.

Sykes skipped up the mast as only a fourteen-year-old boy who did it every day could, with an apparent total disregard for his own safety. He got to the masthead barely out of breath and brought the telescope to his eye after adjusting the focus ring to his mark.

He scanned the horizon from beam to beam then reported.

"Deck there! Endellion about a mile ahead and to port closing fast, the Nymphe is a mile and a half ahead and to starboard also closing fast. The frigates are three miles ahead about half a mile apart and converging on us."

"Come down, tell the lookout to keep his eyes open."

Sykes was halfway down the stay when a cheer went up from the bow. They had scored a hit and he had missed it!

They had actually scored more of a glancing blow as the ball had hit the corner of the stern on the port quarter. It had stove in some timbers but that was about all and didn't impede their progress at all. Fozzard, the schooner's skipper, had realised he had enemies closing in on all sides and knew he had to do something radical.

"We could try and split those frigates," his first mate Robert Ryefield said.

"No, they have staggered so they can hit us without fear of hitting each other, their commander knows what he is doing," Captain Fozzard said. He quickly evaluated the ships closing in on him.

"Steer us directly for that Corvette to Starboard. Make sure the sail handlers keep on the ball, I don't want us to lose any speed."

Marty watched their prey change course,

"What's he up to?" he said.

"I think he means to go head-to-head with the Nymphe," Wolfgang replied.

Marty looked around, the Leonidas was two ships' lengths behind and two cables to port, the Eagle was a half mile or so behind the schooner which was two miles ahead of them, which wasn't much, given the closing speed of around twenty-six to twenty-eight knots.

The Endellion was to the South and coming up fast and the Nymphe was to the North.

"You have to admire their sail handling he hardly gave up anything in that turn," Wolfgang said.

"Signal the Leonidas to close with the enemy," Marty ordered.

The signal was given and acknowledged. The Leonidas turned towards the North. Marty kept the Unicorn on her previous course in case his adversary tried to run South.

It was a game of chess; he and the schooner's skipper were manoeuvring to gain position. He to checkmate him, the schooner to escape. Now he had given him a choice, try to pass the Nymphe or Leonidas. Marty had planned the whole thing to limit the privateer's options and close down his sea room.

The Leonidas closed the range and would soon be able to bring his bow chasers to bear. The Nymphe had none but was ready to fire either of her main batteries as needed.

On the Silverthorn it was strangely quiet. Fozzard was hanging from the mizzen ratlines so he could see both the corvette and the frigate. He had seen that the frigate had bow chasers and the corvette had none.

"Ease her a point to starboard."

His helmsman trusted his skipper with his life and obeyed without question even if he didn't understand why. Another ball from the clipper behind them splashed down to their starboard side.

They were only a quarter mile from the corvette and the range was closing fast.

"Starboard guns ready, fire as you bear. Ready to wear to port!"

The range was a scant cable and closing very fast.

"Wear to port, steer South by Southeast!"

The nimble schooner swung to port right across the bow of the Nymphe. It was a manoeuvre right out of Marty's book of tactics.

Marty realised what the schooner was going to do a moment before he did it. It was audacious and caught Andrew Stamp completely by surprise. His helmsman instinctively swung the wheel to port to avoid a collision and sent the Nymphe into irons as they were sailing as close to the wind as they could already.

As soon as they cleared the Nymphe, the privateer swung back to due West which should just keep him out of the Leonidas's reach. None of the guns on the Nymphe scored a hit although they tried.

"That was a damn fine piece of sailing! He sacrificed almost a quarter mile to the Eagle to get past the Nymphe and behind us." Marty could only admire the professional skill of the captain and crew.

"Wear ship we can only try and chase him down now."

But he knew that if they didn't stop him by nightfall, they would lose him as tonight there was no moon.

The next morning proved him right; there wasn't a sign of the schooner anywhere. The Eagle was missing as well so they reduced sail and slowly started back to Jamaica.

The Eagle reappeared the next day. Marty hove to and requested Archer to come aboard.

"We stayed with him until full dark, but with the cloud cover an' no moon it was as black as pitch out there and we lost contact. My guess is that he headed towards Juventud Island or one of the smaller islands to the East of it. Wherever he is, he is well hidden as we searched for him and could find no sign," Trevor Archer reported.

"You did what you could," Marty said then turned to Philip Trenchard. "I want you to take a cruise up along the coast of Cuba. Look into every nook and cranny for evidence that it is being used as a base for privateers." Archer looked to protest. "The Eagle is needed to support the teams in Colombia and Venezuela. Get back to your ships, we are heading back to Jamaica. We have a clerk to question."

The squadron, less the Endellion, made its way back to Jamaica, picking up their men from the Devonian on the way. It was a thankless voyage against the wind and current and when they dropped anchor, they were thankful it was over. Marty gave the Eagle time to replenish and sent her off to check on the teams on the mainland. In the meantime, he had the Shadows fetch him a certain clerk who he wanted to have a long chat with.

"Search his house, thoroughly," he told John Smith and Wilson.

Jennings was brought onboard hooded with his hands tied behind him. He was dumped unceremoniously onto a hard wooden chair.

"Who are you? What do you want with me?"

Marty had Wolfgang, whose voice Jennings didn't know, ask the questions.

"We hear you've been a bad boy," he said. "That tip you gave our friends was a trap. The Silverthorn was nearly taken."

"What? How?"

"The navy put a load of marines with swivel guns onboard the Devonian. The captain isn't pleased he lost a lot of good men. He wants me to make you pay."

"What?" Jennings squeaked.

"Put his hand on the block."

Antton untied his hands, forced his left arm out and rested it on a wooden block while Matai held him down in the chair.

"This won't hurt much, the axe is nice and sharp and you can still write with your right hand," Wolfgang growled, and rested a blade against his wrist.

"Stop! Stop! Let me talk to Fozzard take me to Siguanea and I can explain everything."

Marty, who was sat with Mallory in his club chairs, nodded to Wolfgang.

"What are you going to tell him that's going to keep you your hand?"

"I've got information on the commodore who's in charge of the new squadron."

"Oh, yes?"

"I will tell Fozzard, only Fozzard."

"You have enough to hang him," Mallory said.

"Yes, but he is an asset we can use. Let's save him in case we need him and hang him later."

Marty stood and pulled off the hood.

"Now what is it you were going to tell Fozzard about me?"

"Siguanea is tucked away at the bottom of this inlet on the island of Juventud. It has a mangrove swamp which conceals a further inlet where they hide the Silverthorn." Marty said to the collected captains.

"How do we know that?" James asked.

"We persuaded their informant to tell us everything he knows," Wolfgang said with an evil grin. "He couldn't explain the cache of doubloons he had hidden in his house."

"Now we don't need the whole squadron to dig them out of there so we will divide it in two. The Unicorn with the Nymphe will go after the Silverthorn and the Leonidas and Endellion, when it returns, will proceed to Haiti and San Domingo and start a search of the South coast ports and bays for French or American ships that could be privateers."

When will Philip get back?" James said.

"Any day now," Marty said. "When you have finished report back here, you have three weeks."

"And if we find any?"

"Burn, sink or take them."

They wasted no time in getting the Unicorn and Nymphe back to sea. Marty had just enough time to report to the governor and leave a letter for Caroline as she was up country visiting The Den. He told her that he suspected that Spencer's plantation was originally one of her family's.

The Unicorn had a full complement of marines and soldiers as did the Nymphe. Marty wanted to at least be able to match the Silverthorn for men. Goodman was in charge and gnashing at the bit to have another crack at the Americans. He was drilling the men relentlessly.

They slipped through the channel just to the West of the Bay of Pigs to take them to the North of Juventud Island at dusk and crept along the reef to the island itself. They had to feel their way under minimum sail, maintaining just enough headway to be able to steer as they let the current push them along.

The island was shaped like a tadpole with its tail curled to the North. The space between the tail and the body formed the inlet where they thought the Silverthorn was hidden.

They followed the coast as it turned South and as the sun rose, they were positioned to block the smaller bay surrounded by mangroves. There were two channels leading to the West where the Silverthorn could be hiding.

"If the Silverthorn is in there, she cannot get out while we are parked here. However, we can't get in there to dig them out with our ships as we draw too much water. The survey boat we sent in sounded the depth and it's too shallow for even the Nymphe to go up there." He looked at Goodman and Beaumont. "You will lead the marine part of a joint cutting out force under the command of Lieutenant Hart up the inlet and take the schooner."

"How do we know which inlet to take?"

Marty grinned, "That's where the Shadows and me come in."

There were two canoes stowed on the Unicorn that were left over from their activities in the Mediterranean. Marty and the Shadows dressed in dark inconspicuous clothes and armed to the teeth rowed them into the bay and towards the inlets. They took one each.

Marty had the Northern inlet which, not far in, suddenly swung to the South and the next thing they saw was the other canoe coming towards them.

"It's a bloody island," Wilson said, a hint of disgust in his voice.

"There are two more channels heading East, both big enough to get a schooner up," Marty said and waved to the other canoe to proceed up the Southerly one.

The channel turned out to be a river with a chain of islands running down the middle and more islands along the Northern side all covered in trees. They paddled against the current staying to the centre of the channel. The first island was about three hundred yards long, as was the second, they had gotten a hundred yards along the third which seemed to go on for a lot further when a bird call sounded from behind them.

Wilson looked back. "It's the other canoe, Sir, they are waving."

Marty stopped paddling and let the sluggish current carry them back towards them.

"The schooner is moored up against the far bank in a bay on the South side. There are a number of rough buildings on shore," Antton said.

"How close did you get?" Marty said.

"Not very, we couldn't see any lookouts but didn't want to chance being spotted."

"Is the ground cover the same as on these islands?"

"Same everywhere, rainforest and swamp."

Marty looked up at the sun. "About three hours to sunset, we will circle around this island and find a landing spot to the West of the encampment. Then we get to do a ground reconnaissance at night."

The terrain was everything they expected, muddy, covered in scrub and thorns an inch long. The trees were a mixture of hardwoods, magnolias, walnut and palms. They made their way through without chopping a path so not to make any noise.

After an hour or so they smelt cooking and dropped to their bellies to crawl forward. Wilson stifled a curse as he slipped into a mud hole, the rest edged their way around it. Thorns caught in their clothes and scratched their skin.

Marty stopped as they came to the clearing, they could see men moving around in the firelight and hear the laughter of at least one woman.

"A proper home from home," John said.

Marty replied, "Spread out and estimate how many are on shore, what the buildings are used for and where any guards are. Avoid contact and be back here in thirty minutes."

That was all the instruction they needed, and they melted into the dark in pairs. Marty and Wilson were together and took the direct route in.

They slunk forward in a crouch to the nearest building. Marty eased along the wall in the shadows to an open window and listened. The sound of snoring drifted out and he slowly raised his head until he could see inside. It was a bedroom, three beds all occupied by men. He looked around the room; weapons were piled in a corner. Suddenly one of the men gave forth a thunderous fart that would have done a foghorn justice. Marty ducked. "Jesus, Kinley what the hell did you eat!" a man cursed and threw something.

Marty rolled his eyes at Wilson and they moved on to the next window. From that one came the sound of rhythmic movement and a woman moaning.

"Get a move on, Pete," a man said, "leave some for the rest of us."

Wilson raised his eyebrows and made an obscene gesture. Marty grinned and nodded before leading the way to the next building which was open sided. It was a cookhouse, covered pots stood atop a cold stove and when he looked inside saw one contained porridge and in others dough left to rise overnight. *Breakfast,* he thought and dug into the body belt he had tied around his waist under his shirt. He found the small glass bottle he was looking for that had a rough texture and carefully drew the cork. He sniffed it to make sure it was what he wanted then emptied it into the pots.

He gestured to Wilson and they retreated back the way they had come. They were the first back and, when the rest arrived, led them into the trees thirty yards before stopping and debriefed them.

"Wilson and John, go back to the boats and take one back to the Unicorn. I want the cutting out party to follow the route we took up the river to circle the big island to come at the schooner from the East. They are to time the attack for ten o'clock tomorrow morning. The rest of us will stay here and prepare a little diversion."

After the two men left, Marty told Sam, Antton, Matai and Chin to get some sleep. He would take first watch.

An hour before dawn they were all up and moving. They circled the camp to a building Matai had identified as an armoury and broke in. Inside were muskets and barrels containing shot, swords and pistols. Marty searched and found what he was looking for, a coil of fuse and a cask of cartridges. After setting a timer/igniter in a barrel of powder, they left, relocking the door behind them.

Back in the forest they tied cartridges a foot apart along lengths of fuse then strung them from the trees. Marty sat himself down at a place he could watch the camp and waited. While he sat, he checked his weapons, he didn't like the loads he had in his pistols, so he pulled them and reloaded with fresh powder. Sam, who was ever near, followed his example.

The cook and his helper had the stove going before dawn. They heated the porridge and baked some bread ready for when the men came to get their morning meal. The smell of fresh bread and coffee made Marty's mouth water. He took a strip of dried meat from his pouch and chewed.

The other members of his team were spaced out around the perimeter each with his own string of cartridges. They sat hidden from the camp suffering the bites of insects stoically, refusing to move. It was four hours from dawn to the attack and they watched for any sign that the attack force had been spotted.

At around nine o'clock men started to look uncomfortable, by a quarter past the latrines had a queue and by nine thirty men were running into the trees. At ten o'clock a shout announced that the boats had been spotted. Marty used one of the Toolshed's flintlock-based igniters to light his fuse. As soon as he was sure it was burning, he took out his pistols and moved to the edge of the clearing.

Men were responding to the alarm and coming out of the trees pulling up their trousers as they ran. Confusion grew as the cartridges strung on the fuses in the trees started to go off giving the impression they were being attacked from the land as well. Marty and the boys helped that by picking off selected targets with their pistols then drew their blades and got stuck in.

On the water, Goodman was in the lead boat, they hadn't been spotted until they were just fifty yards from the Silverthorn. He fired his musket as the alarm was raised, hitting a sailor who was looking over the rail. There was only a slight breeze and it was coming off the land,

"Jesus fucking Christ, what is that stink?" marine Laycock gasped.

Wilson chuckled, "I think the boss has been busy."

Half the boats hooked onto the schooner and men swarmed over the sides. The other half went straight to the bank to attack the camp, resistance was stiff but unorganised, the ship wasn't heavily manned and the men on shore seemed confused as to where the threat was coming from. Then a building exploded. The soldiers and marines had little trouble and ruthlessly knocked men down or bayoneted them, surprised by the lack of resistance.

Demoralised and sick, the privateers gave up. Their captain had been wounded early on and lay in a pool of his own blood near to the hut he had run out of when the alarm was sounded. Goodman saw Marty and his men and went to meet him.

Marty was stood over Captain Fozzard who he had shot in the thigh,

"Sorry about that, not very sporting I know, but I needed to take you out of the fight," Marty said.

Fozzard looked at the dishevelled, scratched and insect-bitten man in front of him who was dressed in black.

"Who the hell are you?" He saw Goodman approaching in full uniform. "I'll only talk to your commander."

"You already are, old boy," Goodman grinned. "May I present Commodore, Viscount Purbeck, Lord Martin Stockley."

"You're Stockley?"

"At your service. Now if we can get you on your ship we can get you to our surgeon."

"What is that stink?" Goodman asked.

"His crew had an attack of the runs," Antton said as he walked up.

"Did you poison my men?" Fozzard said.

"Just added a bottle of concentrated magnesium citrate to your breakfast dishes. The effects are effective but temporary."

Goodman and Fozzard looked puzzled.

"It's a very effective laxative. Probably best we wait for it to wear off before we put the prisoners back on the ship."

"Should we put the fires out?" Goodman said.

"No let them burn we don't want to leave anything behind that can be used."

"Oh, in that case," Goodman said and went off to burn the rest of the camp.

The Silverthorn came out from behind the island under foresails to the cheers of the sailors on the Unicorn. They tied up alongside and started transferring the wounded across. Fozzard was first and Marty accompanied him down to the surgeon's quarters. The Unicorn was unusual in that it had a dedicated infirmary attached to Shelby's cabin. The infirmary had a modern operating table with straps to hold the patients still while Shelby performed whatever surgery was required.

"Shot in the thigh," Marty informed him as they placed Fozzard face down on the table.

Shelby cut the trouser from his leg and swabbed the wound with raw alcohol causing Fozzard to curse him. Shelby ignored him and palpated the wound.

"Restrain him."

His loblolly boys expertly strapped Fozzard down.

"You'll not take my leg! You butcher."

"Oh, shut up and be a man. I'm not cutting your leg off."

He took a probe and pushed it in the wound, feeling for the bullet. Then took a pair of long-nosed forceps and slid them in. Fozzard went rigid with pain but made no sound. A little bit of pushing and twisting later he started to pull and bit by bit drew the ball out until it emerged with a wet slurp. He dropped it in a bowl with a clink then pushed his finger into the hole.

"Aha!" he said and took up the forceps again. This time he drew out a piece of cloth, "a piece of your trousers, can't leave that in there. Brace yourself." He poured more spirit over the wound, when it had evaporated, he took a hot iron and cauterised a bleed, finally he dusted the wound with sulphur powder and packed it with a herbal poultice before binding it.

"All done, release him and take him to the ward."

"No take him to my quarters, have a cot set up for him there."

Shelby raised an eyebrow in question.

"He's the captain of the schooner."

Marty stripped and had a thorough standing wash before dressing in a clean uniform. Fozzard watched him from the chair he had been placed in with his leg propped up on a foot stool.

"You are a fighting man."

Marty looked down at one of his numerous scars. "When necessary," he said as he pulled on a shirt. Last of all he buckled on his belt with his infamous fighting knife.

"That makes you look like a frontiers man, where did you get it?"

"That is a long story,"

"I'm not going anywhere."

"I will trade you, the story of my knife for the story of your activities in the Caribbean."

"I bet you would."

"As you said, you aren't going anywhere and as a prisoner of war we will treat you decently until the war is over when you will be sent back home. So you have nothing to lose in telling me."

"I thought you would hang me as a pirate."

"Why? You have a letter of marque which makes you a legitimate combatant. I found it in your cabin along with all your other papers. Your diary made very interesting reading."

Marty looked at the uniform coat he was about to put on then threw it over the back of his chair before sitting. "Too hot for that."

"What will you do with my ship?"

"I will make it part of my squadron and when the war ends, if it's still afloat, you can have it back. If you cooperate."

"That is a highly unusual offer."

"His Lordship is a highly unusual man," Adam said as he entered from the pantry with a tray of coffee and a cold lunch.

"You aren't a typical British officer either."

Marty looked at him, he could quite like this man if they were on the same side.

"I came from very humble beginnings and got a title by marriage then by the friendship of the Regent."

"Now that is a story I will trade for the story of my activities in the Caribbean."

The two men sat and talked, Bartholomew Fozzard, or Bart as he insisted Marty call him, slightly woozy from the laudanum Shelby had dosed him with, told Marty how he came to be privateering.

"I was running fishing boats out of Jacksonville back in 1811 and doing alright, when I was approached by a schooner owner to skipper a ship carrying cargo between there and New York. It was easier than fishing and better money, so I jumped at the chance. When the war started in 1812, he decided that there was more money in privateering and got me my letter. I built up my crew and moved down here. At first we just wandered around looking for British or Spanish ships to take."

Marty interrupted, "What did you do with the crews?"

"Put them ashore or let them go in their boats if we were close enough to somewhere they could land. I'm no killer, I will fight but killing unarmed men or setting them adrift isn't my way."

Marty nodded it was what he expected.

"Anyway, after a while I figured that this was doing it the hard way and started looking for sources of information. I soon found one after a visit to Jamaica posing as a trader."

"Jenkins."

"You know him?"

"We arrested him and he confessed."

"Shame, he was useful. Anyway, he was in a bar moaning about how little he got paid as a clerk to a shipping agent. He was on the way to getting drunk, so I started talking to him and buying him drinks. The next evening, he was back, and I made a point of sitting and listening to his moaning. I started to hint that I might be interested in information. It didn't take him long to offer to supply it for a price. I paid him in gold for the name of the first ship and his eyes when he saw it were like plates, he couldn't take his eyes off it. That's when I knew I had him hooked."

"When did he start offering ships with hidden supercargo?"

"About four months ago. He told me one of those ships was worth any two other ones and charged accordingly. He was right, so that is when I set up the base here on the island. We could wait here until we got the sailing details of our next target. Then one of the planters instructed his skipper to take the route up past Haiti. So I teamed up with a skipper out of Tortuga who had a clipper and he covered that route."

"That's what I thought from the pattern of losses. You seemed to have heard of me when the good major introduced me."

"Ha, ha, yes. You are a bit of a legend."

Marty was surprised.

"Your taking of the Spanish treasure ships is every privateer's dream. You are an inspiration!"

Fozzard collapsed in a gale of laughter at the incredulous look on Marty's face.

Chapter 11: Tortuga

The trial of Jenkins was short, he was given a defence lawyer who wasn't that interested in defending him as they had his and Fozzard's confession, the conviction was a foregone conclusion.

"Gregory Alphonsus Jennings you have been found guilty of treason and selling shipping information to the enemy. Do you have anything to say before I pass sentence?"

"It's all Mallory's fault. If he paid me better, I wouldn't have been tempted."

"That is no defence or excuse." The judge put on his black cap. "Gregory Alphonsus Jennings you will be taken from this court to a place of execution and hung by the neck until dead. The court is adjourned. My Lord Stockley will you join me for lunch?"

Marty had a pleasant lunch with Judge Mellwood who was also the master of the local Freemason's lodge. Marty had been invited to join the Freemasons several times but had never taken it up.

"You know we have been supporting that fellow Bolívar in Colombia," Mellwood said proudly. "The Freemasons around the world have been helping them."

"Bolívar is a mason?" Marty said.

"Oh yes, he is a master."

"Is that the same as you?"

Mellwood laughed, "No I am a grand master. You have never joined?"

"I have been invited but I never had the time between missions."

"It does take time to learn the rituals and go through the initiation, I don't suppose you have the time to join here?"

"I am afraid not, as soon as I see Jennings hung, I will be taking the squadron on patrol then returning to Aruba."

Jennings was taken from his cell under army guard the next morning to Prison Oval where a scaffold had been erected in his honour. There was a substantial crowd who jeered and threw everything from rotten fruit to rocks. Jennings was defiant and walked with his head up.

Caroline had returned from her trip up country and had some news she was holding back until the execution was over. They sat together as witnesses in the front row of the dignitary's bleacher which had been erected especially for the occasion.

"The carpenters worked well into the night to finish all this; it's not often they get to hang a traitor," Marty said.

Mellwood arrived and took his seat beside Marty after bowing to Caroline.

"Good turnout," he said as if they were at a wedding or a parade.

"Gives the commons some entertainment," Marty said.

Jennings had reached the steps to the scaffold where his dignity failed him, and he made a bolt for freedom. The soldiers in his escort were ready for that and a foot tripped him before he got more than two paces. He was grabbed by the arms and hauled up the steps by main force. At the top he was held up by the same two soldiers as a priest gave him the last rights.

The executioner had the soldiers position the condemned on a stool then placed the rope around his neck, the knot at the back of the head. The rope was only a foot long from the knot to the gallows meaning the victim would strangle to death once the stool was kicked away. A hood was placed over his head, not to save his dignity but to hide the agonised contortions his face would undergo even to the point of biting his own tongue off. Once he was ready the executioner looked to Mellwood as the presiding judge for permission to proceed. He waved his hand languidly and the stool was kicked away.

Fourteen minutes later Jennings finally expired, his trousers were soiled and shit was running down his legs. He was left hanging for the rest of the morning then cut down and buried in an unmarked grave.

"That was unpleasant, there must be a more humane way of executing people," Caroline said to Marty as they sipped tea at the reception held by the governor in celebration of this particular threat being removed.

"Firing squad is the only other way and that is reserved for service men or officers who are condemned," Marty said.

"Oh, never mind," Caroline huffed quite out of sorts with the whole affair.

"What were you going to tell me?" Marty said

Caroline brightened, "I have bought a plantation."

Marty inhaled his tea and had a coughing fit. When he recovered, he said, "Where?"

Caroline's mood had shifted from morose to mischievous. "In the mountains, the blue ones."

"Blue mountains? A coffee plantation?"

"Yes, with mature plants that are producing crops and a coffee processing plant that is used by several of the local plantations."

"Blue Mountain coffee! That's marvellous, our own supply. I must tell Shelby."

He paused as he had a thought. "Why did they sell?"

"Masters, the former owner, is the last of his line. His son was killed in a horse-riding accident and his wife died of fever years ago. He wanted to retire to the coast and live out his life fishing. There is a manager in place, and they treat their slaves humanely. They adopted The Den's method of tattooing the slaves with a mark rather than branding years ago."

Marty was pleased to hear that as he wasn't a supporter of slavery. He hadn't gone as far as openly supporting the anti-slavery movement because of his position as an officer in the navy and had to support government policy. However, he had a choice when it came to his own property and he would be damned if he would be classified as a slave owner.

"We need to free them at the earliest opportunity."

"Yes, I know, and I worked with the manager to come up with a way that they can be freed and employed. Interestingly when I talked to the workers they really liked working and living on the plantation and if given the chance would stay on as free men."

"That says a lot for the previous owner."

"It would be like the way the estate workers are treated in Cheshire and Dorset." Marty smiled, on some estates the workers were treated as little more than slaves, some were even indentured, but on their estates they were treated with respect.

The squadron sailed the next day. Caroline decided to stay in Jamaica and would charter a sloop to take her back to Aruba once she had completed her reorganisation of the plantation. She gave Marty a sack of coffee beans as a parting gift.

"Good luck, and happy hunting!" she said.

Marty sat with Shelby in his cabin savouring a cup of the Blue Mountain coffee that had been freshly roasted and ground by Adam then infused in the apothecary's pressure cooker.

"From your own plantation?"

"So, it seems. I have a question."

"Ask away."

"Is there a better way to hang someone than the way they do it now? What I mean is, the victim is strangled to death and we wouldn't do that to a dog."

"I understand your concern, it can take twenty minutes."

"In Spain we saw a man garrotted it broke his neck. A quick clean death."

"Let me have a think about it. What is your plan for this patrol?"

"The Leonidas and the Endellion didn't find any American ships along the South coast of Haiti or San Domingo but our American friend, Fozzard, let slip that there is a fellow over on Tortuga who he was working with. By the way, laudanum is a great tongue loosener."

"So, Tortuga is our next target?"

"Yes, then we will run down the Atlantic side of the islands."

There was a knock on the door and Wolfgang stuck his head through, he was about to say something but sniffed instead.

"That coffee smells wonderful."

"Come in and grab a cup."

"No time, just wanted to tell you that the winds shifted more to the North so we will have to go around Cuba rather than take the direct route to Tortuga."

"Thank you, carry on," Marty said.

After Wolfgang disappeared Marty called Adam, "Prepare a pot of coffee for the quarterdeck please and present it with my compliments."

Marty came up on deck an hour before sunset, the setting sun shone straight down the deck and was just dipping under the main sail. He looked astern, the sun was shining on the Leonidas's sails making them glow and behind her the Nymph. The Endellion was making her way back to the squadron and would soon drop in two cables to windward of the Unicorn.

The Silverthorn, with a crew made up from all the ships in the squadron and commanded by Terrance Howarth with Terrence Shepherd as his midshipman, was tagging along at the rear to give her crew time to bed in.

Sam was sat on a carronade making something out of a rope end, the rest of the Shadows were either on watch or getting ready for the change in watch after the evening meal. Third Lieutenant, Keith Farrell had the quarterdeck and was pacing the windward side. The wind, capricious as ever, had swung to the East-Northeast as soon as they got far enough past Cuba to make it impossible to turn back.

Marty looked at the glory of the setting sun and thought about the prisoners they had taken off the Silverthorn. Several were obviously runners from the royal navy and Marty had given them the choice, re-join under his command or hang. Suffice to say they all accepted his offer under false names. The Americans were housed in a prison camp on Port Royal. He had the word of the port admiral they would be treated fairly.

A familiar figure came on deck. "Hello, Richard," he greeted the acting fourth.

"Commodore, good afternoon," Richard Brazier said, touching his forelock in salute.

"How is your swordplay?"

"Greatly improved, Sir, according to Chin and Lady Caroline,"

"You are off duty?"

"Yes, Sir."

"Good I could do with some exercise."

Jackets were shed and arms loosened. The two faced off and sparks flew.

"Well done, Richard, you have come on a lot since I last tested your arm," Marty said at the end of the session. Richard had scored once and Marty three times, but Richard was as pleased as punch to have tagged his commodore.

"Will we be looking into the French ports, Sir?" Richard said as he put on his jacket.

"Yes, we will, the Silverthorn will be useful for that as she is a known American ship."

"I hope we find some privateers; I don't care if they are French or American, I just want some action." Richard grinned.

Marty patted him on the back, "Don't worry you will get your fair share."

Sam met Marty at the top of the stairs and handed him his coat. "He is good."

"Yes, and as keen as mustard, he will go far."

"If he do live."

"There is always that, Sam, always that."

They approached Tortuga. All the ports were along the South coast and accessible via the Tortue Canal, as the passage between Tortuga and Haiti was called.

"Signal the Silverthorn to come alongside," Marty said after ordering the squadron to heave to and all captains to report aboard.

The schooner came up as graceful as a swan and hove to under the Unicorn's lee.

"Be ready to bring a boat alongside to transfer me and the Shadows across. Sam, let the boys know we will be going over and probably going ashore."

"That explains why you aren't in uniform," Wolfgang said. Marty was dressed in clothes that would pass for those worn by Fozzard. The captains assembled on the Unicorn's quarterdeck.

"I will take the Silverthorn down the canal and into the ports. I want the Unicorn and Nymphe to stay at this end of the canal to prevent any ships escaping in this direction. The Leonidas and Endellion are to sail around the North side of the island and blockade the other end. With the wind from the Northeast privateers can run in either direction."

The Shadows were assembled at the entry port, checking their weapons. They were a fine example of professionalism, calm and ready for anything. Marty waited until the captains had returned to their ships then asked for the boat to be brought up and manned. He was last in, of course.

"We will give the Leonidas and Endellion time get in to position then head in to the first port," he said to Captain Howarth. "That will give you time to get out of uniform, I want this ship to look like the privateer she once was."

Marty had upgraded the schooner's eight-pound cannon with a couple of twenty-four-pound carronades on the fore deck. They had shifted the forward eight pounders to the stern to maintain the ship's trim. They would alert anyone who saw them that this was a navy ship, so he had them covered in canvas to hide them.

The crew always enjoyed dressing up and Marty's ideas for fooling the enemy. They all knew about his and the Shadows undercover work and the occasions when they were included were to be enjoyed.

The schooner had been kept well by Fozzard who ran a tight ship unlike some in his profession, so they didn't need to 'dirty her up.' The crew dressed in a variety of gaudy clothes to match their privateer persona and lounged around the deck. The sail handling was more relaxed than the navy demanded, but as Fozzard had a well-drilled crew, they kept it reasonably sharp.

Marty decided for the purposes of this exercise he would pose as the owner of the ship and leave Howarth as the captain. The main reason was Marty didn't look anything like Fozzard, even from a distance. Howarth at least had the same fair hair and was the same height which would pass as long as he stayed onboard. The story would get him ashore and enable him to look around before springing his trap. If there was a privateer in port that is.

The first bay that was deep enough and had a town, or rather, a village was Mare Rouge. They sailed slowly up to it and had a very good look. Nothing except a few small fishing boats. They continued without stopping. Far behind them the Unicorn and Nymphe were advancing in line abreast to seal off the canal.

Marty knew that the main port was overlooked by quite a powerful fort which the French maintained so he didn't want to tip his hand too soon. They were flying the American flag and hoped that their enemies believed it but it was a nervous approach through the barrier reef and past the island that protected the port.

Howarth had never been to Tortuga before and neither had his master, but they couldn't feel their way in as Fozzard had been there many times before. He trusted his charts and the eyes of his lookouts and boldly entered as if he did it every day. The crew breathed a collective sigh of relief as they dropped anchor with their bottom intact.

"Well done, Mr Howarth," Marty said, "Please get a boat around to take me and the Shadows ashore."

He looked around; the port of Tortuga wasn't much more than a bay with a wooden dock sticking out into deep water. The fort was inland and built on the top of a hill, with the French flag flying proudly above it. Through a glass he could not see any activity on the battlement or even any sentries. Anchored in the bay were a brigantine and a brig flying the French flag and tucked in behind them, a Baltimore Clipper that was the twin of the Eagle flying no flag at all.

They stepped onto the dock and made their way along the street. Men took one look at his escort and stayed out of their way even crossing the street to avoid them. Street urchins followed them. Marty flipped a penny to one and asked, "*Any Americans* in town?"

The child, wise in the ways of the world, held out his hand for more money so Marty flipped him a silver thruppenny bit.

"Four doors down says he is a shipping agent."

They stopped at a door identified by a brass plaque and walked in.

"Are you the agent?" he said to the man behind the desk in French.

"No, Sir, I'm his clerk. Mr Stenson is in his office."

"Stenson? That doesn't sound as if he is French."

"Oh, he isn't, Sir, he is an American, but he speaks French."

"Tell him Charles le Boeuf is here and wishes to see him."

The clerk looked at the Shadows who were exuding a sense of threat without trying and practically ran through the door to the back of the building. He returned and beckoned Marty to accompany him, when the boys made to follow, he said, *"He will only see you. Your men must wait here. Please."*

"Antton, you come with me, the rest wait here."

Marty was surprised when they climbed stairs to the second floor. The clerk knocked and they entered. The room was well lit by a pair of French doors that were open giving a view across the harbour.

"Mr Stenson, Mr le Boeuf," he said and left them to it.

"You are an American," Marty said in French-accented English.

"That I am."

"May I ask what you are doing in Tortuga?"

"Running my business."

"Which is?"

"My you are full of questions, how about you answer one for me?"

Marty shrugged and nodded.

"Who are you? And I don't mean your name."

"That is simple I too am an American, out of New Orleans. I own some ships that I have letters of marque for. It occurs to me that it would be more efficient to have an outlet for my goods locally rather than shipping them back to our home port."

"How many ships do you have?"

"Five."

"That's a decent fleet."

"I am always looking for more, for example that clipper. Who owns it and is it for sale?"

"It's not for sale, it is my ship."

"You captain it?"

"No, I am the owner, someone else skippers it."

This was all Marty needed to know. He pulled a pistol and pointed it at Stenson, the click as he cocked it was very loud.

"I will see your letter of marque."

"What the hell? What are you doing?"

Antton moved over to stand behind him and told him to stand. He patted him down thoroughly, removed a small pistol and a belt knife, then opened the drawers of his desk and removed a pistol.

"I am Philip Du Pont of the Department of Internal Affairs. I am here to investigate the leaking of shipping information to the British.

"America is at war with Britain!"

"I am very aware of that, but I have to ask myself why an American would chose to be a shipping agent on Tortuga?"

"Because I have a lead on when British ships are going to come North rather than around Cuba to the West." He said it with a hint of smugness. He handed over a letter taken from the drawer the pistol had been in. Marty cast a cursory eye over it noting the letter was in Stenson's name.

"That is convenient. Who is your source?"

"There is no way I'm telling you that."

He looked out of the window and frowned.

"Barrington said you came in on that schooner."

He looked at Marty quizzically.

"That's the Silverthorn, Captain Fozzard's ship."

"Is it?"

"Yes, I'm sure of it."

Marty went to the window, there was a crowd gathering up the street towards the end where the clipper was moored. The urchin was pointing to the ship brokers' building. About thirty men started moving in their direction. He dropped the French accent.

"I think there's a storm approaching. Secure his arms and gag him, Antton."

"What the hell? Who are you? Mmpphh."

Antton used a neckerchief as a gag and then expertly tied his hands behind his back.

"You, are coming with us."

Marty pulled both his Mantons and cocked one barrel on each.

"Please go in front of us down the stairs. Do not attempt to run as I will not hesitate to shoot you somewhere extremely inconvenient and painful."

They quickly descended to the ground floor where the boys had Barrington restrained.

"There's a rear exit, boss," John said and led them towards the back of the building. A door led them out into a courtyard with a stable, a double gate wide enough for a cart stood open.

"I thought we might want to make a quick getaway," he said.

The Shadows formed up into pairs. Antton and Matai took point alternatively advancing while the other covered. Wilson and John dropped back as rear guard and Chin and Sam stayed close to Marty.

They worked their way up the street moving carefully yet quickly until there was a shout and a shot. Marty could see Antton duck then snap off a shot in return. He was rewarded by a scream. The two retreated back towards Marty. Matai made a signal.

"That way is blocked, Chin, see if we can cut through one of these alleys."

Chin slipped away as there were more shots from ahead. "That one is clear but not for long."

Marty whistled and signalled with a wave of his arm. Antton and Matai retreated until they were almost to the alley then took up defensive positions. Marty dragged Taggart into the alley. As soon as they were in, Chin and Sam took point and Matai and Antton assumed the role of escort.

"There's about twenty men advancing down the street," Antton reported.

Wilson and John had reached the alley and fired a couple of rounds up the street.

"Reload," Marty said.

Chin beckoned them forward and Marty pushed Farnell ahead of him.

Suddenly bullets were smacking into the wall at the end of the alley, Sam dove for cover. Chin fired back.

They were trapped.

Marty cursed,

"Damn it. I should have given that brat pesos not pennies."

It was pointless blaming himself, he had to find a way out of this.

He looked up and down the alley. The walls were blank, devoid of windows or doors. He looked up, no help there either.

"Spare your shots, fire when you have a clear target."

Sam loaded for Chin who took careful aim before he fired. Wilson at the other end did the same for John.

Suddenly there was a volley of musket fire from the seaward end followed by shouted orders, a second volley and a figure appeared at the end,

"Commodore, if you would accompany me, we'll get you back to the ship." Terrance Howarth said.

"We need to take that clipper."

"They are already making sail. We don't have the fire power to stop them."

"Then it's up to the others."

As they climbed into the boats, Marty could see the clipper edging around the barrier reef and making all the sail they could carry.

Marty took the gag off Stenson.

"Was that really necessary?"

"It was to start with, then I was too busy to think about it, my apologies. Your ship seems to have run."

"Standing orders, if there is any trouble in the town they are to go to sea. I heard that officer call you Commodore."

The sound of cannon rumbled in the distance.

Howard looked West and said, "That was the Unicorn's foredeck carronades."

"Followed by the Nymphs broadside."

Stenson looked morose. "A trap, you said you had five ships. You weren't joking were you."

Marty smiled.

"Make him comfortable," Marty said to Sam as he led Stenson into his cabin. "You are the second American I have entertained here. It's becoming a habit."

The clipper, The Pride of Orleans, was visible through the stern lights.

"She put up a fight," Stenson observed. The clipper was missing the top of its mainmast and had an ugly gap in its quarterdeck rail.

"Tried to run past my ships, the forward carronades would have taken out the mast as she approached and then the Nymphe took her quarterdeck."

"Were many killed?"

"You care?"

"They were my men." Stenson snarled.

"The captain was killed as was the helmsman. The first mate was wounded but should recover after treatment."

Stenson looked wounded himself,

"Can I see him?"

"Yes, after we are finished. Is he someone close?"

Stenson looked like he would stay quiet then with a sigh said, "My younger brother."

"And the captain?"

"He was a friend, a brave and loyal friend."

They sat silently for a long moment each reflecting on the friends they had lost.

"What will happen to my ship and crew now?"

Marty noted he didn't ask what would happen to him.

"You will be taken to Jamaica where you will be held until the war between America and Britain ends; then you will be repatriated. Your ship will be sold off as a prize."

"Held in some hulk I suppose."

"No, a prison camp in the interior, you will join your old friend Captain Fozzard."

The sound of the main battery being run out echoed through the ship.

"Have you found another victim?"

Marty looked up through the skylight where Wolfgang was calling orders.

"We will sink every ship in Tortuga that could present a threat to British shipping."

Stenson winced at the thought and jumped when the guns fired.

"You are not used to being on a fighting ship."

"My first time, apart from being ferried to Tortuga and then they didn't shoot at anything."

"Normally they would clear this cabin so those guns could be used." Marty pointed to the two great guns tied down in the cabin. "The walls all come down and everything else is moved into the hold, it takes about ten minutes."

Stenson looked suitably impressed.

"Come with me," Marty said.

He took him up to the quarterdeck just in time for the second broadside to roar out.

Stenson had his hands over his ears.

"My god," he shouted.

Marty laughed,

"Impressive, isn't it?"

"We hung Jennings."

"Who?"

"You don't know him?"

"Never heard of him."

"Really?" Marty said thoughtfully.

"Who were you getting your information from?"

"I won't tell you that."

"Why? He is of no use to you now."

"True, but all the same I won't give him up."

"Because they will hang him?"

"Partly."

The guns fired a third time and Marty took a glass from the rack and focussed on the brig and brigantine that were in the harbour. The brig was the target, and her hull was showing how accurate the Unicorn's eighteen-pounders were. The Nymphe joined in; targeting the brigantine, her twelve-pound long cannon slightly less devastating but damaging all the same. He swung the glass to the fort. There was still no sign of any activity. He panned down the wall to the gate that was open and followed the road towards the town. A group of about forty men was rushing towards the fort on foot.

Marty handed the glass to Stenson; the Brigs main mast went over the side and smoke started to come out of the rear hatch.

"She is burning."

"Either the galley fire was lit or there was a lantern burning belowdecks, does our job for us."

Thirty minutes later both ships were hulks and sinking. Wolfgang asked permission to make sail. A cannon fired on the wall of the fort, the shot splashed down a cable away.

"Bring us up to the rest of the squadron," Marty said.

As the Leonidas and Endellion came into sight Stenson said,

"That is some force you have, when you said five ships, I didn't think you meant three frigates and two schooners."

"Technically two frigates, a sloop and two schooners," Marty said, then relented. "The French call the Nymphe a corvette; I suppose the English equivalent is a jackass frigate but officially she is rated as a sloop of war."

"The British ever complicated things," Stenson looked at Marty, "you haven't given me your real name yet."

"Haven't I? That's very remis of me." He sketched a bow, "Commodore, Viscount Stockley of Purbeck, Commander of this squadron and Governor of Aruba, but you can call me Martin."

"A real life lord? I'm honoured."

"Titles are useful but in the end it's the work that is important."

Stenson watched the other ships drop into formation.

"My name is Barnabas but I go by Barny."

Wolfgang stepped up, "Orders, Sir?"

"We will check the ports down the North side of Haiti and San Domingo then I will take the Silverthorn as escort to the Pride of Orleans back to Jamaica. The rest of the squadron can continue its patrol."

Wolfgang looked mildly surprised. Aye, aye, Sir. Will you re-join us?"

"Probably in a week or so."

Wolfgang left to give the orders and Shelby joined them,

"This is Shelby, our physician. Shelby this is Barny Stenson owner of the clipper we took."

"Stenson? Are you related to the first mate?"

"He is my brother," Stenson said as they shook hands.

"Then you should come down to the ward and visit him."

"Lead on, Doctor," Marty said.

Marty let Shelby take Stenson away then walked over to Wolfgang,

"We still have a spy in Jamaica."

"What makes you think that?"

"I told Stenson that we hung Jennings and he was totally ignorant of the name."

"He wasn't bluffing?"

"No, he didn't give as much as a flicker."

"Could be just a good actor."

"Maybe, but we can't take the chance. I will go back and try and find whoever it is. We know there is a limited list of suspects."

The Dorset Boy book10 - Silverthorn

Chapter 12: To Plug A Leak

They found a couple of French ships in Samina Bay, one of which they cut out and the other they burnt. As they reached the East end of the island Marty transferred to the Silverthorn.

They split the prisoners between the two ships and set off; the wind and current on their sterns. A day and a half saw them back in Jamaica tied up at the navy dock on Port Royal. Marty went to the port admiral's office.

"Is Sir Fredrick in his office?" he said to the secretary in the outer office.

"I will announce you, my Lord," the midshipman said jumping to his feet. Marty was in full uniform and instantly recognisable.

"Admiral, Commodore Stockley to see you," the boy said and bowed him into the room.

The admiral stood and sketched a bow which Marty returned, careful to match it.

"Commodore, welcome, take a seat. Did I see you come in with a prize?"

"Sir Fredrick," Marty said as he sat in the proffered chair.

"Yes, took her in Tortuga. It's the second ship that was targeting our shipping."

"Excellent! Problem solved then, I shall instruct the prize court, unless you want to buy her in?"

"No, I have a clipper and don't need another. However, I may want to use her before the court gets their hands on her."

The mid came in with a tray of tea. Marty waited until he left the room then continued. "There is probably a second person in Jamaica who has been passing information to the Americans and I might want to set a trap."

"A second? Dash it! I thought you had rid us of the traitors when we hung that Jennings chap."

Now I understand why you are a port admiral, Marty thought but said, "Yes, I am afraid so, but with your help I am sure we can winkle them out. I need to ask a favour of you."

Marty's next visit was to the governor's residence to bring him up to date and see if Caroline was still on the island. He borrowed the port admiral's carriage and hunkered down so he couldn't be seen through the window. When he got to the residence his uniform was covered in a plain boat cloak and he wore a nondescript broad-brimmed hat to hide his face. He walked with a limp to disguise his usual gait. The house slave who answered the door was very surprised when he saw who it was.

"Lord Martin, this is a surprise, I thought you were at sea," William said when Marty entered his study.

"That's the way I want to keep it, I believe there is a second informant on the island, and I do not want them to know I am back. The Silverthorn will put to sea in the morning as if she has delivered a prize and gone back to the squadron. She will in fact just go over the horizon and wait there."

"I see, do you think whoever it is, is in Kingston?"

"They might be, I have a list of suspects and want to investigate them incognito to start with. Now is Caroline here?"

"She is at your new plantation."

"Good that keeps her out of the way, she would only want to help if she were here. My men are on shore and are already watching some of the suspects."

"Who are they?"

"Mallory, the harbour master and his assistant, the agent in Montego Bay and his wife."

"Well, if I can do anything to assist."

"Be sure, I will let you know if I need anything from you."

In his room at the residence, he changed his appearance. He took clippers to his hair, cropping it short, this assignment had cost him all his dark locks, and he added a scar to his cheek. He applied some kohl makeup under his eyes and accentuated some of the lines on his forehead making himself look older, dressed in nondescript clothes. He assumed the name of Gregory Stanwell and became a trader.

He left via the servant's entrance and got a room in a cheap hotel. The Shadows all had their own assignments and knew where to find him. That evening he left the hotel and made his way down to the docks to the tavern where Jennings had met his contact. He took a seat in a corner with a glass of rum in front of him and just watched the room.

Babbage came in with his assistant cheerfully greeting several drinkers; the 'boy' went to sit with some friends. Babbage took a place at the bar and chatted to the bartender while he got a glass of rum. He turned as he took a sip and scanned the room. His eye settled on Marty for a second then moved on. Apparently, there was no one in the room that interested him enough to go and talk to and he settled back to chatting with the bartender.

Marty watched the assistant. He was a young man of around twenty-five years of age, slim, fair hair and a surprisingly pale complexion. Amongst his friends he stood out like a lantern. Marty kept an eye on him out of the corner of his eye. Nothing more happened for a good half hour until a man came in who was obviously a sailor who had just landed. He wore a salt-stained coat and had long greasy hair.

"John! Thought I'd find you here, you old seadog," he said loudly.

Babbage, turned and looked at the man,

"Raymond Burk as I live and breathe. I didn't think you would have the nerve to show up here after the fuss you caused on your last visit."

Burk laughed. "Oh, come now what's a boat between friends."

"It was my boat you poor excuse for a captain."

Marty was intrigued and wondered what had gone on so finished his drink and went to the bar to get a fresh one. He stood behind Babbage, his back to him.

The two men shared a drink and talked quietly. "I will replace your damn boat, but I got some news I think you should hear."

"Must be important if'n you risked me shooting you."

"You never would. Tortuga was raided by a British squadron. They sunk the French ships in the harbour and took the American clipper, The Pride Of Orleans. They also raided the town and took Barny Stenson. The men tried to stop them but a load of marines came ashore and drove them off."

"Why did they take him? I thought he was an honest trader."

"That's the mystery, no one knows."

"Well, I can make a good guess as to who did it. There's a new commodore in the Caribbean with a strong squadron of fast ships. Took an American privateer a couple of weeks ago who was hiding out on Juventud Island. Took his ship an all."

"Hmm thought it was too good to be true when the admiral went off to raid the American ports."

"Don't tell me you have slipped back into the old ways."

"No, I gave up buccaneering along with the rest of yus. I just don't like having a lot of navy ships around."

Marty went back to his seat. The rest of the evening was quiet and Marty left as the bar started to empty. He walked slowly for about one hundred yards when he became aware someone was following behind him and catching up rapidly. He slipped a blackjack from his pocket its loop around his wrist and the handle snug in his palm.

The steps approached rapidly, and a hand grasped his shoulder. He spun; dropping into a crouch the blackjack connecting with his assailant's midriff. The man grunted and folded up as he fell backwards to land on his arse. His blond hair shone in the moonlight.

It was Babbage's assistant, and his friends were coming up fast. Marty put the blackjack away and pulled a pistol. He pointed it at the young man's head and said, "You will stop right there, or he gets a bullet through the brain." The click of the hammer being pulled to full cock emphasised the point. A chuckle came from an alley and a figure stepped out into the light of the lantern burning above its entrance.

"Put the gun down, if you hurt the boy I will kill you."

Marty kept his gun just where it was.

"Just like being a Buccaneer again eh?" he said.

The double click of a hammer being cocked sounded from behind him.

"And that would be Mr Burk."

Marty raised his pistol and let the hammer down to half cock. He raised his hands above his head letting the pistol dangle by the trigger guard from his finger.

Babbage walked over and without a word, punched him in the stomach, then clubbed him across the back of the head with the pistol barrel as he folded over.

The world returned and Marty squinted at the sunlight coming through a window. His head hurt and he felt sick. He was securely tied in a chair.

"You are awake at last; thought I might have killed you."

"You have a strong arm, Babbage."

"And you have a hard head, Commodore."

"Darn you recognised me."

"Not until we got you back here."

"That's one thing."

Babbage stepped around until he was in front of him. He lent over so he could look Marty in the face.

"What is a commodore doing wandering around pretending to be a trader and carrying this much weaponry?"

He pointed to a table which was covered in most of Marty's weapons. He stood and used a finger to move them around. "Two very nice Manton pistols, a pair of barkers, knives of various description and a cosh." Not a very gentlemanly selection.

"Why aren't you with your ships and why are you here?"

"That's easy. There is still an informant selling shipping details to the Americans."

"And you think that's me?" Babbage said incredulously.

"You are a suspect yes."

The light of realisation suddenly shone in his eyes, "That's why you took Stenson,"

"Well done."

"He was taking British ships?"

"Uh hu."

"And he won't tell you who is nark is."

"Right again."

Babbage picked up Marty's fighting knife and slipped it from its scabbard.

"That is one fine blade, Damascus steel if I'm not mistaken."

He stepped behind the chair and Marty braced himself. The ropes dropped away parted by the razor-sharp blade. The rope around his wrists was next and then Babbage freed his ankles.

"Well, it's not me or any of mine."

Marty worked his hands to get the blood flowing in them.

"That I already knew." He nodded to the window. Across the street on the opposite rooftop was a figure holding a rifle. Marty waved and the figure waved back.

Babbage's eyes widened, "He was there all the time?"

Marty nodded then collected his weapons putting them back where they belonged.

"If I thought you were the one you would be dead already."

Babbage sat in the chair Marty had recently vacated.

"Damn you are a cool one."

"You are no murderer; you might kill if attacked or threatened but not in cold blood."

"That's a hell of a gamble."

Marty didn't reply, he felt the back of his head which had a substantial lump. He had the mother and father of headaches.

"Who in Kingston apart from you and Mallory would know what a ship was carrying and its planned route?"

"No one I can think of. You think it was Mallory?"

"No. He has too much to lose."

"Then who?"

Marty went back to the residence after a week of snooping around the town incognito. Neither he nor the Shadows found anything. He returned to the residence to find a slightly tetchy Caroline waiting for him.

"The only reason I knew you were back was because your uniform was in the wardrobe. Why didn't you leave a note? And what have you done to your hair!"

Marty turned his head to look in a mirror a quip on his lips. Caroline gasped, "You've been hurt! There is a lump on the back of your head and a scab."

She prodded it.

"Ow!"

"Who hit you?"

"A man with a gun."

"Did you kill him?"

"No. I need to change clothes."

"It's a bit early for dinner."

"I need to take the clipper around to Montego Bay."

That confused things even more and by the time Marty had straightened it all out and explained what was going on it was time for dinner.

William and Susan were too polite to ask what had happened to his hair and just nodded wisely when he told them he had to leave again that evening. They weren't even surprised when he refused the use of their carriage.

Marty met the Shadows at the navy dock where the Pride Of Orleans was tied up out of sight of the general public. The prize crew was aboard, topped up with some men from the Silverthorn.

"Get her ready, we sail first thing in the morning," Marty said to Lieutenant Keith Farrell who had command of her.

"Are we going far, Sir?"

"Just to Montego Bay. Get out of uniform and have the crew dress like American privateers."

Marty paced the quarterdeck as Farrell got the crew organised thinking through his reasoning. He still had a headache from the blow on his head and in the end only ended up arguing with himself. As soon as Farrell reported they were ready whenever he was, he went to bed.

He was woken early by Sam who presented him with a coffee.

"One hour to dawn, Sir."

"Thank you, Sam," he winced as he sat up, a spear of pain running through his head.

"You alright, Sir?"

"I'm fine Sam, let me get dressed and we can get this mystery solved."

The clipper sailed like a witch and was a joy. Marty was seriously tempted to buy her for himself. She was fast, responsive and sailed closer to the wind than even the Bethany. They made Montego Bay in record time and made a show of anchoring in sight of Trowbridge's house. They waited.

"Boat pulling out from the dock," a lookout said quietly.

Marty waited in the cabin.

There was a bump as a boat hooked on the chains.

The sound of someone coming up the side and asking to see the captain.

Marty frowned.

The sound of someone coming down the steps from the main deck.

The door opened,

"Who are you?" Marty and the girl said at the same time.

She turned as if to run up to the deck but found Sam blocking the door.

"Please come in, you were expecting to see the captain of this fine craft?"

"Where is he and where is Olaf the first mate?" She had an American accent.

"First of all, tell me your name."

She looked frightened. "Why should I tell you that?"

"Because I have news of the two men you thought you would be meeting here."

The colour drained from her face. "Imelda Stenson."

"Then the first mate is your brother?"

"Yes."

Marty wrote his report, the girl was Mrs Annabel Trowbridge's personal maid. She had brought Imelda with her from America.

Stenson and the captain of the Pride had worked for Annabel's father and when she sold off the company went independent as privateers. Imelda passed them tips about cargos which she picked up in the house and from gossiping with the staff from the plantations when the owners visited.

Marty hated the thought of hanging a woman and decided to treat her like her brothers and have her interred for the duration. However, that wasn't so easy. There wasn't a woman's prison and there was no way she could stay in the same place as the men. They were on their way back to Kingston and he would try and figure it out by the time they got there.

He went to stand up, a pain lanced through his head making him cry out, the world spun and he fell to the deck. He tried to get to the door but darkness closed in on him and he lost consciousness.

Sam found him twenty minutes later.

"We must get him to Kingston as soon as possible," Farrell said as they got Marty into his cot.

"No, Sir, you got to get 'im to Shelby, he de only one who can help him," Sam said.

"That will take days!"

"It take twice as long for you to get a message to 'im and for 'im to get to Jamaica. This is a fast ship. Get the boss to Shelby."

Sam loomed over the much smaller man then the door opened and the rest of the Shadows came in.

"Sam is right," John Smith said, "There ain't no sawbones on Jamaica who has half the knowhow Shelby has."

Faced with the collective will of the Shadows, Farrell did the sensible thing and gave in.

The Pride was driven harder than she had ever been by a captain and crew determined not to lose their leader on their watch. Imelda was conscripted as a nurse and Sam and Matai hardly left his side. Marty drifted in and out of consciousness over the next four days. They bathed his head, keeping cool damp rags against the swelling.

Sam was worried, if he looked at Marty's eyes the pupils were different sizes. He had no idea what it meant but he knew it had to be a bad sign. He fretted and it was huge relief when the lookout shouted that he had the squadron in sight.

Shelby examined Marty in his cot. "Get a litter ready we need to get him onto the Unicorn and tell that damn German that we need to get somewhere out of the waves. I have to operate."

The Shadows strapped Marty to a litter and oversaw him being lifted onto the Unicorn's deck. They carried him down to Shelby's domain and refused to leave. Shelby ran out of curses and gave in.

"If you won't leave you can damn well act as assistants. Matai, you have had some training in field medicine, you will assist me. The rest of you help Armitage to set up the operating table."

"What are you going to do?"

"I suspect that the blow he took has fractured his skull, depressing the bone and put pressure on his brain. I am going to open his head and relieve the pressure. Now get to work and give the back of his head the closest shave you can."

Shelby went up on deck and found Wolfgang.

"How long?"

"We will be entering English Harbour in an hour. That is the closest sheltered anchorage."

"I will operate as soon as the anchor drops, there is no time to lose."

The Unicorn swept into English Harbour with no salute, swung into the wind and dropped anchor. The port admiral in a fit of offended pique, send a flag officer to see what the hell was going on.

Down on the Orlop the air was heavy with the smell of lamp oil as Shelby had a full half dozen lamps burning to give him enough light. Matai stood at his shoulder and the rest of the boys stood in a half circle prepared to help if Marty so much as twitched. All of them had bathed and put on clean clothes. Matai had also washed his hands in raw spirit and helped Shelby clean his tools.

Marty lay face down. Shelby took a scalpel and made an incision. After peeling back, the skin he carefully worked his way down through the layers until he got to Marty's skull. At first there was a lot of bleeding and Matai was kept busy mopping out the wound.

"There it is," Shelby said. Matai looked over his shoulder and saw the star of cracks and the slight depression.

"What are you going to do now?" Matai asked.

"Trepan it to remove the bone."

"That will leave a hole in his head!"

"We will cover the hole with this." Shelby held up a square of yellow metal with eight holes in it.

"Brass?"

"Pure gold."

"How is it fitted?"

"Watch maker's screws into the skull."

Up on deck Wolfgang was facing down an outraged admiral who had come aboard as soon as his flag officer had reported to him.

"No salute, no side party and no ceremony and now you tell me you will not let me see the commodore?"

"With all due respect, Sir, Lord Martin is being operated on by Mr Shelby our physician. I am told it is an extremely delicate procedure and have been given strict instructions about creating noise on the ship."

"You take orders from a sawbones?"

"In this case yes I do and I can assure you Mr Shelby is much more than a sawbones as several of your fellow admirals will testify."

The admiral calmed down a little. "You have a lot of faith in the man."

"I have seen him perform miracles. I pray he can pull another out of the bag now."

The admiral started to pace, forcing Wolfgang to follow. He said nothing, and after a few minutes stopped by the rail to the main deck.

"I have never been on such a quiet ship; you can feel the sense of anticipation."

Wolfgang said nothing but he felt pride that the men respected 'the boss' as much as they did.

An hour and a half later and three hours after he had made the first cut, the doctor came up on deck. There was a collective intake of breath as he made his way to the quarterdeck. Wolfgang met him at the top of the stairs, Adam hovered within hearing distance and the admiral watched from the windward side.

Shelby smiled; he looked tired. "The operation went well, I have relieved the pressure on his brain and he is sleeping."

The word went around the ship like wildfire, the men grinning and nudging each other, whispering about how Shelby had pulled off another miracle.

"The commodore is well?" the admiral said.

"We will see in the next days, there are many things that can go wrong with this kind of wound. If we can avoid infection then he stands a chance of recovering, but there is a chance that he may be impaired in some way even then."

"Would he be better off onshore? We have a hospital," the admiral said.

"He should not be moved. We will care for him here," Shelby said firmly, then turned to Adam.

"Do you have any of that excellent coffee ready? I could kill for a cup."

"I will bring a pot for all of you," Adam grinned as he had heard every word.

The three men stood together sipping the rich coffee, goat's milk and sugar was available for those that wanted it. The admiral had gotten over his spat,

"I had a letter from Admiral Turner telling me that the commodore and your squadron was coming and to aid him in any way he asked. Which is a rum way of putting it. There were hints he was here to do more than chase down privateers. Turner is head of the intelligence group, so I assume you and your commander are part of that."

Wolfgang and Shelby looked at each other, then Wolfgang said, "The squadron is under Admiralty orders and within Admiral Turner's command."

"Ha! I knew it." The admiral had enough sense to leave it at that.

Wolfgang sent the rest of the squadron back on patrol with orders to return to English Harbour in a fortnight. Marty stayed in the hospital for a week, sedated, fed by a tube pushed down his throat. Imelda came over from the Pride and along with one of the Shadows nursed him. He was never alone.

After a week the wound on his head seemed to be healing nicely, Shelby removed the drain he had left in it and gradually reduced the drug he used to sedate him. He woke fully after ten days to see Caroline bent over him.

"Hello," she said.

"Hello." He looked around.

"Where am I?"

"In the sick bay of the Unicorn, you have been very ill."

"What happened? The last I remember is being in Montego Bay."

"You are in English Harbour now. The boys brought you to Shelby when you collapsed."

"I collapsed?"

"That bang on the head, fractured your skull and put pressure on your brain."

Marty raised his hand to feel the back of his head, but Caroline stopped him.

"Shelby has mended it; you have a gold plate under your skin. He will take the stitches out later today."

Now he was awake Shelby had him moved up on deck so he could get fresh air and sun. The Shadows carried him with the utmost care as if they were moving a fragile, priceless object.

Imelda was supplanted by Caroline and was left to her own devices. She found that the crew were amiable and friendly. She started to plan. Step one was to get one of the crew under her control and to do that she was going to seduce him. She chose a reasonably good-looking mate, there was no point in not having some fun while she did it.

She waited until he was on watch one night and slipped up on the deck. He was pacing up and down the port side watching even though they were in a friendly harbour. When he was at the far end of his pacing she went to the rail and pretended to be crying. He found here there as he walked back up the deck.

"Here now, Miss, what's the matter?" he said.

"Oh, nothing I was just thinking about my brother, I would do anything to see him again."

"He's the first mate off the Pride isn't he?"

"Yes. I miss him so."

She pretended to break down again and moved towards him, he stepped forward and held his arms out, she looked up into his eyes, pleading with a look.

He held her relishing the feel of her body against his and the smell of her hair.

"I suppose you wants me to help you get off the ship so you can go to him."

"Could you?"

"Aye I could, but I won't."

"What?"

"I'll not help you nor will any man on this ship."

She stepped back and swung a hand to slap his face. He caught it without effort, spun her around and slapped her on the backside.

"If you want a rumble come see me again." He laughed.

Marty was sat on the quarterdeck in a canvas chair with a low table beside him.

"Why are you mollycoddling me?" he said to Caroline.

"What do you mean?"

"Don't act innocent, it's been a week since I was allowed up on deck and you haven't let me do anything myself."

"I just want you to take your time recovering."

"The stitches came out three days ago, Shelby says he is satisfied with what he sees."

"But you have not yet fully recovered."

"Nor will I, sitting here."

He stood, a little unsteadily and took a few steps. He was aware that everyone on the quarterdeck was watching with concern. He squared his shoulders and walked across to the windward side of the deck. The men cleared it automatically. He rested his hands on the stern rail, his legs were weak, but he didn't want to show it. He straightened again and walked the length of the quarterdeck to the forward rail. His legs felt stronger, so he turned and walked back to the stern.

"Well done," Shelby said.

"I didn't see you come up."

"I was waiting for you to lose patience."

"Am I that predictable?"

Shelby laughed and stood in front of him.

"I want to carry out some tests if you don't mind."

"Go ahead."

Shelby looked into his eyes, shaded them and exposed them to the light. Then he had Marty reach out with each hand in turn and touch a finger he held out. He had him squeeze his hands then said, "Squat and stand back up."

Marty did and only wobbled a little.

"Now walk the length of the quarterdeck along that seam."

Again, Marty did it without wobbling too much.

"Now play a game of slaps with me," Shelby held out his hand palm to palm inviting Marty to do the same. When their fingers were touching, he attempted to slap Marty's hand. His hand hit empty air. It was Marty's turn and he made contact.

"You do not seem to be adversely affected by your wound in any way I can see."

"Oh, so that was what you were all worrying about. You've been like a bunch of old hens."

Caroline blushed. Marty laughed.

"I thank you for your concern, but I am fine, as far as I can tell."

"Just avoid getting hit on the head again," Shelby said and stepped aside so Marty could go back to Caroline.

"One thing I do want to know. How did you find out I was hurt and how did you get here?"

"Wolfgang sent a message via the admiral's packet and I got Terrence to bring me on the Silverthorn."

Chapter 13: Recovery

Marty and Caroline sailed the Pride back to Aruba to continue Marty's convalescence. He gifted Wolfgang with the Silverthorn for the squadron and decided to buy the Pride for his personal use. She would be renamed the Pride of Purbeck. They took Imelda along with them as Marty had heard of her attempt to subvert a member of the crew. She didn't know it, but she chose the wrong man, he was happily partnered with Wolverton the gunner although not averse to a bit of female company from all accounts. Aruba wasn't where Marty wanted to keep Imelda but his options were limited so he decided to put her into the care of the army under house arrest.

Marty continued to exercise; he was amazed how much condition he had lost during his illness. He also noticed that his ability to concentrate was lessened. To counter that he started playing chess with Keith Farrell. It was hard, he kept drifting off to stare out of the window and had to drag his attention back to the game, but with persistence he got better.

They anchored at Oranjestad and Caroline insisted they take a carriage back to the mansion. The sight of a shaven-headed governor would have set tongues wagging and she didn't want that.

Once back safely in the grounds Marty climbed down to be met by seventy pounds of ecstatic Dutch Shepherd as Troy pushed him down onto a bench and proceeded to wash his head. Marty couldn't push him off and Caroline was too busy with the children to help.

When he got a chance to take a breath he said, "Better now? Got all that nasty outside world of my head?"

Troy sat on his lap his front paws on Marty's shoulders and grinned into his face, his tongue lolling out of his mouth.

"I know, you missed me; I will have to take you with me next time."

Troy agreed by giving him another sloppy lick.

"Martin! Come and say hello to the children," Caroline called.

"Come on, boy, let's go see the kids."

Troy fell in beside his left leg, it somehow made him feel complete.

"Daddy! Daddy!" yelled the twins when they saw him. He was soon trapped by their arms around his legs. He picked them up and kissed them.

"What did you do to your hair?" Edwin asked

"How did you get so big?" Marty countered. The twins were seven now and he could only just pick them up together.

The twins giggled and after a bit of snuggling he put them down and looked at the beautiful girl who had walked out of the front door.

"Edwin is right, you look terrible," Bethany said.

"Who are you and what have you done with my little girl?" Marty asked feigning astonishment. Beth was twelve, almost thirteen and was blooming into the image of her mother.

"Oh Daddy," she laughed and ran into his arms.

"I had a letter from James, you and Mummy have one too. What did you do to your hair?"

"Your father forgot to duck and got hit on the head, Mr Shelby had to mend it," Caroline said.

"Tittle tattle," Marty smiled.

"He needs to rest."

"That'll be the day," Wilson quipped as he carried Marty's sea chest up the steps to the door.

"Take that man's name!" Marty laughed.

"See 'e caint e'en remember his own men's names," John Smith said as he followed Wilson up the steps with one of Caroline's many trunks.

Marty sighed and rolled his eyes as he allowed Beth and Caroline to lead him into the house.

Marty sat with Bethany after the two completed a light fencing practice.

"You have improved, who have you been practising with."

"Ensign Rupert Colepepper has been partnering me for fencing practice he is very accomplished."

Marty stiffened ever so slightly and forced himself to say casually, "That's good, I don't think I have met him,"

"He is sixteen years old and awfully handsome," Beth said a slightly dreamy look on her face.

"Really, I shall have to meet this dashing young man." There must have been a slight edge to his voice because Beth turned to look at him, blushing, a dangerous glint in her eye that he recognised.

"Why would you want to meet him?"

"Well, to see if he is of good family, has his manners and is a suitable suitor."

"What?"

"Well, you seem quite taken with him and you will be sixteen in, what, just over three years. My sisters were all married off at that age."

"Married?" she gasped.

"You can't start looking too soon you know." He couldn't keep it up and laughed.

"Oh! You, you, aargh," Beth spluttered.

"Oh, come now I'm only teasing. I'm sure he is just a friend and a nice lad at that."

Beth stood her eyes wide then they narrowed,

"It's your head wound. You have overexerted yourself; it has patently made you infirm, let me get you a cup of tea and a comforter." She stalked off indignation leaking from every pore.

Marty chuckled, but made a mental note to check out Ensign Colepepper the next time he came calling.

Relations with Beth returned to normal after she cooled down, she had her mother's temper and her ability to hold a grudge, so he was still watchful for retaliation of some sort. Ensign Colepepper turned out to be a very competent fencer and Marty spent some time practising with him to improve his coordination. His hair was growing back and the latest editions of the newspapers that arrived on the packet (only two months old) were full of the latest fashions.

"I think your hair would look good like this." Caroline held up a picture of a man whose hair was trimmed to collar length was curled and had a quiff that dropped down across his forehead to his eyebrows.

"Won't do."

"Why?"

"For one he looks like a bloody rooster and second I need to get back the style I had before I shaved it."

Caroline glanced at him,

"That sounds like you are planning on going back to the mainland."

"The Eagle will be back soon and now we have the Pride and Silverthorn—"

"The Pride is our private ship." Caroline had every intention of using the Pride herself.

"Alright, now we have the Silverthorn plus those two schooners we can double up the operations."

"Once you have found me a crew for the Pride."

Marty sighed, why couldn't life be simple?

His main problem was he couldn't use the squadron's men to man his private ship. If he got caught doing that even Prince George wouldn't save his hide. He thought it through. He had four schooners: Silverthorn, Endellion, Mayfly and Robin, a Boston Clipper, The Eagle, Two frigates and a sloop.

He barely had enough men to man them all. What he needed was more men or fewer ships. They had delivered the guns to the rebels, so he didn't really need the Mayfly and Robin. The two best schooners were the Endellion and the Silverthorn.

Decision made the Mayflower and Robin would be laid up in case they were needed. That brought it down to the frigates, sloop, clipper and two schooners.

He wrote down on a piece of paper what he needed each part of his squadron to do and the split was obvious. The schooners were the ideal ships for his insurgency, the Silverthorn was American built and the Endellion, although Cornish built, could pass for being American any day of the week. The Eagle with her bigger guns was much better suited to be with Wolfgang hunting privateers.

Now how did he man the Pride? He was sat in his study by the open window that looked out onto the garden and watched a gardener deadheading roses. He realised he recognised the man. It was Stan Philpot a veteran hand who had been part of the crew of the Queen. As she was in port the crew had been reduced to a harbour watch and the rest of the men had shore leave.

Marty took a walk out into the garden and found Stan.

"Good morning Stan. I didn't know you were a gardener."

"Your Lordship," Stan greeted him with a tug of his forelock. "I caint stand loungin' around doin' nuttin, so I volunteered to help in the garden. Suits me as me bones ain't what they used to be."

"Feeling your age?"

"Aye a warship is a hard life, I been thinking of retiring from the service and maybe do something easier."

"You have enough prize money to do anything you want."

"Aye but giving up the sea will be hard."

Marty had an inspiration,

"How would you like to sail in one of my private ships?"

"A merchant ship?"

"No, the Pride, we will use it as our personal ship."

"That would be an honour, Sir."

"Good, I will get you registered as retired, and you can report aboard. Once you have finished here that is," Marty said with a wink.

Aruba had its fair share of sailors looking for a berth, some were runners, others, merchantmen who had lost their ships. Marty had some handbills made for recruitment and had the available midshipmen travel the coast, visiting the ports and villages.

The hand bill read:

EIGHT POUNDS A YEAR AND PRIZE MONEY

JOIN COMMODORE STOCKLEY

AND THE ANTILLES SQUADRON

ABLE SEAMEN

LANDSMEN

WAISTERS

A CROWN FOR SIGNING

HAPPIEST SHIPS IN THE NAVY

NO PRESSED MEN.

They left full of enthusiasm with a pair of burly bosun's mates and four marines. Marty provided a purse to pay for accommodation and food with a strict warning against drunkenness.

The Eagle returned from her latest tour of Colombia and Venezuela. Trevor Archer visited and brought written reports from their men on the ground.

"Bolívar is very pleased with the training and advice our men have given, he is planning a sortie or two to harden his men up at the suggestion of Captain O'Driscol."

Marty read O'Driscol's report which mainly dealt with the numbers of men they were training and in what. He mentioned several men who had performed well, recommending one for promotion to sergeant on their return.

"How are things going in Venezuela?" Marty said once he had finished.

"Garai sent this," Archer handed over a packet of papers. Inside was an encoded report and a map.

"Very well, that will be all. Oh, I am recruiting some new men, if you have any that are thinking about leaving the service, please send them to me as I need a crew for the Pride."

Archer looked puzzled.

"She is a clipper that we captured in Tortuga, I'm buying her and need a crew. Stan Philpot gave me the idea that I could offer the men that are thinking of retiring from the service a berth. Some of them are getting too old to serve on active warships."

"I see, Sir, there is only one that I know of on the Eagle, but I will put the word around." Personally, he thought that, swapping raw recruits, even if they were able, for experienced hands was crazy. Then he realised that Lady Caroline and the children would probably be using the ship and understood why Lord Martin wanted known hands.

Marty decoded Garai's report. It started with the same kind of information that O'Driscol had provided. Piar had been busy raising an army and Sergeant Bright and his men were busy whipping them into shape. They were being trained as guerrilla fighters in the main, but a certain amount of square bashing was going on to prepare them for a traditional battle as well.

Garai reported he had formed a relationship with the servant girl, Catalina, in Piar's house and she was a fine source of information. Stefano had forgiven Antonio for his betrayal and the two were living in harmony. Piar, however, didn't trust Antonio and had a permanent watch on him.

The men that had followed the wounded Lianos had returned. He had evaded them with the help of some natives. They suspected that there was a large force somewhere to the Southeast of Angostura and were sending out scouts to try and locate them. There had been several raids on farms that were attributed to that group and Piar wanted to eliminate them.

Marty sat back and thought about the situation in Venezuela. There must be a way he could help the rebel cause. He pulled out a chart and tried to put himself into the mind of the Llanos.

Caroline had her own ideas about how he should be recuperating, she let him work in the morning and then made sure he rested in the afternoon. He was still getting headaches and when she saw the tell-tail signs, she ensured he was left alone to rest or sleep it off. She banned him from drinking any alcohol other than a single glass of Madiera a day. He was impatient but she was determined that for once he would recover properly.

Marty exercised first thing every morning. A brisk walk, escorted by one of the Shadows under orders from Caroline to not let him break into a run, followed by a ten-minute fencing session and shooting practice. When he complained to his escort, he invariably got the response, "Lady Caroline's orders, Sir." He made steady progress and after three weeks Caroline decided he could increase his work time by an hour a day.

The recruiting party returned, followed by twenty men, not as many as Marty wanted but a start. They would be signed on to their ships when the squadron returned to port and would replace any men who took up Marty's offer to 'go private'.

They still had a month before the hurricane season started but Marty woke up to a feeling of oppression. The air was heavy and still. He climbed out of bed and went to the window that opened to the East. He threw open the shutters and looked at the sky.

"What are you looking at?" Caroline said.

"The weather, I feel a storm coming."

"A hurricane?"

"No, not this far South. It's probably a tropical storm, just as dangerous to ships."

The storm had been building in the South Atlantic and travelled North passing over Trinidad where it met the warm water of the Caribbean and got supercharged. The squadron were near the Virgin Islands and were about to make the run across to Aruba when they noticed the waves were building and coming from the Southwest.

"That's odd," Arnold Grey sucked his teeth as he alternately looked at the sky then the sea.

Wolfgang heard him mutter,

"Is there something wrong, Arnold?"

"That sea is coming from the wrong direction and building."

"Could be a storm to the Southwest."

"Will have to be a biggun to send waves all the way over here." He took a telescope and looked at the horizon. Seeing nothing he called up to the mainmast lookout,

"Franky, what can you see to the Southwest? Any weather?"

Franky turned and had a good look. "West-Southwest there is some cloud but nothin' else."

Arnold paced up and down, went back to the side and looked at the waves again.

"I don't like it, we should delay the crossing. Whatever is going on down there is something I don't want to sail through."

He was right the storm was moving West and would pass the Lesser Antilles just to the North and by the time it got level with Aruba it had seventy-mile-an-hour winds gusting to ninety.

The wind was rattling the shutters. Marty and Caroline sat with the children playing a game of Spillikins to distract them as it had frightened the twins. It was girls against boys and Edwin had the honour of dropping the bundle of sticks. He tried to drop them from too high and immediately Constance remonstrated with him.

"That's too high, he's cheating, Mummy!"

Marty gently told his wayward son to lower his hand when there was a drumming on the door. Tabetha went to answer it and a moment later a drenched soldier came into the room,

"Good God man, what is bringing you out in this foul weather?" Marty said.

"Begging your pardon, milord, but there is a ship run aground on Colorado point. She's a British warship."

"Antton!" Marty shouted as he leapt to his feet. Then to Caroline. "We need to get down there fast."

"What are you thinking? You are in no state to go out in this storm!" Caroline cried.

"I am well enough," he took her by the arms, "men's lives are at risk. If they're aground on the point they will need our help to make it to shore."

Caroline knew that his sense of duty wouldn't let him sit by while others risked their lives.

Antton quickly gathered the rest of the Shadows and Marty ordered the soldier to alert the crews of the Eagle and Pride. They would have to take horses the ten miles across the island to the point and would need some special equipment. They got the horses and headed down to the dock.

"We need a cart or a carriage, messenger cable, a couple of swivels and boarding grapnels. Thirty strong men should do it." The Shadows 'acquired' a couple of carts and teams and emptied the local livery of horses.

They piled the equipment into the carts, topped them off with men who couldn't ride and set out. The weather was foul, the rain driving in the gale force winds stinging any exposed skin. Ten miles looked an awful long way on roads that were washing away.

They made five miles an hour, better than walking but much, much slower than Marty wanted. Just over two hours after setting out and exhausted from wrestling the carts through the mud they got to the point.

She was an armed brig and was hard up on the reef some fifty yards offshore. The waves were huge hitting her on the stern and she was listing about twenty degrees. Men were on the deck waving their arms.

"She must be holed," Marty shouted into Trevor Archer's ear over the wind.

"Aye, there's no way they will get her off and those waves will break her back."

"We have to get them off before then. Get the swivels ready we need to get a line across."

Marty had realised that the only way they would get a line to the ship from the shore was to use a swivel fired grapnel. But the wind was against them and it would be a lucky shot that made it. The gunner from the Eagle was one of the men that had joined. A bull of a man, he stood, braced, knee deep in the sea, a swivel in his hands. A second hand stood beside him with an open crate which contained the carefully coiled messenger cable, and a second stood the other side shielding a burning slow match.

The swivel fired and the hook shot across the gap, but the wind veered and took it to the side of the stranded ship. The gun and crate were abandoned and replaced with another set.

He waited until there was a lull in the wind before he fired. Again, a gust caught it and took the cable away from the ship. They had one more set prepared.

Marty stepped into the sea and took the crate from the seaman, he stood beside the gunner and smiled encouragingly.

"Take your time," he said.

There was a rending groan from the brig and her fore mast went over the side. They could hear the shouts from the crew. A man jumped from the bow and attempted to swim for the shore only to be overwhelmed by the waves and smashed on the reef.

The gunner braced himself and aimed more to the right. He nodded and the slow match was applied. The grapnel shot out of the barrel with the messenger trailing behind. It looked like he had over compensated, but the wind played its part again and the line dropped across the bow. Marty took the bitter end back onto the beach and the men tagged on ready to haul.

On the brig the crew spliced a two-inch cable onto the messenger and waved for the shore team to haul away. A wet two-inch cable is heavy, and it took all the men to pull it to shore and secure it so that the brig's crew could tension it with their capstan. A man started down the cable another messenger secured to his waist. He struggled along the cable, slipped, hung by one hand, recovered and carried on. He reached a point where the men on shore could reach him. He practically fell into their arms.

The second messenger was attached at the ship end to a pulley block from which a bosun's chair was suspended. A man sat on it and the shore team hauled him across. Marty decided he needed to organise things on the ship and rode the chair on to the brig's deck.

"Who is the officer in charge?" he said.

A young lieutenant stepped forward and saluted. "I am, Commander Burnley, and you are?"

"Commodore Stockley. What is the state of your ship?"

"Holed amidships, her back will break soon. We need to get the men off fast."

"Get a second chair and block mounted linked to the first."

"Aye, aye, Sir." Burnley shouted orders.

The next haul two men went across.

"How many injured?" Marty asked.

Burnley led him to the stump of the mainmast. There he found half a dozen injured men. He quickly assessed their condition.

"You two go forward take the forward chair and have the man behind hold you," he told the men who had broken arms.

"Those two will need to be strapped to boards which we will secure across the two chairs. They will go last before you and me. This man is dead and that one will be before we can move him."

The brig sailed with a crew of seventy-five; thirteen were lost during the storm when their mainmast went over and two died as a result of their wounds. That left sixty souls to be saved plus a ship's cat. The big black and white tomcat was tucked inside the shirt of a sailor and made it safely to shore.

They had gotten two thirds of the men ashore when the ship's back broke. The capstan went down with the stern and they were left with the cable tied to the stub of a foremast. What was left of the ship moved with every wave and each time it did it threatened to jam the pulley blocks.

The last able man left and Marty helped Burnley tie one of the wounded to a board. They pulled the blocks back aboard and got the man lashed to the bosun's chairs. He started his trip across and was twenty feet from safety when the bow shifted. It rolled throwing Marty, Burnley and the last injured man into the water.

Marty felt the deck move and drop out from under him, he fell awkwardly, landing on his back in the water. The last thing he saw before he went under was Burnley falling directly towards him.

His back hit sand, Burnley followed a second later and hit him in the chest. His breath rushed out and it took every ounce of control he had not to try and breath in. He shoved Burnley off of him and got his feet against the bottom, shoving with all his might he shot for the surface.

It seemed to take forever but was no more than a few seconds before his head broke the surface and he dragged in a breath. Burnley appeared a few yards away a second later eyes wide and started thrashing the water in panic. Marty started for him but a wave engulfed him and it was all he could do to get back to the surface again. Burnley had disappeared.

Marty trod water and looked around; the bow of the ship was still there although now on its side. He was buried by another wave and when he surfaced knew he had to get to the ship as it was his only chance. He struck out, fighting the waves, tiring fast but would not give up. His hand struck wood and he clung to a piece of rail that was still attached to the now vertical deck. He clung on; he had to get out of the waves or they would beat him to death. He braced himself and started to climb when a strong hand gripped his wrist and pulled him up.

"Wilson! What the—"

"No time, Sir, here let me tie this around you." He passed a line around Marty's waist and tied it off then helped him onto the bosun's chair.

"There's only one!" Marty cried.

"No problem," the big man said and slung a block over the cable behind Marty on which he had tied a pair of ropes. He wrapped the ropes around his wrists then waved towards the shore.

The men on the shore heaved, half latching onto the line and running to pull the line in, the second half ready to latch on and continue the pull. In this way, Marty and Wilson fairly flew to the shore. As they got closer, they could hear the men's calls, "Latch on! Haul! Faster you swabs!"

"You did what?" Caroline said in a worryingly quiet voice.

"We rescued sixty men," Marty repeated trying to avoid the coming storm.

"And you felt you had to go aboard?"

He hadn't meant to tell her that, but it had slipped out.

"Well yes I needed—"

"I do not want to know," she said. "Tabetha, get a bath prepared, make sure it is good and hot. You," she prodded him in the chest with a finger, "get upstairs and get undressed. Adam watch him, his mind is still addled and he cannot be trusted."

Adam grinned and took Marty by the arm.

Caroline didn't let Marty out of her sight until she was convinced he was fully recovered which was about a week after the squadron finally returned.

Chapter 14: Toro Toro

"We have signed on all the able men from the Rose so even with the men who chose to retire to the Pride we have enough to man the Silverthorn fully as well," Marty said.

"Yes, there were a few pressed men on the Rose but we gave them the option to volunteer and take the sovereign. They all took it which surprised me, our previous sorties into this region gained us a certain fame it seems," Wolfgang said

"Infamy more like," Shelby chipped in.

"Ha, ha, yes that's true," Marty said.

"Now you have everything reorganised, what do you want us to do?" Wolfgang asked.

"The Eagle will re-join the squadron. The Silverthorn and Endellion will stay here to support our efforts on the mainland. I will recall most of the men from Colombia as their job is all but done and I want most of your marines as well."

"Sounds like you have something big in mind," Shelby said as he poured more coffee.

"There is a force of Llanos South of Angostura that needs to be eliminated, I have a mind to catch them in a pincer."

"Will you use the army?" Wolfgang said.

"Tricky, I have no doubt that Goodman would jump at the chance but having to explain to Horseguards any casualties would be difficult."

"Training accidents," Shelby said.

"A limited number could be," Marty conceded.

"Sounds like I have my job to do and you yours. I will ask Goodman if we can borrow some more of his men for this patrol," Wolfgang said.

The next morning Goodman appeared at Marty's study door,

"Good morning, Major, what can I do for you?"

"I hear you are going to do a land battle in Venezuela."

"You have talked to Captain Ackermann then."

"Yes, and I think you are making a mistake."

Marty sat back and looked at him, he was red in the face and obviously in a passion. "Please, sit down and relax. I will hear you out." He rang a bell and when Adam appeared asked him to bring some coffee and once it was served said, "Now what is on your mind?"

Goodman had calmed down and took a breath,

"You are going to take your sea soldiers into a battle on land. Now I know they are good and have experience but if what Wolfgang is telling me is correct, my men would be better suited."

"Can you expand on that?"

"You are going to attempt to encircle and eliminate a force of Llanos correct?"

"So far."

"Trying to encircle a force on their own ground is a very bad idea as your own marine captain would tell you if he were here. You need to choose the ground and then force them to make battle on your terms."

Marty nodded, "Carry on."

"Wolfgang said you would have a second force from Angostura. These should act as beaters to drive the Llanos toward your trap which would be a well-prepared defensive position. Then the chasing force can come up behind them and eliminate them."

"Hammer and Anvil."

"Exactly."

"I agree that your men would be better suited and can understand you wanting to get involved but I cannot risk having British soldiers killed in a battle that effectively will never officially happen, in a land where we are not at war, against a foe that is officially an ally."

"I think I can form a force of volunteers who will take leave of absence"

"They will still be British soldiers."

"Like your men are British sailors and marines. There isn't a difference."

"My men know what they were getting into when they joined the squadron."

"So will mine."

"Can they keep it a secret?"

"Have any of your exploits ever stayed a secret?"

"Touché. They are not acknowledged as official navy actions and sometimes get no mention in official quarters or in the Gazette."

"Well, this will be the same for us."

"I will insist on compensating the dependents of any casualties."

"That would be too kind, and more than the army would do in an official action."

"I will probably regret this if it goes horribly wrong, but we will use your volunteers topped up with marines."

Goodman looked relieved, "You will not regret this. I will let you know how many men tomorrow."

Marty wondered how many that would be. The major had a battalion at his disposal but how many would willingly volunteer for this?

"You are worried about something; you tossed and turned all night, and your worry line is back on your forehead," Caroline said over breakfast.

"I am waiting to hear from Major Goodman."

"Well, you won't have to wait much longer. If I'm not mistaken that is him coming down the drive on that big white charger of his."

She was right, the major made a magnificent sight as his high-stepping stallion carried him in full uniform towards them. The sun glinted off his highly polished buttons and brass work on his tack.

A groom took his horse as he dismounted, Adam met him at the door and escorted him into the dining room.

"Good morning, milord, Lady Caroline." He bowed to them both. Marty rose and returned his bow, "Please join us, help yourself to breakfast." He swept an arm towards the sideboard which was covered in dishes.

Goodman helped himself to a plateful and Adam poured him coffee.

"This is a damn fine brew," he said after sipping it.

"From our own plantation," Caroline said proudly.

"You have news?" Marty asked, trying not to sound impatient.

"What? Oh yes, I almost forgot. I have the men you need."

"How many?"

"Three platoons, non-commissioned officers and officers."

"Good grief that's, what, sixty men."

"Sixty-six actually. Sixty-seven with me."

"That's half your company."

"Just under to be exact."

"How are you going to explain that?"

"Exercises."

"Exercises?"

"Yes, training exercises. It will be entered into the company diary as a training exercise. Lieutenant Peters' idea."

"Resourceful young man, will he be coming?"

"Couldn't stop him if I wanted to."

Marty relaxed, this might just work.

"We will be transporting a hundred troops and marines so we will need the Mayfly as well," Marty said as he briefed Goodman, Howarth and Trenchard. "But first, I need to contact Matai and Piar to find out where we need to go."

"You will go to Angostura yourself?" Howarth said.

"Yes, I need to give Lady Caroline a rest from caring for me," Marty said with a completely straight face.

"She has been rather taken up with your recuperation," Trenchard said also with a straight face.

"Yes, I owe it to her to give her time to herself."

Marty was rather proud to have kept a straight face during the whole exchange. He was eternally grateful to Caroline for caring for him, but it was time for him to get back to work.

"I will take the Silverthorn to Angostura tomorrow, I should be back in two to three weeks. Have the force ready to embark as soon as I return. Major, please liaise with Captain O'Driscol. He has a touch of swamp fever, but I hope he will recover sufficiently to take his part in the exercise."

"If I come with you, I can better coordinate our force with the rebels," Goodman said.

"A good point, get your gear aboard. I will join you presently; I wish to visit O'Driscol now."

Marty went to the house the captain was recovering in. Shelby was there and he waited until the doctor had finished his examination.

"The good captain is on the road to recovery. I have dosed him with Jesuit bark and his fever has broken. He will be weak for a while but with care should recover completely."

Marty sat beside his bed.

"You aren't worried you will catch it?" O'Driscol said.

"No, I've seen it before and am sure that it's not transferable by sitting in the room. We will leave tomorrow for Angostura to talk to Piar and coordinate the attack on the Llanos. We will be back from there in two weeks, then we will load up the troops and start the exercises."

"Exercises? I thought it was an attack?"

Marty chuckled, "|That is what Goodman is calling it to justify us using his troops. Joint training exercises. Will you be fit?"

"I will or die trying."

"Let's not push it that far. You will have another week on the voyage where you can train with the men."

"Goodman is coming?"

"Yes, he is very keen."

"He is a good man, listen to him."

Marty could see that he was tiring and made his excuses.

Shelby was waiting outside.

"He feels terrible right now, the fever has taken his strength, but he is over the worst and should start recovering soon. He won't be left behind, but don't let him push too hard."

The Silverthorn sailed at first light and headed towards Trinidad. They were wary as although the hurricanes normally ran much further North, there was always the chance that one or a tropical storm would dip down to them.

As it was, they had the best of the seasonal weather, that is it rained, and the wind came from the Northeast. The schooner fairly flew in those conditions her gaff rig sails booming. It was most exhilarating. They passed Trinidad and entered the Orinoco which was in flood.

"We are going to need all sail to make progress against that," Howarth said eyeing the river, "and there is a lot of debris washing down it."

"I don't see any boats risking it," Marty said and as he watched an entire tree came down on the current. "I won't risk the ship by ordering you to travel up that, we will have to wait until after the rains have ended." He knew it was the right thing to do but he hated waiting. It was a wasted trip and that annoyed him.

Back at Oranjestad they settled down in the expectation that they would have to wait until the storm season passed. However, the arrival of a Dutch ship changed all that. The master insisted he speak to Marty.

"Are you the commodore?" the man asked after he was shown in. He was a big built fellow with wavy brown hair and a rugged face.

"I am, Commodore Stockley at your service. What can I do to help the Dutch merchant marine?"

"I'm Captain Reginald De Boer, of the Zeeland, I saw you when you came to Curaçao to end the privateering years ago. I hear you are here to stop the Americans."

"I am. I'm afraid I do not remember you."

"You wouldn't I was a first mate then. I have some information you might find useful."

"Please sit down and tell me what you know."

"We have been sailing between Bluefields and Curaçao for some time now carrying trade goods, and timber. On this trip we noticed something odd as we passed Bocca de Torro so on the way back I had extra eyes in the tops."

"What did they see?" Marty said.

"Masts."

"Masts?"

"Ya, masts of at least four ships."

"Why would there be four ships in the Bocca de Torro?"

"That's what I wondered, and the only thing I can think is it's someone laying up until the hurricane season is over."

The Bocca de Torro was a mass of small islands and mangrove swamps on the North coast of Panama. It started at the Chiriqui lagoon and continued for about thirty-five miles West. Most of it was too shallow for anything bigger than a canoe but there were deep-water inlets and streams where a larger ship could hide.

Marty dug out a chart, unrolled it on his desk and weighted the corners with stones.

"They were there behind the Northern of the Bastimentos islands, we caught a glimpse of them on our way out and managed to get a better look on our way back. Two masted ships, four that we could see."

"Two masted? Cutters or schooners."

"Probably."

"It's well out of the way of everywhere. Thank you for the information we will look into it. You are based in Curaçao?"

"Ya, I am."

"Then I know where to find you. If this turns out to be American privateers, you will be due a reward."

"They take our ships as well, Commodore, but our navy does nothing. If you catch them it helps us as well."

Marty wrote some notes and called Sam, "Get this to Wolfgang. Tell him we will sail this afternoon." He sent a second note to Major Goodman inviting him to partake in an exercise if he had two platoons of volunteers available for immediate departure.

He was in his room with Adam packing a small sea chest when Caroline found him.

"Are you going somewhere?"

"We have a tip that there might be some Americans hiding on the coast of Panama."

"And you need to personally lead the flotilla for that?"

He stopped packing and took her in his arms, "I need to get back into action, this is probably nothing, but it will get me back into trim. I'm not cut out to sail a desk."

She smiled, "No you are not, go lead your valiant men and come back safe to me. I am not in the mood to nurse you again."

"Witch, you will be in the mood when I get back."

She knew he wasn't referring to nursing and kissed his nose, "We will have to see won't we."

Adam coughed, "All packed, milord."

Marty gave her one last hug then patted her behind, "Until later, wench."

Caroline gave him a 'you know what you will be missing,' look and led him down the stairs leaving Adam to bring the trunk.

The Unicorn, Leonidas, Nymphe and Silverthorn left port and headed West. They were out a day when a storm came in from the East and they had to shelter in Ciénaga Bay until it passed. The ships were full of marines and soldiers, manned more like privateers than navy ships. The storm adversely affected the soldiers who were seasick to a man.

The rest of the trip enabled them to get their sea legs and to get to know their marine colleagues. This time the marines had the upper hands and schooled their land-based colleagues in some of the finer arts of ship-to-ship combat especially the manning of swivel guns and cannon.

Marty had to smile at the sight of ten burley soldiers under the command of a marine corporal going through the firing steps for an eighteen-pound cannon.

They hove to before the Bastimentos islands in the shelter of what was marked on the chart as Ensenada Bay and Marty called for all captains to attend him.

"If our friend was correct and they haven't sailed we should find the mystery ships behind this island here." He pointed to the island on his chart. "There are two ways to get to them, from the East through this channel between the islands and to the West through this other channel."

"Ah now I see why you need four ships! You will take them from both sides at once," Goodman said.

"I doubt it," James said, "the timing would be too difficult. The chances of everyone arriving at the same time would be practically zero."

"James is correct, we will, in fact, employ your idea of beater and shooter."

Goodman looked puzzled.

Marty took a pencil and drew an arrow on the map.

"This is the current wind direction which is unlikely to change in the next twenty-four hours. That makes it impossible to sail out of the Eastern channel so if they run they will have to head up the Western one."

"Ahh, I see. I think," Goodman said making the others laugh.

"The Nymphe and Silverthorn will take on board most of the marines and sailors and take the East channel. They will board, capture or burn the ships, if they turn out to be French or American, but there is no way they can take all four simultaneously so we can expect at least one, probably two, to get underway.

The Unicorn and Leonidas will sail up the outside of the islands and when the shooting starts blockade the Western end. I do not expect them to give up without a hell of a fight," Marty said. He asked for questions then dismissed them.

The captains returned to their ships and the marines and soldiers were transferred. It was dark by the time they were done, and the men settled down to rest as Marty wanted them under sail at false dawn.

The Nymphe and Silverthorn had to feel their way up the channel which ran almost due South. In the early dawn light, it was a tricky bit of sailing and their progress was slow.

The Nymphe led the way. She had bigger and more guns being effectively a small frigate and a stronger hull so could absorb more punishment than the lightly-built Silverthorn.

"Keep those men swinging the lead," Andrew Stamp instructed Stanley Hart.

"Aye, aye, Captain."

"By the mark, three fathoms two feet," Sam Samwise called followed a minute later by, "By the mark three fathoms one foot, mud bottom," from Gareth Williams who had the second lead line.

"Shoaling gently, Captain," Stanley said.

"Ease her a point." Andrew said to the helm.

He watched the trees pass by.

"If they don't see us coming, they are blind."

"I 'ope they don't have any guns set up to cover the channel," Bob Goldup the helmsman muttered.

Andrew grinned as he heard that. He had his ship ready for action, his carronades loaded with small ball. The six, four-pound round shot per gun were a good compromise between smashers and grape. Heavy enough to do damage to the rigging and hulls of lightly-built privateers.

"Masts to starboard. Looks like three two masters and a three master," the lookout called down.

They emerged into a lagoon.

"Captain, there appears to be a marked channel," Stanley said and pointed out two rows of markers that curved through the lagoon to the anchorage. The privateer ships, they could see American flags flying from their sterns now, were anchored in line and Andrew could see that he would have to take them one by one. He went to the stern rail and called to the Silverthorn.

"Terrance! I will take the second in line; you take the first behind me."

Terrance waved in acknowledgement.

The privateers had woken up and were rushing to arm themselves and man their guns. They approached the first ship, a two masted schooner.

"Guns! Give her one to soften her up for the Silverthorn!" Andrew shouted. It would also keep the privateer gunner's heads down.

The starboard battery roared as they passed a scant fifty feet from the ship. The effect was devastating,

"Good God!" Goodman gasped as he watched the schooner's upper deck being flayed.

"Reload. Take the rigging of the next one!" Stanley shouted.

"Get your men ready, Major, we will close with that one and board her."

Ahead they could see the three master and the third two master sprout sails and could hear the thud of axes cutting anchor cables. Then there was a thud as the ships came together and the world dissolved into violence, blood and death.

The Unicorn led the Leonidas slowly around the windward side of the islands and, as soon as they heard the Nymphs guns, turned into the Western channel where they anchored in line astern. The two big ships effectively blocked the channel, their guns run out and ready.

"Ships coming around the island!" a lookout called.

Marty stood by the rail with Troy by his side; the two of them well out of Wolfgang's way. It was hard but the Unicorn was Wolfgang's now and he could manage quite well.

"Larboard battery ready!" reported First Lieutenant McGiven.

"As soon as they are a cable away fire as you bear," Wolfgang said.

The main guns were elevated to take down rigging. The big bow carronades and the smaller aft carronades would sweep their deck fore to aft. Marty wasn't bothered about how many of the enemy they killed he was only interested in keeping his own casualties to a minimum.

The three-masted schooner came around the island and as soon as they saw the frigates fired bow chasers.

"They are going to try and force the gap between us," Wolfgang said calmly as the balls few over their heads.

The schooner was piling on sail and with the wind on her beam was picking up speed.

"Ready there," McGiven called to the gun crews whose captains all had their arms raised, lanyards extended and taught.

The American must have been up to ten knots when both frigates fired, the Unicorn first followed a scant second later by the Leonidas. The chain howled across the two-hundred-yard gap in a storm of destruction. Her fore mast folded in two, cut through. Rigging along her whole length parted, blocks and yards tumbled. Her deck was swept with a hail of canister as the carronades fired. Men were shredded.

"Lookout, she will hit us amid ships," Wolfgang shouted as the schooner swerved to port as her foremast dragged her off course."

"Prepare to board!" McGiven shouted.

Marty had his pistols in his hands before he even thought of it, the Shadows formed up around him.

The schooner hit the Unicorn just forward of the quarter deck at an angle that ran her down their side, rigging entangled, the deck tilted under the impact.

"Boarders away!" McGiven shouted and led the charge.

"Come on, lads," Marty shouted and headed for the rail.

Wolfgang was beside him, wielding a new weapon for him, a falchion, a brutal broad-bladed chopper of a sword. Heavier than a cutlass but completely suited to his style of swordsmanship.

Marty leapt on to the rail and down onto the schooner's deck. He fired his pistols at the first body he saw with a weapon in its hand and the man dropped his chest sporting a pair of holes.

The second barrels were cocked and fired instinctively, then it was sword and knife work. The Americans fought bravely, refusing to give up. Marty was at the point of a wedge made up of the Shadows with Troy at his side.

The big dog leapt forwards biting a man in the armpit and pulling him down. Marty stepped around his legs that were kicking as he tried to get the dog off of him. Sam stabbed down with his spear and that struggle was over.

Marty was toe to toe with a man who was a more than fair swordsman, but he was in no mood to fence. He parried a thrust with his knife, kicked him in the balls and nearly took his head off as he went down.

A warning growl from Troy and he spun to face another attack, he went high, Troy went low. The man, hamstrung, started to fall. Marty slashed backhanded with his knife finishing him.

There was a cry behind him and he turned to see Sam stagger back a boarding pike in his side.

"SAM!" he shouted as he attacked Sam's assailant stabbing the man in the back with both sword and knife.

"Sam," he said as he held the big man and gently lowered him to the ground, "we will get you to Shelby, stay still." He didn't try and pull the pike out he could see it had penetrated about halfway up the blade.

Matai arrived beside him; he was the Shadows medic when they were in the field, and tore open Sam's shirt.

"You might be lucky my big friend, unless you've been wiggling that around it might have missed anything you can't do without."

Sam had hold of the shaft in a rock steady grip.

"It ain't gonna wiggle anywhere."

Marty looked around, the fight was all but over. A few determined men fought to the end but were outnumbered and cut down. The Americans never struck.

Marty had Shelby brought to Sam,

"We can't move you with that sticking up, can you pull it out when I tell you?" Shelby said.

Sam nodded.

Shelby took a freshly boiled piece of linen and wadded it up and held it beside the blade.

"Right, now pull the blade out nice and straight we don't want to do any more damage than we can avoid."

Sam gritted his teeth and tried to pull on the shaft but stopped sweat dripping from his face.

"Help me, boss," he said to Marty.

Marty moved around until he was directly in line with the pike and grasped it carefully.

"Are you ready?" he said.

Sam nodded.

"On three. One, two, three!"

He pulled the pike as straight as he could, and it slid out with a wet sucking sound.

"I swear you look pale," Antton said from over Marty's shoulder as he took the pike from him. Sam glared at him.

Shelby pressed the linen on the wound.

"Make yourself useful and hold that firmly on his side," he said to Matai. "The rest of you get him down to my sickbay."

Troy was covered in blood. None of it his own as far as Marty could tell. With Sam being repaired by Shelby he had the task of washing the dog himself. It kept him from bothering Shelby down in the sick bay. A crewman manned the deck pump and Marty directed a stream of water over the dog, rubbing his fur to shift any dried-on bits. Troy loved the attention, especially having his back rubbed. He went all stiff legged and had his nose in the air, a big doggy grin on his face.

Wolfgang waited until he had finished. "Happy to report all four ships taken. Although we will probably have to tow the three master home. I will carry out an inspection and let you know."

Marty was surprised, he hadn't seen the Nymphe or Silverthorn approach with their prizes. He had been so worried about Sam he had lost track of everything else.

"Pass my congratulations to them for a job well done."

"I will, and Mr Shelby has sent a message that he has finished with Sam and you can visit him if you wish."

Marty turned towards the stairs to the lower decks.

"He isn't down there, Antton and Matai moved him up to your cabin."

Troy chose that moment to shake himself violently and both men got sprayed.

"You can stay here." Marty told the still dripping dog, brushing water drops from his face.

Matai was sat beside Sam, who was laid out on Marty's cot. When Marty came in Sam tried to get up.

"Stay there," Marty said and stood next to them. "Well?" he said to Matai.

"Nothing damaged inside. He grabbed the shaft before it could be pushed all the way in. Shelby had a good nose around in there to be sure. He had to cauterise a couple of bleeds and flushed the wound with spirit and dusted it with sulphur before he stitched him up. Three layers of stitches would you believe. Our friend here has really thick stomach muscles."

"How long has he to stay in bed?"

"About two weeks as long as there isn't any infection. There is a herbal poultice on it which should keep it good."

"Where will you sleep boss?" Sam said.

"They can make me another cot or sling me a hammock. You are staying there."

"Shelby has given Adam instructions on what to feed him," Matai said.

"What was the butcher's bill?" Marty asked Shelby at the first opportunity.

"On the Unicorn, four dead, twenty-five wounded all of which should recover. I don't know about the others in detail but casualties were light."

"And the Americans?"

"That is a different story. Almost the entire crew of the Dawn's Light were killed or wounded, that's just on a hundred men. Most killed by shot from our carronades. The schooner that the Leonidas took on gave up when they saw the damage the three master took."

"I'm sure all that will be confirmed when Wolfgang has gathered all the reports."

Wolfgang did indeed confirm the information and added, "The schooner that the Silverthorn attacked gave up without a fight. There were a dozen casualties from the Nymphe's broadside that she gave as she passed. The Nymphe's main target put up a bit of a fight and they killed ten, including the captain before they gave up. The Silverthorn suffered only one casualty, the gentleman in question will be doing extra duty on the range to learn how to handle a pistol safely without shooting himself in the leg."

Marty didn't ask.

"The Nymphe's suffered three casualties: two walking wounded and one who will probably lose his left arm below the elbow. He was a topman; the arm was shattered by a ball."

"Not a bad day's work, when will you bury our dead?" Marty said to Wolfgang.

"This evening at dusk. Will you take the service? The men would appreciate that."

"Certainly. What do you want to do with the three master?"

"We could repair her but to be honest it would take days. The combined broadsides ruined her rigging and neither of her remaining masts would survive a blow over a stiff breeze. Her hull is still sound with practically no damage. She is also loaded with goods they have taken from British ships."

"Tow her then, we will be taking the prizes to Jamaica."

"That will slow us up a lot."

"True and there is the risk of hurricane or storms." Marty considered the options, "I hate to do it, but I think the only option is to unload and burn her."

They sailed out into deep water and the service for the British dead was done in the age-old way. Each was sewn into his hammock, the last stitch through his nose to make sure he was dead and not just sleeping. An eighteen-pound round shot was placed at the foot end to make sure they reached Davy Jones' locker.

Marty read the service and finished with Psalm 130:

Out of the deep have I called unto thee, O LORD;

Lord, hear my voice.

O let thine ears consider well

the voice of my complaint.

If thou, LORD, wilt be extreme to mark what is done amiss,

O Lord, who may abide it?

Fore there is mercy with thee,

therefore shalt thou be feared.

I look for the LORD; my soul doth wait for him;

in his word is my trust.

My soul fleeth unto the Lord before the morning watch;

I say, before the morning watch.

O Israel, trust in the LORD,

for with the LORD there is mercy,

and with him is plenteous redemption.

And he shall redeem Israel

from all his sins.

The dead were committed to the deep and the men, generally not a religious group, appreciated this verse as it sounded nautical and responded with a loud, "AMEN."

Marty allowed the Americans to bury their dead themselves. The service was very much the same only they had a preacher who took the service. The smoke from the burning ship a fitting backdrop.

Chapter 15: Hammer and Anvil

"Now the grandmother lived away in the wood, half an hour's walk from the village; and when Little Red Riding Hood had reached the wood, she met the wolf; but as she did not know what a bad sort of animal he was, she did not feel frightened."

Marty read the latest Grimm's fairy tales to the twins for their bedtime story. His hands on approach to his children was unusual. Most aristocrats farmed their children out to nannies, only seeing them during the day then sending the boys to boarding school or the girls to one of the fancy finishing schools to make them ladies. However, Marty was an aristocrat only by title, his blood was decidedly red and from a long line of peasants.

"Is the wolf like Troy?" Edwin asked.

"A little bit bigger, and he has grey fur."

Troy, hearing his name, lifted his head from where he lay on the rug.

"But they both have great big teeth." Troy yawned showing his canines.

Constance giggled. "Would he eat us up?"

"I would fight him with my sword or shoot him with a pistol," Edwin said with all the belligerence a six-year-old could summon.

Marty laughed and went on with the story, he had received the book from his sister, Jane, along with letters from her, his brother Arthur and Ryan Thompson. The estates in both Cheshire and Dorset were in good order and their tenants doing well. Caroline had received letters from Louise, the ex-French spy who helped her run her mercantile empire, and from Bill Clarence, the head of her wine 'importers' in Deal.

Marty was waiting for the Endellion to return from the Orinoco estuary to tell him that the river was navigable. The Silverthorn was on standby to take him to Angostura and General Piar. The hurricane season was almost over, and this year it had been particularly stormy and wet. That meant the river had been in flood for the last few months and impassable.

He had recovered from his wounds and, more importantly to him, Sam had recovered from his too. The big man's wife, Hannah, had taken him in hand when they had returned and made sure he was fully healed before she allowed him to get back into action. Consequently, he had put on a few pounds.

"We both need to train harder," Marty joked when Sam complained about his slightly flabby waistline. Sam took him at his word, and they were soon sweating on the training ground. Staff fighting, swordplay, strength training.

Halfway through November Marty was stripping off ready for bed when Caroline looked him up and down. "My you have toned up," she said as he pulled his shirt over his head. Marty assumed a pose that flexed his muscles then dropped his trousers and leapt on the bed. Caroline squealed then giggled as his lips started to explore.

The following day they got up late and had just finished breakfast when Philip Trenchard was shown in by Adam.

"Good morning, Philip, good to see you back," Marty said.

"Good morning, milord, Lady Caroline. I beg to report, Sir, that the Orinoco is passable."

"Excellent news!" Marty said, "Grab yourself a plate and join us for breakfast."

Philip noticed that Caroline had a healthy glow about her.

"I must say you are looking particularly well, Lady Caroline."

Caroline glanced at Marty and blushed. "Thank you Philip I am very well thank you."

Marty coughed and said, "You can prepare the Endellion for an amphibious operation as when I return, I expect we will be embarking the marines and a contingent of the army."

"Is the Silverthorn also taking part?"

"Yes."

"I will prepare the stores and boats for them as well."

They had brought the whaler-based landing boats with them as deck cargo and they had been stored on shore, the marines and their army colleagues had been practising embarking from ship to the landing boats using the two redundant schooners. They had achieved a level of proficiency that surprised Marty. It seemed that the enthusiasm for the action wasn't restricted to the officers.

The Silverthorn left port the next morning; Marty and Major Goodman stood at the rail and waved goodbye to their womenfolk. Caroline stood with Femke van Drenth. The beautiful Dutch woman and the major had become a couple in the time he had been posted there.

"I hate it when he leaves," Femke said tears in her eyes.

"In the navy our men are always leaving and away for long periods, but one never gets used to it."

"Does he often come back wounded?"

Caroline turned to her and could see the fear in her eyes. "Sometimes, but they have the best surgeon in the fleet in Shelby and his two nurses here on the island are very well trained."

"You can use a sword, why?"

"It makes me feel closer to Martin. He thinks it is because I want to be independent but that is only half of it. Being able to use a sword and shoot somehow makes me feel— I don't know how to explain it."

"Could you teach me?"

Caroline was surprised. "Yes, I suppose I could."

The two men watched the dock until it was out of sight.

"Will you two get married?"

"I have asked her."

"And?"

"She hasn't said no."

"But she hasn't said yes either?"

"How long to we get to Angostura?"

Marty took the hint. "Two weeks."

"Two weeks there, two weeks back and a week in between. It will be at least nine weeks before we can take the war to the Llanos."

"That's the way of it."

"I wonder if there will ever be a faster way?"

"Only if we can speed up travel or find a way of communicating faster. The signal tower relay has sped up communications on land, but there is no way to speed it up at sea. We have some short-range ways of signalling with flags, rockets and lights but nothing that goes farther than the eye can see."

"The distances at sea are so great, everything seems to happen so slowly," Goodman said.

Terrance Howarth had approached to report to Marty and barked a laugh. "That's until we come to action and then it all happens very quickly."

"Quite right, Mr Howarth, what have you to report?" Marty said.

"We are under full sail and making fourteen knots, Sir, heading West by Southwest."

"Very good, Captain. Thank you."

Goodman looked thoughtful. "I have been meaning to ask, you talk of speed in knots. What is that?"

"We measure speed with a log, which is effectively a triangular shaped piece of wood on a line that has knots tied at fixed distances. We cast the log over the side and allow the line to run out for twenty-eight seconds as measured by a glass. The number of knots that run out in that time gives us our speed. A knot equates to one and a quarter land miles an hour."

"Makes perfect sense," Goodman laughed. "So, we are travelling at seventeen and a half miles an hour."

"Ah, but in this case our land speed is not the same as our sea speed."

"Why is that?"

"Because the Caribbean current is running against us. That means we are swimming against water that is travelling at just under a mile an hour in the opposite direction."

"Pfft, travelling on land is much simpler."

"But you go so slow on land and a ship never gets tired," Marty said with an artful grin.

"Touché, Commodore."

The made it to Angostura in twelve days and once tied up made their way to General Piar's residence.

"Mr Stockbridge and Mr Goodings to see you, Sir," the maid announced showing them in.

Piar stood and held out his hand to Marty as they greeted.

"You have arrived at an opportune moment; we have found that band of Llanos."

"Opportune indeed, how many of them are there?"

Piar referred to a paper on his desk. "Close to two hundred, if the scouts are to be believed. A substantial force."

"Do you have enough men to beat them?" Goodman asked.

"Thanks to the instructors Mr Stockbridge provided, yes, but that isn't the problem."

Marty and Goodman looked at him expectantly. He sighed, "Bringing them to battle is the problem, if we approach with anything larger than a squad they move away. This is a very big country, and they can escape easily."

"Can you show me where they are on the map?" Goodman said.

Piar moved to the large map he had on the wall picking up a yard-long ruler from his desk on the way which he used as a pointer.

"They are here camped between the rivers Oris and Paragua in this valley."

Goodman looked at the map closely then asked if they had a magnifying glass. Piar took one from a drawer and handed it to him.

"Is the river Paragua fordable this time of year?"

"It isn't fordable at any time of year along that stretch."

"And these hills to the West are they high?"

"More like mountains."

"So, if you approach from the North they have no choice but to run South."

"That is true."

Goodman looked expectantly at Marty.

"If we were to place a force across that valley to the South of their camp then we could catch them in a trap forcing them to fight on our terms."

"But how would we get a force there without them knowing?" Piar asked.

Marty stepped forward and pointed to a large river to the East of the Paragua that ran parallel to it.

"This river, the Caroni, is navigable?"

"Yes, you can get a large boat up it."

"How about a schooner?"

"Up as far as there, where there are rapids," he indicated a point on the map where the river was joined by another river called the Uriman.

"That's about as far as we need to go." Marty sat back in his chair and said, "I will provide a force of men and get them dug into a fortified line between the mountains and River Paragua that will stop the Llanos and provide an anvil which your hammer can smash them against."

"What will that cost?"

"Consider it a gift, but I will need the advisors returned to me immediately."

Piar looked at Marty with a calculating look. "I still think there is more to you than you are telling, but there is an expression that one should not check a gift horse's teeth, so I accept your offer."

There followed a detailed planning session with Piar's officers. Goodman automatically took the lead and showed that he was much more than a garrison officer, showing tact and an ability to sell tactics to the most sceptical of Venezuelan officers.

The voyage back to Aruba was full of anticipation and a measure of impatience to get on with the job. The Silverthorn seemed to feel it too and flew along with the wind on her starboard quarter until the island came into sight.

"Skipper! A cutter is signalling us."

"Get up there and see what they are saying, Mr Shepherd," Captain Howarth said.

The young midshipman grabbed a glass and shot up the mainmast that was sitting at a twenty-five-degree heel.

"Our number and 'Follow me to Savaneta.'"

"Damn odd," Howarth said, "Fipps, give the commodore my compliments and tell him that we are being guided into Savaneta."

Marty came up on deck and studied the cutter through a glass. "If I am not mistaken that is young Reynolds commanding the cutter."

Trenchard focussed his own glass and said, "I believe you are right, Sir."

"Follow them in, I think Trenchard has been busy."

The cutter led them into the cattle dock. "If you would be so kind as to tie up at the dock opposite the Endellion, Sir," Reynolds called across.

Men appeared on the dock and looped the thrown lines over mooring bollards. The Endellion was tied up on the other side, her deck covered in boxes of stores. Trenchard walked down the gangplank and raised his hat in greeting.

"You appear to have been busy, Philip," Marty said as he shook his hand.

"Yes, Sir. The troops have assembled here and are ready to embark. The Endellion is provisioned and loaded. The provisions for the Silverthorn are ready to be loaded as are the stores for the troops."

"Excellent. We can have a fast turnaround. We have three weeks to get our men into position. This will give us an extra few days," Marty said.

Men were already bringing crates and sacks of provisions along the dock. Marty realised that they were a mixture of marines and soldiers.

"Captain Howarth! Please resupply and get the army's stores aboard as soon as possible."

Goodman joined him on the dock. "Where are my men bivouacked?"

"Follow me, Sir, I will show you to them and your quarters. I took the liberty of securing shore quarters for you as well the commodore."

"Lay on MacDuff!" Goodman quipped getting inquiring looks from the two navy men. "Shakespeare? Macbeth?" he said to them.

Marty and Trenchard looked at each other, then at Goodman,

"Never read him," they said in unison.

The troops were camped in well-ordered lines of tents a short distance away from the dock in an area normally used for cattle. They were greeted by Lieutenant Peters.

"Good to have you back, Sir, the men are keen to get into action."

"Looks like you have them well set up."

"Yes, Sir. We had to clean out a lot of cow shit but once that was done this place is a regular home from home."

"Marines and soldiers all in one place?" Marty said.

"Not quite, the marines are over the other side, closer to the sea. Their idea of a camp is somewhat different to ours."

Marty concealed a smile by pretending to wipe his nose, he had a feeling he knew what was coming.

They walked over and the dividing line was quite clear. One side were precise rows of tents. Neatly tied-back flaps revealed folding camp beds with soldier's packs neatly stacked at the end. Soldiers were partly dressed in uniform as they relaxed and guards in full uniform stood at parade rest. On the other side of the line, were angled sheets of canvas supported by oars or booms. Bed rolls were laid out in rows under them with sea chests at their foot. The marines were not in uniform, so it was hard to tell who an officer was.

There were central cooking fires in both camps but that was about the only similarity apart from the weapons stacked within easy reach.

"We need to get your men in to civilian clothes," Marty said to Goodman as Captain O'Driscol walked over to them the image of an Irish gentleman at large.

"Good afternoon, Commodore."

"Welcome back, Captain, I hope all is well?"

"Mission accomplished, my report is on your desk at the mansion."

"Excellent. I am looking forward to reading it when we get back."

They made their way to a house, a large colonial-style pile with a columned porch which had been acquired as temporary officer country. The drawing room had been turned into a wardroom by the navy and a steward was ready to serve drinks. Glasses of Madera were distributed, and Marty brought them all up to date.

"So, we have three weeks to get into position to block the Southern end of the valley and act as the anvil for Piar's force to smash the Llanos against," Marty said. "He will be setting out in a week and drive them ahead of him."

O'Driscol looked up at the ceiling.

"It would be best if we could create a fortified line, some kind of bank with redoubts every thirty yards or so."

Goodman nodded. "I agree, what would you put in the redoubts? I don't think you can haul cannon across that terrain."

"We did in Italy," Marty said, "but we had horses and could create road carriages for the guns."

"Swivels and mortars," O'Driscol said.

"Where do the mortars come from?" Marty asked.

"The Toolshed has come up with a way to throw a three-and-a-half-inch grenade a decent distance. We can lob one two to three hundred yards."

"How big are they?" Goodman asked.

"When we have finished our drinks, I have arranged for a demonstration."

"Can't wait," Goodman said, drained his glass to heeltaps and stood. The rest laughed and followed suit. O'Driscol led them to an area to the rear of the town which was just brush and sand. A three-man team of marines had set up one of the mortars.

"Corporal Wells, please explain to our guests the weapon and how it is operated," O'Driscol said.

Corporal Wells snapped to attention.

"At ease, Wells, in your own time," Marty said.

He visibly relaxed and said, "The boys in the Toolshed were experimenting with ideas for throwing grenades when one of them remembered the bombs at the Basque Roads. He took a scrap six pounder from one of them schooners that are laid up and cut off the barrel, so it left the breech and about four inches. Then he got a carpenter to make up a mount so that it sits at forty-five degrees. After some refinement and experimentation, they came up with this."

He pointed to the stub barrelled gun where the barrel was clamped in a block. Either side of the block were a pair of steel hoops.

"If you put spars through them 'oops, four men can carry it comfortably. Now we will send a couple of grenades down range."

He turned to the gun crew who were knelt beside it.

"Ready to load. Load!" One man dropped in a cartridge of powder, followed it with a wad, which he tamped down, then dropped in a grenade with the fuse sticking out the top.

"Prime!"

The second man shoved a priming pin down the touch hole then inserted a quill and pulled the flintlock back to full cock, straightened out the lanyard and raised his arm. The second marine had a slow match on a short linstock ready to light the fuse.

"Stand back, gentlemen, we will fire three rounds."

They stepped back to be at a safe distance and Wells shouted, "FIRE!"

The fuse was lit, the lanyard pulled, the mortar chuffed, and a black blob left a trail of smoke in the air. Three seconds later the grenade exploded about two hundred and fifty yards distant about twenty feet above the ground.

They reloaded. They didn't rush but thirty-five seconds later a second grenade left the barrel. It hadn't reached its target before they were reloading for the third.

Marty noticed the explosions were walking towards them. "Are you reducing the charge?"

"Aye, Sir, we have prepared charges to throw grenades from one hundred yards to the maximum in twenty-yard increments. The same for the grenades, we have pre-cut the fuses.

"Please fit the carry bars," Marty said, and once they were in he turned to the assembled officers.

"Major Goodman, Captain O'Driscol and Lieutenant Peters, if you would be so kind."

The four men lifted the mortar and rested the bars on their shoulders.

"By the left, march," Marty said and the four preceded to walk across the rough terrain in a loop back to the firing site.

"I think four men could carry this for an hour especially if the shaft was wrapped in padded leather," Goodman said.

"How will you transport the ammunition?" Marty said.

"Handcarts, Sir. We have one for every gun."

"Why not carry the guns that way?"

"Not enough wheels available, Sir, we could only requisition enough for the carts and don't have time to make any more. The Toolshed think they could come up with a way to attach a pair of wheels for transporting them, but they need more time."

"Excuse me for asking," Goodman said, "but what or who is the Toolshed?"

They all got a good night's sleep, aided by an excellent meal and ample wine, and saw to the loading of the men onto the Silverthorn and Endellion. The ships were very crowded, but the men made the most of it. They set sail just after midday.

Four days saw them entering the Orinoco and another two days saw them enter the River Caroni. Then things slowed down as the current was strong and against them, forcing the use of sweeps to supplement the sails when they lost the wind.

"It's a good thing we gained a few days, we are hardly making four miles an hour," Captain Howarth said.

"According to the chart we should soon find the junction with the River Uriman," Marty said.

The land through which they travelled was grassland scattered with brush and trees. They saw plenty of game and Marty tasked a team to get them fresh meat once they landed. He and the Shadows would scout towards the last known position of the Llanos.

They eventually came to the junction of the rivers that designated their debarking point. They tied the ships up to the bank and started unloading.

"Major Goodman is in charge of the march and setup of the defensive line. Captain O'Driscol is second in command. Lieutenant Peters, I believe you are fit, would you like to accompany me and my men on a scouting trip?"

"Oh, rather, Sir!" Peters said then remembered to look to his commander for permission.

"I think you may regret your enthusiasm, Peters, but you can join the commodore and his band of cut throats."

Marty tossed him a pack. "There are provisions for three days in there."

Antton passed him a canteen with a long strap, a cavalry carbine and pouch of cartridge.

"Leave your sword it will get in the way. Do you have a dagger or long knife?" He didn't, so Antton gave him one of those as well.

"Right, we will be back in no more than four days. You need to be in position and dug in by then," Marty said in parting to Goodman.

Peters thought he was fit, but he soon found that Marty set a punishing pace across the wild terrain. They headed West following a tributary of the Caroni until they found the larger River Paragua running South to North. The river was smaller than the Caroni but wide enough and deep enough to make crossing difficult.

"How do we get across that?" Peters asked as they stood on the bank.

"According to the scouts we talked to in Angostura there is a place upstream at the head of some rapids, but we will cross here."

"I can't swim."

"I have no intention of swimming it," Marty said.

The Shadows were busy cutting poles from the many trees that lined the bank and Wilson unlimbered a crossbow that was strapped to his backpack. He took a specially-designed bolt and lashed a thin, strong line to it. He placed his foot in the stirrup on the front of the crossbow and used a lever to crank the string into the loading position. Peters noted that even the huge Wilson's muscles bulged with the effort. He fitted the bolt and made sure the coil of line was free, raised the crossbow to his shoulder and fired.

The heavy bolt flew across the river into the trees on the other side trailing the line behind it. It bounced off a couple of branches and a trunk becoming tangled.

"Perfect," Wilson murmured and bent the other end of the line around a tree, pulling it tight.

"Line secured, boss."

The other Shadows were busy lashing the poles together into a serviceable raft.

"We will raft across using the line to stop being washed downstream. The first ones across will run out a heavier rope which we will secure across the river. The troops that are following us will use the raft and line to ferry the rest of the men and supplies across."

"They could even make more rafts!" Peters said enthusiastically.

"Indeed, how are your feet?"

"I have a couple of blisters."

"Take your boots off. Matai, please have a look at Mr Peters' feet."

Peters opened his mouth to object but a look from Marty told him that this wasn't a request. He took off his boots and stockings while Matai knelt to check his feet.

"I need to treat these, or they could go bad," He said after checking the blisters on Peters heels and beside his big toes.

"Your boots could be better designed."

"Never expected to do other than march on parade or ride a horse. This running across country isn't in the job description."

"We have an ex-shoemaker in the squadron, he can make you a proper pair of boots more suitable for this type of work."

Peters tensed and suppressed a yelp of pain as Matai rubbed something into the open blisters.

"This is benzoin gum in alcohol. It will clean the blisters and seal them." He took a knife and poured some alcohol over the blade.

"I will vent the unbroken blisters and apply the tincture to them as well."

Peters could only nod as tears ran down his face.

"There you are all done. I have put clean cotton wadding soaked in tincture over the blisters. Try to keep it in place when you put on your stockings. I will see you again when we camp tonight."

The raft was finished, and the first three men went over. A rope was attached to the stern to drag it back and the men would attach another to the prow to help pull the next load across.

"How will Goodman and the main force find the crossing?" Peters asked.

"Didn't you notice that we left markers along the trail?"

"I was too busy keeping up."

"Well, we left markers that our men know and can follow. Once they are this side of the river, they can choose their own path." Marty showed him how the marker was made.

"I will have to remember all this when I get back to the regiment, I will be taking over the skirmishers soon and this is all wonderful."

With everyone across they set off again at the same punishing pace. Peters' feet were much less painful, and he found he was adapting to the loping gait the Shadows adopted that covered distance so quickly. It wasn't a run, nor a walk, but a sort of trot or lope that they could sustain for hours.

They camped before dark. John Smith and Wilson dug a deep fire pit that concealed their fire and made tea and boiled rice. They boiled a thick concentrate of beef stock with dried beef strips, dried peas, herbs they had foraged locally, with water to make a nourishing meal.

"I will take the first watch with John. Antton and Matai will take the second, Wilson and Garai the third and Peters and Chin the last," Marty said.

Peters looked surprised.

"Something bothering you, Lieutenant?"

"I was just surprised that officers took a watch."

"In this outfit everyone takes watches and helps clean up after dinner, you can help John wash up."

He slept like a log; the bedroll that had been tied to the top of his pack was surprisingly comfortable. He was woken by Wilson who shook his shoulder.

"Your watch, it's all quiet."

He rose and pulled on his boots, shaking them first in case something had crawled in overnight.

"Keep back to fire," Chin whispered, "you stay this side I go other side." He faded into the dark.

This is a rum crew I've got involved with here, no sense of rank at all! Officers taking watch and washing dishes, whatever next. I wonder if this is what Sebastian experienced? he thought as he stared into the dark. The moon had gone down an hour before and the world was waiting for the dawn, the cough of a puma some distance away made him jump. He had his carbine in his hands which comforted him, but he would have to see something to shoot it. *No good asking for a torch,* he mused.

He had been on guard for an hour when there was a rustle in a bush outside the camp. Peters tensed and brought his gun to the ready, his thumb on the hammer ready to pull it to full cock. There was another rustle, whatever it was had moved closer.

He brought the gun to his shoulder and pulled the hammer to full cock.

"I wouldn't do that," Marty said quietly from the dark behind him.

"I heard something."

"So would any Llanos in five miles if you fire that gun."

He lowered the carbine and let the hammer back to half cock.

Marty appeared out of the dark and stood beside him. The rustle came again. Marty pulled his knife and slipped forward into the dark.

Peters waited, straining to see or hear Marty. The rustling had stopped.

"Just a pig," Marty said as he materialized as if out of nowhere.

"Jesus Christ! Do you always sneak up on people?"

"Comes with the territory. It's almost dawn, please wake up the others."

The next phase of the mission was at a much slower pace.

"Chin and Garai take the lead, the Llanos camp should be just a couple of miles ahead."

They stayed under cover as much as they could, moving forward only when they were sure it was safe to do so. Chin and Garai were ghosts flitting in and out of view a couple of hundred yards ahead.

Marty suddenly held up his hand as he caught the unmistakeable odour of unwashed humanity and sank to a knee, the others followed suit.

"What is it?" Peters asked.

Marty put a finger against his lips and shhhhd him. He lent close to his ear, "Can't you smell it?"

Marty flicked a series of signals to the men and they quietly shifted position out to the sides. Peters went to follow but Marty laid a hand on his arm and shook his head.

Chin reappeared and his hands flickered, Marty moved forward in a crouch until they came up to him.

"The camp is three hundred feet ahead, there are at least three hundred men in it including a contingent of Spanish infantry," Chin whispered.

"Any signs of alarm?"

"None, they are very relaxed, and my guess is they have been here a while."

"Let's go and have a look."

Chin led them around to the West and up the back of a low hill, as they got closer to the top they went into a crouch and then into a crawl until they could look down into the encampment.

Marty examined the scene laid out before them. A haphazard collection of tents and rough huts made of unpeeled logs. It had obviously been there a while. A stream ran through it towards the river which he could see sparkle in the distance. The inhabitants were predominantly men, but he could see one or two women wandering around. He followed one with his eyes and she made her way past several of the tents, exchanging comments with some of the men until she came to one of the few wooden structures.

"They appear to have a brothel set up, so they must have been using this site for months. Makes me wonder how they kept it a secret."

Peters nudged him. "There is a coral over there with a dozen or so horses." As he said it a rider came into the camp. He rode to the coral, dismounted and handed his horse over to what must me a liveryman. He then hurriedly made his way to a large tent/wooden structure. He shouted something as he approached, and a uniformed man came out to meet him. There was a waving of arms and an excited exchange with the messenger repeatedly pointing to the North.

The uniformed man called back into the tent and two more uniformed men came out and went to the coral with the messenger. They got fresh horses saddled and set out to the North.

"I believe that indicates that Piar's army has been spotted," Marty said.

"Do you think they will move immediately?" Peters said.

"I doubt it, the army is probably still miles away and as you know you can move that many men probably ten miles a day if all goes well."

"In this landscape probably only six. How far South of here are our men?"

Marty turned to look South, "See that line of mountains? They are setting up the line between them and the river at a narrow point. It's about six miles from here."

Peters groaned.

"I thought you army types were used to walking."

"In our regiment all officers ride."

Marty suddenly looked down into the camp, "Good, Antton and Matai have infiltrated the camp."

Peters peered in the same direction, "Where?"

"Just passing the brothel, Matai is talking to one of the whores."

"You have very good eyesight," Peters said and pulled out a telescope.

Marty stopped him before he could extend it. "If you are going to use that you need to make sure the sun doesn't flash off the lens or the brass work. Try this one."

Marty passed him a small telescope that had the brass blackened and a long shade over the object lens. Peters took it and adjusted it to his eye.

"I say, your chap is coming on a bit strong with that girl, he has his arms around her and is holding her behind."

"Just flirting while he milks her of information probably. He is happily married."

"He has just parted with her and given her a slap on the behind. She is laughing."

"Probably inviting him to come back and dally with her for a discount, women seem to find him attractive."

They watched the two Basques make their way through the camp to the headquarters and settle down within hearing distance. Just before dark a horseman galloped into the camp and rode straight to the headquarters building.

"Piar's army is fifteen miles North. The scout who came in earlier says they were setting up camp when he left them. It would have taken him at least an hour to get from there back to this camp by horse and he had ridden it hard," Antton said.

"They have been in this camp for four months, according to one of the whores. She was worried that the rebels would find them but apparently they lost their commander not that long ago and since then there hasn't been the same level of organisation or activity."

"What happened to their commander?" Peters said.

"The boss killed 'im," John Smith said.

Peters looked at Marty expectantly, but he said nothing.

"Poison dart wunnit, Garai?" John said.

"Yea, right in the face. He was a shirt lifter."

"That's enough of that," Marty said, "did you hear anything about them moving?"

"They are going to wait and see what Piar does in the morning, the bloke in charge doesn't believe the rebels know where they are or that the rebels pose a serious threat."

"Did you discover where they keep their powder?"

"No, it seems that they keep it distributed amongst the men," Matai said.

"They don't have much then."

"A couple of powder flasks per man." He tossed Marty an oversized powder flask made of some kind of gourd. "Took that off a drunk."

"Two of these each?"

Matai nodded. "I think you could get around fifty loads from a full one."

"No cartridge?"

"No, they all have different guns so make their own balls. I bet that every load is different, and no two balls fly the same."

"They all carry a big knife they call a machete which looks like a broad-bladed fascine the Spanish army carry," Antton added.

Peters was amazed. "You found out all this but just wandering around the camp?"

"It's not just wandering," Marty said.

"It's knowing how to wander," the Shadows all said together and collapsed in fits of laughter.

They kept the camp under observation for two more days until there was a sudden burst of activity, lots of shouting and the odd scream.

"They are packing up in a hurry."

"Get ready to move out," Marty said.

The Shadows were ready to move in a matter of minutes and helped Peters who was lagging.

Matai and Chin had performed an early morning reconnaissance and came back into camp.

"We might have a problem, boss," Matai said, "we took a look down a well-used track towards the river and they have set up a ferry down there."

"Like the one we set up?"

"Sort of, they have strung a rope across the river and use that to drag a barge across."

"Chin, Matai you are with me, the rest of you stay ahead of the main body, do not make contact and no shooting."

Marty was about to move out when Peters grabbed his arm. "Take me with you."

"We need to move fast and quiet, you will hold us up."

"I can keep up; I won't be a problem."

Marty looked at him and saw a need in his eyes. "Alright but it's up to you to stay with us. We won't wait for you."

With that he turned and moved out, moving silently but quickly. Chin took the lead, keeping the morning sun at eleven o'clock. They followed a game trail for a mile or so through brush then dropped into a dry arroyo which paralleled the track to the river. They could hear people moving down the track and Marty pushed them to a loping run.

Chin stopped and carefully raised his head above the bank.

"Shit, they already sending a load across."

The others lined up beside him and could see that the barge was coming up to halfway across, heavily laden with people and goods.

Marty studied the setup of the barge. It was as Chin had described; a heavy rope was stretched across the river secured on either bank by stout poles that had been driven into the bank. The barge was held to the rope by loops of leather and the bargemen moved it by pulling on the rope.

"We need to cut that rope," Marty said.

"How? There are a load of people waiting on this bank ready to cross," Peters said.

"You need to learn to think outside the tactics book," Marty grinned.

"Chin, Matai, I need a smokescreen."

The Shadows grinned and slipped over the bank into the brush. The wind was coming from the Southwest so would work in their favour.

Marty took out a cloth and tied it over his mouth and nose. Peters was surprised and followed suit.

"As you insisted on coming along, we will make use of that big knife of yours," Marty said.

A crackling to their left presaged flames that spread rapidly in the dry brush. Marty studied it for a moment, judging its direction and speed.

"Come on."

They set out in a crouched run down the arroyo then slid over the bank on their bellies, then snake crawled through the brush until they were at the edge of the landing. Marty checked the barge; it was over halfway across.

Smoke and sparks were blowing on the breeze from the brushfire and slowly engulfed the landing causing cries of consternation and coughing from the people.

"Now!" Marty said and slipped into the smoke. Peters stuck to him like a leach, worried that if he lost sight of him, he would be lost. Marty's sense of direction took him directly to the post and he crouched beside it while he rummaged in his pack. He pulled out the powder flask that Antton had stolen, pulled both levers to open up the spout and pushed a short length of fuse into it. He took an igniter from his pocket, one of the Toolshed's specials, lit the fuse and after it had burnt to about an inch of the spout threw the flask towards the coughing crowd.

"Cut the rope," he said and pulled a pistol to cover them.

Peters sawed furiously at the rope which was a good inch and a half thick and tarred. The flask exploded, panic ensued, people started screaming and running in all directions. He had gotten about halfway through when a man ran towards them.

Marty let him come and as he got to him, swept his legs from under him and struck him with his pistol butt on the back of the head. He looked at Peters who was sweating as he sawed.

The rope gave with a twang and shot away across the river. The people on the barge would probably get to the other side but no more would. They turned to return to the arroyo when a trail of fire arced from the bank towards the barge, embedding itself in a pile of sacks.

"What the hell?" Peters said.

"It's Chin. He is having fun. Come on."

Marty led them towards the source of the fire as a second arc of fire flew towards the barge.

Chin was just loading a third when they found him kneeling in a depression by the riverbank.

"Nice shooting," Marty said, "but it's time to get out of here."

Chin said nothing, aimed and loosed the fire arrow, unstrung his bow and broke it down into two halves before packing it back into its bamboo tube. They followed the arroyo for a while then broke to the South as a trail presented itself.

They stopped for a second to look across the river. The barge was in flames, the passengers desperately pulling for the far shore. They would make it, but the barge was lost.

They found the rest of the Shadows a mile ahead of the Llanos who were now trying to escape to the South.

"They are moving much faster than Piar and his army can, this explains how they always avoided a confrontation," Wilson said as they dog-trotted along.

"Yes, at this rate they will be on our line by the middle of the afternoon," Marty panted, it had been a busy day and he was feeling it. Peters was manfully hanging on and forcing his tired limbs to keep moving. The rest of the Shadows were moving easily, their fitness wasn't in question.

"Who goes there?" a voice shouted.

The group stopped and Marty stepped forward; his hands above his head, "Commodore Stockley and his men."

"Step forward and be recognised."

Marty moved forward and found Peters beside him.

"Lieutenant Peters, Sir!" the sentry barked and came to attention.

"Stand easy, Harrison. Is the major on the line?"

"Centre redoubt, Sir."

"Thank you, stand easy," they moved away, "oh and stay alert the enemy is about two miles behind us."

They found Major Goodman and Captain O'Driscol in the redoubt. Their force was dug in along a line that stretched the three hundred yards from the mountains to the river. There were redoubts every thirty yards where a mortar and a pair of swivels were mounted.

"Looks like you are ready." Marty said.

"Not our natural way of fighting, they outnumber us and we need to stop them, not get into a hand-to-hand fight. Not until Piar gets here anyway," Goodman said.

"Are we relying on just the guns?"

"No, we have placed mines across our front which can be detonated from the redoubts." He showed Marty a bundle of fuses that led out ahead of the line.

"Excellent," Marty said then looked ahead, "I would suggest you get everyone ready." He nodded toward the sentry who was running for the line for all he was worth.

"The Llanos force is a mile away and we can see the Venezuelans on the horizon," a messenger reported.

"We have a lookout up on the mountain," Goodman explained when Marty gave an enquiring look. "Sound the ready," a bugler spat, moistened his lips then blew the signal.

Rifle barrels sprouted along the line and sergeants shouted orders.

Goodman climbed up onto the front of the redoubt and looked forward. He could see mounted scouts from the Llanos stopped half a mile away. A cloud of dust behind them indicated that the main force was not far behind. That was not what interested him though, he used a glass to see if he could see another dust cloud behind that.

"No sign of Piar yet." He jumped down. "I think the Llanos know we are here and will be getting ready to attack."

"Look, Sir!" a sergeant said.

A scout had ridden forward looking at the ground beside his horse as he rode slowly towards them.

"Looking for pitfalls and traps," Marty said.

"They are two hundred yards away," Goodman said.

Marty unlimbered his Durs Egg carbine and loaded it. The soldiers watched, fascinated by the breech loader's mechanism. He got himself into a comfortable position and adjusted the sight, took a deep breath and slowly let it out.

The rider was three hundred yards away.

He held his breath when it was all out and gently squeezed the trigger.

"Oh, jolly good shot, milord," Goodman cried as if he had taken a game bird.

The rider rolled over the rump of his horse as the bullet took him in the face. A second rider who was a little behind and fifty yards to his left stopped then retreated to a safe distance.

The dust cloud resolved itself into a double line of men a hundred yards wide that stopped four hundred yards away. The scout reported to a mounted officer who rode forward a little and stopped to look at the fortified line.

"About four hundred?" Goodman said.

"There or thereabouts," Marty said.

"We will fire the mortars as they approach the three-hundred-yard mark," Goodman ordered.

Marty and the Shadows moved out ahead of the line to act as skirmishers. Marty paired with Chin and took the centre the other two pairs spread out to either side.

There was a shouted order from in front.

"Avanzar, muchachos."

"Here they come."

A drum started beating, setting the pace for the advance.

Marty waited; his heart rate elevated by the adrenaline running through his veins. He took a deep breath to settle himself and picked a target, an officer that was waving his sword and extolling his men onwards. The rifle barked and the officer folded to the ground. Marty retreated ten yards and reloaded while chin picked off a sergeant.

The Llanos advanced in good order, surprisingly disciplined in Goodman's view. He worried he had underestimated them.

They came on and approached the three-hundred-yard markers.

"Mortars Fire," Goodman bellowed, glad it had started.

Ten Mortars chuffed and the black blobs with their smoking fuses arced through the blue sky. They exploded between ten and thirty feet from the ground sending shrapnel flying. A second volley followed almost as soon as the first had detonated.

The first volley exploded short of the Llanos line but the second was right above it. Men fell as shards of red-hot metal rained down on their heads. Not as effective as howitzers but discomforting and deadly all the same.

They kept on coming.

The mortars continued to fire until they were two hundred yards away.

"Ready the swivels!" the order rang out.

A sergeant lit the fuses to the mines. The fast fuses hissed and spluttered as they burnt and quickly disappeared into the distance. Their timing was off, the mines exploded ahead of the line, knocking over men but not with the devastating effect that the mines should have had.

"Damn," Goodman barked.

Marty moved he and the Shadows had been the other side of the mines. The line emerged through the cloud of smoke, it was holed here and there but still formidable. He picked off another man and ran for their line, Chin right behind him. They slid over the berm into a trench. Marty looked left and right. The line of bayonets on the rifles of the marines and soldiers was steady.

The mortars started again at one hundred and fifty yards raining more death and destruction.

Did the line falter? Shouted commands steadied it, then they broke into a trot. At one hundred feet they fired their muskets and broke into a run, charging the British line.

The swivels barked and swathes of shot from canister cut men down and still they came.

Fifty feet, "FIRE!"

The rifles spat fire and were reloaded as fast as they could be.

Bite, pour, shove the cartridge paper into the barrel spit in the ball, tap twice, present and fire.

The advance stuttered then halted.

A third volley and they started to retreat which broke into a rout.

Marty took a breath then a swig of water from his canteen to get the taste of sulphur out of his mouth.

"Piar is a mile behind them and closing fast," Goodman said.

"Sneaking up on me like that could get you killed," Marty said as he recovered from the surprise.

Goodman grinned, "We can expect another attack and I don't expect they will make the same mistake again."

"How many did they lose?"

"Thirty or so in the charge, hard to say how many to the mortars."

"Still a lot of them out there then." Marty dug into his ammunition pouch and pulled out another handful of cartridges. "Did we lose many?"

"One marine dead, three soldiers wounded."

The second attack was more like what they had expected the first time. A broken line of skirmishers came forward, making best use of the available cover. Behind them came the rest of the force scattered along a broader front they fired and moved.

"Waste of ammunition," the soldier beside Marty grunted.

"Makes them feel braver," Marty said.

A skirmisher got within two hundred yards and knelt to fire his musket. Marty took aim and fired. It was, he admitted later, a lucky shot. His bullet hit the man's musket, knocking it out of his grasp and him on his backside. The mortars started up again at that moment and a grenade burst right over his head. He didn't get up.

"Now that makes me feel better," the soldier grinned then realised who was next to him. "Beggin' your pardon, milord."

"Made me feel better too," Marty laughed.

They could hear drums now as Piar's force advanced. The Llanos knew they were trapped and that made them desperate. They came on with more determination than the first time, zigzagging to make themselves harder targets. Marty knew this time they would end up fighting hand to hand.

He fired, loaded, fired, again and again. The air was thick with gun smoke and his eyes stung. His throat was raw but he daren't stop to quench his thirst. He lost track of time, his only measure the steady reduction of the number of cartridges laid out before him. The noise was incredible, not comparable to a ship's broadside but loud and incessant.

A man rose up in front of him, machete raised, a pistol appeared in his hand without thought and the man fell to be replaced with another. The soldier beside him cried out as he was hit by something, blood ran down his face from a cut on his forehead. It enraged him and he stabbed forward with his bayonet impaling a Llanos who had mounted the berm.

Marty fought another man armed with a machete, his sword in one hand and fighting knife in the other. He parried a vicious swing and drove his knife up under his assailant's ribs. Then he was alone. He looked around and an errant breeze blew the smoke aside. Uniformed men were in front of the berm, Piar had arrived.

Chapter 16: Victory

Christmas came and Aruba celebrated with exceptional enthusiasm. The news from Europe was that Napoleon was in retreat across all fronts. His disastrous campaign against the Russians and the success of the allies on the peninsula made them feel the end was in sight. 1813 was going out with a celebration.

The conflict that never happened in Venezuela had cost four men their lives and twenty-two wounded, of which four would never fight again. Marty covered the cost of care for all and Shelby, with his two nurses, working minor miracles almost every day. It could be said that health care on the island had never been better.

The Llanos threat in Venezuela was reduced but not eliminated, however, the rebel army was now much better equipped to counter it than before, not to mention better trained. Several marines were still there acting as advisors and Marty feared that one or two were going native, but if that was all he had to worry about then he was fairly content.

Caroline had the household decorating the house and gardens for a grand Christmas ball. Chin had shown the children how to make paper lanterns. Bethany had enlisted the children of the staff and had a production line organised.

The Toolshed were busy creating fireworks for a grand display that would be the highlight of the evening. Corporals Dibble and Pew created leather suits to protect themselves when they lit the fireworks including helmets with wire mesh visors. Marty noticed that his officers were spending more time than usual with his creative geniuses but chose to leave them to it. However, he did have to ask them what they were up to, when they were setting out with a covered cart.

"We need to test some of the designs, Sir," Dibble said, "we think they will work but we won't know till we try them."

"Why not do that here?" Marty said.

Dibble looked a little uncomfortable and slitty eyed at that but rallied and said, "The noise, Sir and we don't want to spoil the surprise."

"What surprise?"

"The patterns they make when they goes off, Sir."

Marty let them carry on. He was sure there was more to it than that but let it go.

There were none of the traditional Christmas boughs on Aruba to decorate the house with. Holy and ivy didn't grow there so they searched for alternatives. Caribbean pine, hibiscus and orchids made colourful alternatives and soon the house was festooned just like their house in England would be but with a decided Caribbean flavour.

Special attention was given to the gate, Caroline turned it into an arch of colour, running the gardeners ragged and enlisting men from the ships that were in dock.

They couldn't invite everyone on the island, so Marty made sure that every town had enough booze to hold their own party. He wrote it off as goodwill in the accounts, but it wasn't that much. The

Silverthorn brought a cargo of Mescal back from Colombia and when the squadron returned, they had rescued a cargo of wine and spirits from an American privateer.

Marty employed the Toolshed to create a present for Edwin who would get a set of tin soldiers and cannon that could actually be loaded with a few grains of powder and fire. Beth would get a beautiful new dress and slippers befitting her rapidly-maturing body. Constance was very interested in animals and especially horses so she would get her very own rocking horse. He had a special present for Caroline that he had bought in London before they had left which he would present to her on Christmas Eve.

All in all he was quite satisfied that everything in his world was working well. He had left a present for James in London for when he went home for Christmas, it was a silver bound midshipman's dirk for when he joined the Naval College. Not having James with them was the one thing that left his Christmas incomplete, but the boy needed his education.

Christmas Eve came and for the British this was the main family day of the season. The Dutch celebrated Sint-Nicolaas day on the fifth of December. Otherwise known as Sinterklaas, he delivered presents to good children and supposedly punish those that were naughty. But in the Stockley household Christmas Eve was the big day.

Marty and Caroline decided that as they were all so far from home, the whole household including the Shadows would celebrate together. They erected a pavilion on the lawn with one huge table that sat twenty people. Marty and Carolyn sat at the head with the children. The food was prepared by Roland with the aid of numerous helpers.

Christmas Dinner

Turtle Soup

-

Clams with Orange Candied Onions
Mint Mignonette

-

Honey and Mustard Glazed Ham
Roast Beef
Baked Onions, Carrots Vichy
Roast Yams

-

Lemon or pineapple posset
Plum Duff

-

Cheese, nuts and fruit

Of course, this was all washed down with white and red wines that Roland matched to every course. He fussed over every service like an old hen, refusing to sit and enjoy the meal himself. At the end of the meal Marty called him forward and stood next to him, his arm around his shoulders so he couldn't escape,

"Everyone, I think that you would all like to thank Roland and his kitchen staff for creating and serving this sumptuous feast that we have been treated to this Christmas Eve. The food as always was wonderful. Now give him three cheers and a tiger!"

"Hup hup, Hurrah! Hup hup, Hurrah! Hup hup, Hurrah!" The Tiger was a low guttural growl.

A band from the garrison struck up a popular tune and Marty led Caroline in the dance which everybody else with a partner joined. The next tune was a polka and even if they didn't have a partner, they grabbed the nearest body and stomped around.

Bethany, who was now thirteen, had invited Ensign Rupert Colepepper to the ball. It transpired that he was not only an excellent swordsman but a devil on the dance floor. Beth's face was all aglow and Caroline said, as she and Marty took a breather,

"That is the fourth dance in a row she has had with Rupert, and I do not believe she has accepted a single request on her dance card."

"Should I have a word with her?"

"No this is mother and daughter territory let me deal with it."

"If you think that's best, should I have a word with him?"

"God no! Not unless you want to incur Beth's wrath. Stay well out of it, I will tell you what needs to be done."

Marty ceded to his wife's superior knowledge and expertise in the matter. He had no wish to get on Beth's bad side as she could hold a grudge better than most and could be most vindictive if she put her mind to it.

The highlight was the fireworks display and the Toolshed outdid themselves. It started with a curtain of roman candles that fired a sequence of exploding charges into the air, which in turn sent out globes of sparks. Rockets whooshed into the air to explode in vast chrysanthemums. Volcanoes gushed and strings of crackers crackled, then the finale – a ship of fire sailed across the sky. The cheers echoed and could be heard in the town.

At midnight Marty gave Caroline her present. She opened the box and unwrapped the tissue paper carefully to reveal an exquisite broach that could be adapted to a pendent. The broach was an eagle, wings outstretch talons extended, modelled in gold, studded with diamonds and sapphires It had rubies for eyes.

"Oh, Marty it's beautiful," she sighed.

The ball was, of course, a raging success as were the celebrations throughout the island. It was the talk of polite society, those that were there, being in high demand for coffee or tea mornings to reveal all.

Life was settling down as they waited for the new year to come in when a letter arrived from Charterhouse, the school James was in, in the general postbag.

"What the fuck?" Marty exclaimed over the breakfast table as he read it.

"Marty, language!" Caroline chided then saw the look on his face, "What is it?'

"James has gone missing from school. They don't know where he is. There was an incident where he got into a fight with some boys that were bullying younger lads. Oh God, he put one in the infirmary for a week, and another has been sent home to his parents."

"Why would he run away? When did this happen?"

Marty looked at the date of the letter. "Middle of November, the fools sent this by normal post instead of through the diplomatic bag."

Beth, who had been listening intently said, "He would have gone to one of the houses, is there a letter from any of them?"

Marty searched through the pile and came up with one from Dorset and another from Cheshire. He opened and scanned them.

"Nothing in here, James and Arthur have just sent end of year reports and season's greetings."

"What should we do?" Caroline said.

"I will write to James and Louise; they can organise a search for him. I will also write to Turner and enlist his help to get us sent home. The job is all but done here anyway."

Marty spent the rest of the day writing letters and cursing the inadequacy of the post to get messages sent in a hurry. He was desperately worried for his son and wished that old Tom was still alive to talk to.

New year approached; he was constantly worried but couldn't expect a reply to any of his letters for weeks. He stood on the porch outside his study looking out over the bay. A ship was coming in; British by the look of her and he watched as she turned into the wind and dropped anchor. She was tidily handled, and her sails were furled neatly.

"A well-handled ship," he said to himself.

A boat set off and crossed to the shoreline. The skipper looking for a cargo no doubt. He sighed and went back inside to find Caroline who was in the drawing room keeping herself busy with needlepoint.

"Was there anything of interest in the post?" she said.

"A letter from Wellington. He is having a rare old time of it. Swears he will have Napoleon beat before the end of '14."

"Peace would be very welcome."

"Yes, but I am sure Turner, and the Foreign Office will find something to keep me busy despite it. The government is always falling out with someone or another."

He dropped into a chair and picked up a book, read half a page and put it down. He sighed again, stood and went to the fireplace.

"Why don't you go out and do some weapons practice," Caroline said.

"I would but I can't seem to concentrate. Was that someone at the door?"

"I'm not expecting anybody are you?"

"No. Probably someone lost a cow."

There was a knock on the door and Tabetha put her head inside. She had a grin on her face. "A Captain Francis here to see you."

Marty rolled his eyes, "Show him in please."

A tall tarry man with a weather-beaten face came in and doffed his hat, "Are you Lord Purbeck?"

"I am, how can I help you?"

"It's more like I can help you."

He reached through the door and dragged a boy into the room.

"He says he is yours."

"Hello, Dad, Mum."

"James?" Marty gasped.

Caroline dropped her needlepoint and fainted as she started to stand.

"Found him stowing away after we had left Poole," Captain Francis said. "It were too late to turn back and he told us he was the son of Lord Purbeck and you would compensate me for his passage."

"How did he know you were coming here?"

"We weren't. We were scheduled for St Kitts but he promised me a hundred pounds if we brought him to you here."

"Did he be damned."

Marty went to a picture on the wall which swung open to reveal a safe. He dug a key out from his pocket, opened it and took out a pouch. He tossed it to Captain Francis.

"One hundred golden guineas, a bonus for getting him here in one piece."

"He worked his passage you don't need to pay it all."

"Keep it, he can pay me back."

"He will, he is a fair hand."

Captain Francis turned to go. "Don't be too hard on him, I know he ran away from school; he had his reasons. Hear him out before you act."

James presented himself in Marty's study, washed and dressed in some clothes the staff had rounded up. Marty looked him up and down,

"We will have to visit the town tomorrow and get you some clothes. Now tell me what drove you to leave Charterhouse and stowaway on a ship bound for the Caribbean."

James squared his shoulders looking older than his twelve years,

"It started a year ago when a new master came to the school, his name was Jonas Quin. He was made my house master. From day one as soon as he saw my name, he was watching me and if I put a toe out of line, he would beat me. I soon made sure I gave him no excuse, then the bullying started. He had his favourites; they were the worst sorts and he encouraged them to bully me. As you instructed, Sir, I didn't react and in the end they gave up until after the summer break when they started picking on my friend Matthew Stoneway. He is small and not very brave, they picked on him relentlessly and he would go to bed crying every night.

In the end I couldn't stand for it any longer and made myself a blackjack."

"Where did you get the wherewithal to make that and more important where did you learn how?"

"The leather was from a coat of mine and the shot I borrowed from Professor Dingwell's fishing box and ammunition for his bird gun."

"Borrowed?"

"I gave it back, Sir."

"After you taught the bullies a lesson?"

"Yes, Sir."

"And who told you how to make one?"

"I've seen yours and just copied it from memory."

"The boy that was sent home. Was he badly hurt?"

"Broken fingers on his right hand and a broken wrist."

"And the other boy?"

"Which one?"

"The one in the infirmary."

"Just bruises, well maybe a cracked rib or two."

"There was another?"

"Yes, he ran away when I put down the other two."

"How old were they?"

"Seniors, so fifteen or sixteen."

"This still doesn't explain why you came here."

"I wrote to you several times telling about Quin. I found out his father was a friend of Graves and he had been forced to take a teaching job because you ruined their business. I ran because Quin was stopping my letters and was going to use me to ruin your name."

"Was he, and how do you know that?"

"I found letters in his study." James looked more than a little sheepish when he said that.

"What were you doing in his study when he presumably wasn't there?"

"Looking for my letters, Sir."

"Did he not lock his study?"

"Yes, Sir."

"You broke in?"

"I didn't break in, Sir, the lock was easy to pick."

Marty didn't ask how he knew how to pick a lock.

"Does he know you gained access to his study and read his private letters?"

"No, Sir I left it exactly as it was."

Marty was torn between admiration and pride and a feeling he should disapprove.

"Well, I can do something about Mr Quin and his friends. Go to your mother now, I believe she has a few things she wants to say to you. Take my advice and let her have her say, then apologise."

James left and Marty sat and wondered what kind of son he had sired. Then he started to laugh, the boy had done exactly what he would have done.

More letters had to be written to call off the search for James which Marty sent in the diplomatic bag. He and Caroline still had not decided what to do about their son and it was greatly complicated by the fact they were stuck in Aruba until relieved.

A solution came with a letter from the Foreign Office at the end of January. After all the formal addresses it basically recalled Marty to England. His replacement would be out on the next packet. A second letter in the same envelope was from Turner asking that he leave the squadron there for a few months until ships could be freed up to replace them. It also hinted there would be an important task for him when he got there. *How will they free up that many ships?* Marty wondered.

The next packet was due in two weeks causing the house to go into a frenzy of preparation. They didn't have the Bethany but they did have the Pride. She wasn't as big and couldn't carry as much so some things would have to be left behind to be shipped out later or brought back by the squadron. Caroline made the selections with military precision.

The Pride was captained by Fergus McDonald who they had found in Jamaica, an old salt and retired freighter captain. He enjoyed sailing the Pride and had gotten to know every square inch of her. He worked with Caroline on planning what would be taken. Between them they developed a loading plan that optimised every cubic inch of cargo space.

The two weeks shot by and before they knew it they were greeting the new governor. He was an elderly man with an elderly wife. Sir Cuthbert Harrington-Fitzwilliams was a lifelong diplomat and had all the graces one would expect as well as a core of iron which glinted in his eyes.

He practically shooed Marty and Caroline onto the Pride and waved them off from the dock. Aruba was his now.

"It will be a lot quieter without you around," Goodman had commented at their farewell dinner. "Any idea what they want you back in such a damn rush for?"

Marty didn't then and still didn't when their carriage delivered them to their London home.

He had barely time to unpack when a note came asking him to attend on Admiral Turner at his earliest convenience. It was mid-March and a beautiful day, so he walked to Admiralty House with Troy at his side and reported into the clerks at the waiting room. Troy was well known to the clerks and they all made a fuss of him, finding treats from God knew where for him.

The other officers waiting kept a respectful distance from Marty, partly because of his rank, but more, he suspected, because of Troy.

"Admiral Turner will see you now," a messenger said and led them to his office.

It was the familiar oak-panelled room with its big fireplace, attendant chairs and bigger desk. Admiral Turner stood and held out his hand in greeting.

"Sit down, Martin, can we offer you coffee?"

Marty accepted the offer and sat in one of the club chairs, Troy plonked himself down in front of the fire. Turner fussed over some papers while his secretary brought the coffee and a bowl of water for Troy.

"Some of that wonderful Blue Mountain bean you sent me."

They sipped and savoured for a moment.

"I suppose you are wondering why you were recalled," Turner said. Marty nodded.

"The situation here is changing rapidly and will come to a head by the end of April."

Marty looked slightly puzzled.

"Oh sorry, I am talking about the war with France.

"I heard from Arthur that he was in the final furlong," Marty said.

"Yes, he was quite right. We expect to come to terms with the French very soon as the Russians, Austrians and Prussians are closing in on Paris."

Marty sat upright, "It really is that imminent?"

"Yes, we will accept their surrender on condition that Napoleon is deprived of his rule and goes into exile, and that is where you come in."

"Hold on, you said we are negotiating with the French. We aren't talking to Napoleon?"

"No, he is busy losing the war and we will be in Paris by the end of the month. By the middle of April, he will be on his way to Elba."

Marty sat back and blew out his cheeks. "Phew! Things have moved along."

"What we want is for you to be a member of the commissioners that accompany him on his journey into exile."

"Why me?"

"Because you are known to him and we think he will talk to you. You have been a royal thorn in his side for your entire career and he put a personal bounty on your head. Which, by the way, is still there."

"What about South America?"

"Priorities, Martin, priorities. The South American problem will resolve itself. You gave it a good push in the right direction and that is enough."

"When do I leave?"

"You have a couple of weeks at least but be ready to leave at short notice. I have a ship ready at Dover to take you across."

Troy put his head on Marty's lap.

"You can take him along if you want."

"I think he will stay with the children."

"That reminds me, what is happening with James?"

"That young rogue is going to the navy college, he has outgrown school and needs discipline. The school will, however, need a new housemaster."

Turner knew the look in Marty's eye and chose not to ask.

"As long as you're available to go to France. Now tell me about this battle you had."

The problem of Mr Quin was delegated to the Shadows, Marty didn't particularly care how they solved the problem as long as it went away. His only stipulation was it had to be able to stand up to examination. The Shadows got together to work out a plan and John Smith kicked off the discussion,

"I can create letters that make it look like he is in collusion with French spies, then we can get 'im pulled up for treason."

"Too complicated," Wilson said, "I say just grab him and throw him off a cliff."

"Charterhouse is miles from the sea," Antton reminded them.

"He could blow 'imself up," John said.

"Why would he do that?" Chin asked. "It better he have accident."

"Well blowin' 'imself up is an accident innit?"

"Not one that is believable," Garai said.

"Does he have any hobbies?" Wilson said.

"Not that we know of."

"Why don't we just disappear him," John said.

"We would need to plant something in his room to explain it," Matai said.

"No problem, how about same lascivious letters between him and his boyfriend." John looked at Wilson as he spoke.

"He hasn't got a – Oh! I see."

Antton suddenly perked up, then assumed a thoughtful pose,

"His lover has told him he no longer wants to see him, and he commits suicide. Double bonus, he's dead and the parents will want to know why the school employed a pederast as a housemaster in a boy's school if it gets out so they will hush it up."

"Sounds like a plan, I'll start on the letters," John said.

"A messenger has brought this, milord." Adam held out a silver tray with a message in green ink. It was mid-April and the papers were full of news of the taking of Paris.

"Admiralty, let's see." He took the note and unfolded it.

"Blah, blah, blah, Aah here is the meat."

Marty stood, went to his desk and wrote an answer.

"Give this to the messenger," he dug out a silver sixpence and dropped it on the tray, "tell him to return it to the sender."

As soon as Adam left, he went to the drawing room where Caroline was entertaining several ladies of some organisation or another. He put his head in the door and winked at her before going up to their room. It was a scant twenty minutes before she came in to find him and Adam packing.

"You have had your instructions?"

"Yes, they came half an hour ago, I need to make my way to Dover."

"Is the war over?"

"Yes, it is."

Caroline grabbed him and kissed him fiercely, tears in her eyes. A discrete cough from Adam reminded them they were not alone.

"When he is exile, we can celebrate," Marty said.

"Be better if he was dead," Adam muttered loud enough to hear.

"He will always be a danger if he is alive, a rally point, a focus for the discontented. The Bourbons are not popular."

"Well, you make sure he goes into exile," Caroline said passionately.

Chapter 17: Exile

Marty's carriage pulled up at the dock in Dover a couple of hours after dawn. It was a grey, blustery day with frequent bursts of heavy rain. He was met by a midshipman.

"Milord Purbeck." He greeted Marty through the open door of his carriage. His blond hair shining in an errant sunbeam.

Adam scowled at the boy who had pre-empted him opening the door for his master, but Marty smiled,

"And you are?"

"Oh! Midshipman Johnson, Sir. Compliments of Captain Stanley, I am to escort you to the Kestrel. I have some hands to help you with your dunnage." The boy spoke in hurried bursts and his hair blew in the gusty wind.

"Adam, be so kind as to oversee the transfer of our baggage," Marty said to allow Adam some space from the boy who he appeared to have taken an instant dislike to.

"Milord," he murmured and stepped out of the carriage. He was soon barking orders to the waiting sailors.

"Now, Mr Johnson, fulfil your mission. Lead on!"

The Kestrel was a sloop of war and fast enough to make the passage to Calais in about three to three-and-a-half hours.

At Calais he was met by a coach and whisked away as soon as Adam and his baggage was loaded.

"They seem to be in a hurry," Adam said.

"Yes, almost unseemly haste from a French point of view."

"Where are we going?"

"Fontainebleau, It's Southeast of Paris. Napoleon is there and it is where the treaty will be signed."

"Is it true he has abdicated?"

"Yes, but as far as I can tell he still retains the title of Emperor. The whole thing is very French and I am sure the British will not sign as long as he still has the title or any power at all. I will find out more once we get there."

The coach picked up a British cavalry escort at Amiens where they stopped overnight. The horses were changed every twenty miles or so, the driver after four hours and food and comfort stops were brief. The chateaux at Fontainebleau was a welcome sight after two days of that.

Marty was met by Robert Stewart, Viscount Castlereagh, the foreign secretary, who was in charge of the British contingent.

"Lord Purbeck, welcome. Sorry you had such a precipitous journey, but things have been moving apace y'know."

Marty, being of equal social rank, shook hands and looked up at the imposing building.

"Impressive pile, have the negotiations been concluded?"

"Would you like to walk with me? Your man can take care of your baggage."

Marty welcomed the chance to stretch his legs and the two strolled off together. Once out of earshot of anybody Castlereagh stopped by a fountain that would further mask their conversation and said, "The damn French have given him Elba as his personal possession and allowed him to keep the title of Emperor. Even let him choose the island himself."

"He is a Corsican, an island must be attractive," Marty said.

"Well, anyway," Stewart huffed, "they have also agreed to pay him two million Francs a year."

"Pfft that is some pension. Who has signed the agreement?"

"All the allies except Britain. We will not as long as he holds the title and any lands."

"When will he leave?"

"Tomorrow." Marty grimaced. "Sorry about that but we have allocated you a room here so you will at least get a good night's sleep."

They strolled along silently for a few minutes.

"Who will guard him there?"

"In Elba? No one, at least no one visible. We will have a man on the island, one of our agents, Neil Campbell."

"British Intelligence?"

"Yes, don't think you two ever met."

"No."

Castlereagh gave him a potted background of the agent.

"I know all about your activities as part of Naval Intelligence, you have done a damn good job and I'm sure your career isn't over yet. Turner values you and I wouldn't be surprised to see you take over from him one day."

Marty knew when he was being buttered up for something.

"Look, Napoleon knows of you, he put a price on your head after all. You are also known to his brothers. He has spoken of you with a certain admiration. We want you to use the trip to Elba to talk to him, get to know him, befriend him even. Try and find out what his next move will be or at least get a hint."

Marty nodded; Stewart turned them back towards the chateaux more carriages had arrived.

"The other commissioners. All politicians who are looking for a bit of glory by being able to say they took the monster into exile."

Marty stopped and turned to Castlereagh. "Elba will not be secure, and he will have resources. What is to stop him coming back?"

"Nothing, dear boy, absolutely nothing," Castlereagh said sombrely.

The chateaux was abuzz with activity, servants in livery scooted around with boxes and items to be put in boxes. The palace was astonishing, artworks covered every wall, frescoes by the Fontainebleau school and paintings by every major artist from the renaissance.

"Organised chaos," Adam observed.

"Yes. How is my room?"

"Yours is sumptuous, mine is a dog box. So much for equality, fraternity and liberty."

"Is there a chaise longue in my room?"

"Yes, two in fact."

"Sleep on one of them, it's only one night."

"Viscount Purbeck?" a French Lieutenant of Artillery said.

"Yes?" Marty said switching to French.

"If you will come with me, I am to introduce you to the emperor."

Marty turned to Adam. "Be back in my room for six, I will have to dress for dinner then."

Adam nodded and wandered off.

"Lead on," Marty said.

The lieutenant said nothing more as he led Marty to a large receiving room. Napoleon sat writing, looking small behind a huge ornate desk. He looked up as the two men approached and put down his pen.

Marty bowed and said in French, "Emperor Napoleon, a pleasure to meet you at last."

"Viscount, or should I say Commodore Stockley? You may call me Napoleon. Come, let us sit by the window." He stood; he wasn't as short as the British papers would have it. Marty estimated he was five-foot-six of medium build erring towards overweight, dark hair swept forward to hide the fact he had a widow's peak. He was dressed in an artillery officer's uniform adorned with some of his honours.

"Then you must call me Martin. Do you still have a price on my head?"

Napoleon barked a laugh. "I need to cancel that. It is somewhat superfluous now. You earned it though."

"I tried," Marty smiled.

"You did indeed, was it you who stole the gold for the payroll back in 1797? That is the one incident my intelligence service couldn't attribute to you."

Marty had to think then smiled. "Why yes it was, we were on a training exercise and the opportunity presented itself."

"I should have put a price on your head then."

"Is your wife here?" Marty said changing the subject.

"No, she will take my son back to Austria."

"You must miss them."

"Terribly, I was writing to her when you arrived. I will tell her you and I have spoken. She admires your wife."

"Really?"

"Yes, her marriage to the old Baron, then her public affair with you and eventual marriage was seen as a romantic fairy tale."

"I had no idea; it is strange the French were interested in us."

Napoleon shrugged.

"You are both commoners who made it into the aristocracy."

The conversation continued as the two men got to know each other until an equerry came in to remind Napoleon that it was time to get ready for dinner. A servant showed Marty back to his room where Adam had a bath filled and a suit laid out ready.

"What is he like?" Adam said as Marty shaved.

"Intelligent, thoughtful, arrogant in his belief that he should be leading France. He has a phenomenal memory as well, it's a shame he couldn't put his talents to something more useful."

"Like spying?"

"Touché."

The dinner was a vast, formal affair in the ballroom and Marty was honoured with a seat close to the great man himself. Which as there were at least a hundred people in attendance was significant and a clear indication of preference. Castlereagh sought Marty out before they sat and warned him that Napoleon had been fiddling with the seating plan. This signal of favour wasn't at all a blessing in Marty's eyes as he was immediately targeted by those wanting to move up the social ranking.

He had a dreary Austrian next to him who prattled on about ceramics, to listen to him you would think that pots were the most important thing on earth. Napoleon caught his eye and winked. Marty knew then that he was the subject of a jest, the man had a sense of humour.

After the dinner he was invited to sit and talk with Napoleon's inner circle. Marshal Ney was there as a guest.

"You are not going with him?" Marty asked.

"No, my light has dimmed in his eyes since I refused to attack Paris. I will stay here and serve the king."

"I am surprised, I would have thought you had a dislike of the Bourbons."

"I do, but I serve France, whoever rules. The same can be said for all the senior officers in the French army."

That was interesting. *So, you would shift allegiance if you thought someone else was better suited,* Marty thought.

The next morning, Napoleon left his apartment and exited from the chateaux, the imperial guard formed up in farewell. He gave a speech, thanking them and praising their courage:

'Soldiers of my Old Guard, I bid you farewell. For twenty years you have been my constant companions on the road to honour and glory. In these latter times, as in the days of our prosperity, you have never ceased to be models of courage and fidelity. With men such as you our cause would not have been lost; but the war would have been interminable; it would have been a civil war, and France would only have become unhappier still. I have therefore sacrificed all of our interests to those of la patrie; I shall depart. But you, my friends, continue to serve France. Her happiness was my only thought; it shall continue to be the object of my desires. Do not lament my fate; the only reason I have allowed myself to survive was so that I could further serve our glory. I want to write down the great deeds which we have done together. Adieu, my children! Would that I could press you all to my heart. Let me at least embrace your standard!'

There was silence only broken by the sobs of some of the soldiers. General Petit seized the standard and brought it to Napoleon who kissed it. Then he said in a loud voice:

'Once again, adieu, my old companions! May this last kiss pass to your hearts!'

He burst out of the group which had formed around him and threw himself into his carriage. The theatre of the occasion carefully orchestrated. Marty watched the whole thing then got in his carriage for the journey to Marseilles. At the first stop to change horses Marty was summoned to ride with Napoleon.

"Travel with me, Martin, your company will be more interesting than those other oafs and make the journey less tedious."

"You honour me, Sir," Marty said and climbed in.

"You didn't bring that famous dog of yours," Napoleon observed as a pair of hunting poodles climbed in and made themselves comfortable on the floor. The dogs were easily as big as Troy their coats clipped short showing off their athletic build.

"He is at home with my children and wife. He would be too much trouble given the temptation of so many bitches." He had noted that both dogs were female.

Napoleon laughed, he had several mistresses in his time, his current wife being the last of them. "The opposite sex can get you into trouble, but they are such a joy and distraction from the cares of life."

The talk turned to the countryside they were passing through and Napoleon asked about Marty's lands. He knew that he had estates in Cheshire and Dorset, Marty explained how he ran them.

"You make cheese on the estate? And the dairy is run by the women? You are a true revolutionary, Martin; we French could learn from you that not all the aristocracy are leaches."

"Like you I didn't start out as what I am now," Marty said and went on to tell his history.

As the journey progressed, change of horses after change of horses for four days, they talked of many things, Marty carefully injecting questions about the future and Napoleon's remaining ambition. Napoleon deftly parrying the thrusts. Marty had the impression he enjoyed the sparring.

They arrived at the port and their transport. The Undaunted was a thirty-eight-gun fifth rate frigate that had a distinguished record mainly in and around the Mediterranean. Ussher was her latest captain and had taken something like seventy ships since he had taken command earning him the nickname Undaunted Ussher.

Marty and Napoleon were greeted by him at the top of the gangplank. His first impression was of a high forehead and long straight nose. A friendly face but eyes with steel in them.

"Commodore Stockley," he greeted in a soft Irish accent.

"Captain Ussher, pleased to meet you. May I introduce his excellency Emperor Napoleon."

"Imperial Majesty, my first lieutenant will show you to your cabin."

Marty was interested to see how a crowded frigate would be rearranged to accommodate not only an emperor but the commissioners as well.

The answer was typically pragmatic. The trip from Marseille to Elba was around two hundred and sixty sea miles which would take the Undaunted and her consort twenty-four hours to make. Napoleon would get the captain's cabin. Marty as the senior officer would be in the coach. The rest of the commissioners and the captain would overnight in lieutenant's cabins. The ships officers would move to the cockpit and the mids. would sling hammocks. Napoleon's entourage would sail on the Euryalis, only his hand servants would travel with him.

Napoleon was not interested in ships, apart from the guns, and was not a good sailor so went to his cabin. Marty stayed on deck to watch the loading as he had enough of being shut in for the time being. The sea air blowing in off the Mediterranean refreshed as well as soothed him. Castlereagh found him on the quarterdeck,

"Did you enjoy your time shut up with the emperor?"

Marty motioned to the skylight and led him along the main deck to the fore deck.

"You can hear every word spoken on a quarterdeck in the captain's cabin if the skylight is open," he said when they were alone.

"I shall bear that in mind. What have you found out?"

"He has not said anything specifically of course because he isn't a fool."

"I hear a 'but'."

"Yes, from what he's revealed about how he feels and what his ambitions were, I feel he will try and return to France and take back the throne for his son."

"He will need a full army to do that."

"That's the other thing, if he returns and the army thinks it's for the good of France, they will follow him."

"That's your assessment?"

"Yes, it is after speaking to Ney."

"Blast. The job is not finished then."

The crossing to Elba was textbook and when they arrived Marty was surprised to see there were no cheering crowds. Napoleon had stayed in his cabin for almost the entire journey only coming on deck for the entry into Portoferraio. He looked depressed and a little pale but as the ship came to the dock, he squared his shoulders and looked more the man Marty was used to seeing.

A delegation appeared and as soon as the gang plank was down, came aboard. It was the mayor of Portoferraio and his councillors. Marty stood close enough to hear what they were saying.

"Welcome your Imperial Majesty. Emperor Napoleon of Elba, you grace us with your presence, and we welcome you in the name of the people. On behalf of all of Portoferraio I present to you the keys to the city and the freedom of the Island" was a condensed version of a speech that went on for a good fifteen minutes.

"Well, that gives him the whole island," Marty summarised for Castlereagh.

"Ah, here comes Campbell," Castlereagh said.

"Milords," Neil Campbell bowed.

"Hello, Campbell, may I present Sir Martin Stockley, Viscount Purbeck."

"Commodore, it is a pleasure to meet you." He looked around. "I don't see your infamous team anywhere."

Castlereagh looked at him quizzically.

"Sir Martin has a team of men who are, I believe, called the Shadows. They are experts in everything from larceny to outright murder and are commonly employed by the government to, unofficially, sort out problems."

Marty didn't like this loose talk of his team, or the way it was said with an almost sneering tone. He decided he didn't like Campbell at all. His tone said it all as he said, "You are here to keep a watch on the emperor I believe. Do you have a network?"

"Oh no," Campbell said cheerfully missing the hint, "I work alone. It is only a small island after all."

Castlereagh seemed satisfied with Campbell and the two chatted about people they both knew.

"Will you be staying on the island?" Campbell asked Marty.

"No, I will return to London."

"Sir Martin's mission is complete," Castlereagh said. "By the way, how will you get back?"

Marty pointed to an American clipper anchored in the harbour. "That is my ship the Queen of Purbeck. If you want to meet the Shadows Campbell, they are on board."

"But that ship has been in harbour for a week at least," Campbell said a look of surprise on his face.

"I know and the Shadows have been on the island all that time and you didn't notice." The admonishment was clear and bit home.

"I say!"

"You can say what you want but I daresay that I will know more about the feelings of the locals than you do by the time we get back to London."

"How come I wasn't told you were putting a team on the island?" Castlereagh said. He was a mite put out at the disclosure; he was the de-facto head of British Intelligence after all.

"Because no one but me knew."

"Not even Turner?"

"No, not even him."

Castlereagh blew out his cheeks. "I should object but I expect you have your reasons."

"Join me tonight on the Queen and we can debrief the men together, then you will understand."

Ussher made his barge available to shift Marty and Adam over to the Queen. They were met at the gangway by five grinning faces.

"Hello, lads, where are Antton and Chin?"

"Hello, boss, they'ms ashore. We've found a few discontents who are willing to pass on any information to us about what old Boney is up to and they are making sure they know how to use the pigeons we brung with us," John Smith said while the crew swung up the baggage.

"I have to attend a farewell dinner with 'old Boney' this evening. When I return, I will expect a full report on what you have found, but I will have someone with me that I would prefer did not hear that we have established our own network on the island."

"Understood, boss, I will make sure that's kept shtum."

Sam had Marty's trunk in his arms and was making his way to his cabin followed by Adam who carried a much smaller leather bag. Marty smiled as it looked rather comical.

"I had better go and get changed. Oh, by the way, have you been watching that British agent – Campbell?"

"Yes, boss, took care of him meself." John said.

"I don't want that mentioned either."

The dinner was not as lavish as Fontainebleau but was superb all the same. Napoleon was in a hurry to get started and it finished when he left at ten o'clock. Marty knew the man didn't need a lot of sleep and would probably work well into the night. They parted on friendly terms and promised to correspond.

The Queen's boat was waiting for Marty and Castlereagh when they got to the dock and as soon as they were aboard Marty had the boys gather in his cabin.

"This is Viscount Castlereagh who led the British contingent at Fontainebleau and is the foreign secretary. I have invited him to hear first-hand what you have found."

Antton started, "In general, the people are happy with having Napoleon as their ruler, he is seen as the true leader of French Republic. There are, however, a significant minority who object to being removed from France and another faction that believe they should be part of Tuscany. The merchant classes are waiting to see what happens. Will there be additional taxes? Can they still freely export to France? That sort of thing.

There is a standing army which are expecting to be directly under his command and the beginnings of a navy. There are about thirty thousand people on the island."

Wilson looked up and added, "The local government has already voted to support him by a large majority, only two voted against and four abstained."

"Are there any specific pockets of dissenters?" Marty asked.

"No, we worked our way around the entire island and there are dissenters but they ain't organised."

The conversation continued and concluded with Castlereagh asking, "If Napoleon asked, could he raise an army of any significance here?"

Matai answered. "He could form the core of one, the question is how many will travel from France to join him?"

"Thank you, lads that's all." Marty dismissed them.

"I get the feeling there is something they are not telling me," Castlereagh said once they were alone. "But all the same, that was a comprehensive summary."

Marty ignored the comment, "You should have Campbell monitor for men coming in from outside to join the army."

"I will. Are you finished here?"

"Yes, we will leave tomorrow."

Chapter 18: The Warning

Marty was back in the admiralty and sat at a conference table full of the great and the good. The ones he cared about were Admiral James Turner, The Most Honourable Robert Stewart (Lord Castlereagh) – Foreign Secretary, The Duke of Wellington and Robert Jenkinson, the Prime Minister.

"So let me get this clear," Castlereagh said, "it is your considered opinion that Napoleon will attempt to retake France and the role of Emperor."

"Yes, Foreign Secretary,"

"But my man on the spot says everything is stable and he is just concentrating on building Elba up."

"With all due respect he would."

Castlereagh got a dangerous look in his eye. "Are you saying Campbell is a traitor?"

"Not at all, Sir, it's just that he will be seeing things from close up and only what Napoleon wants him to see. He is well aware of who Campbell is," Marty said.

That mollified him a bit. Arthur stepped in before Castlereagh had a chance to respond. "I have had the privilege of working with Lord Purbeck a number of times in the past. Martin, what measures have you taken to maintain a watch on old Boney?"

Marty smiled his old friend knew him too well.

"We have recruited a number of dissidents amongst the population and, more importantly, in the civil service. They are instructed to only make direct contact if they see anything significant."

"How will they make contact?"

"We left homing pigeons that will return to my Dorset estate and I have arranged for a ship to call at the island regularly, ostensibly to trade but in reality, to collect messages left at dead drops."

"Does Campbell know this?"

"No, it is important to have independent sources of information."

"Marty is right, milord," Turner interjected, "it is good intelligence practice if not common sense."

The Prime Minister sat forward in his chair,

"Tell me, what is your estimation of when Napoleon will make his move?"

Marty considered that; he didn't want to panic them into doing something stupid but at the same time wanted to keep the urgency.

"I believe he will make his move in the next six months to a year, sooner if the French king proves to be unpopular with the army. He has already started building up the navy to 'protect' Elba by buying ships and he is recruiting an army. Ships arrive from France every week carrying soldiers who have been disbanded by the king. Especially his old guard."

Robert Stewart shuffled through a number of papers. "I don't see any mention of that in the reports I have."

Marty just looked back at him apologetically and Stewart sat back in his chair with a resigned sigh.

The meeting broke up after the members were reminded that everything they had heard was considered to be top secret and not to be repeated to anyone.

Marty and James Turner returned to his office and were joined by the foreign secretary.

"I should be angry at you," Castlereagh said, "you didn't trust me in Elba to tell me everything you had done."

"I am sorry, but I couldn't take the risk, I don't know Campbell or how he would react, and we need a second, independent source of information."

"You seem to know more about how he is operating than I do," he scowled.

"My men observed him both before and after Napoleon arrived, he was far too visible and connected to the wrong people. They have been feeding him what they want him to know. He hasn't done much field work in the past and his lack of experience shows. I am sorry if that is a bit blunt, but people die in this game if they make mistakes."

"It is true he has little field experience, but he is held in high regard for his analytical expertise."

"You can only make a good analysis if you have good information you can rely on. Getting that in the field is an expertise in itself." Turner said.

"Yes, and Martin here is the best we have in any service," Castlereagh conceded which was rich praise indeed.

Marty reached into his pocket and pulled out a sheet of very expensive paper.

"There is something else we need to keep an eye on. This is a letter from Napoleon to me." He smiled at Castlereagh, "You did ask me to befriend him. Now, in it he complains that the French government are very slow at paying his enumeration, in fact have yet to make any payment at all. The letter was dated two weeks ago."

"The Fontainebleau agreement states he will receive two million Francs divided into monthly payments, that is," Castlereagh did the math in his head, "just under sixteen-thousand seven-hundred a month and he has been there a month and a half."

"This is increasing the chance of him doing something, he could conclude that the French have reneged on their part of the deal if it continues."

Marty returned home to his London house; Turner had told him that he was going nowhere until they were sure Napoleon wasn't a threat anymore. Marty replied that they had better lock him in the tower or kill him if that is what they wanted.

That evening he said to Caroline, "I think it's time we spent some time in Dorset, I haven't seen my family for a long time."

She wasn't fooled. "That has nothing to do with the fact that those pigeons will return there?"

"A happy coincidence," he grinned.

"I would love to see your brothers and sisters again. When shall we leave?"

"I suppose tomorrow would be too soon?"

Caroline's look was all the answer he needed.

"Saturday?"

"You are due to read the lesson at church on Sunday."

"Alright Monday then," he said, exasperated.

"Perfect!" Caroline smiled sweetly.

Marty had to be honest and admit that the few days in London were useful. He wanted to take gifts for his brothers and sisters and their children, so a shopping trip was scheduled.

Before then he had an unexpected visitor, Gordon Graves, the cousin of the slaver he had killed in Tortuga.

"I came here to ask you face to face if you had anything to do with the death of Jonas Quin."

"Who?" Marty said, then remembered, "The school master! He committed suicide, didn't he?"

"That is what someone would have everyone believe and that he was a pederast. Which was frankly untrue."

"I have no idea as I never met the man, why do you suspect I had anything to do with it?"

"Your son."

"My son?"

"Your son. Jonas wrote to me about him said he was afraid the boy would try to incriminate him as he was friends with our family."

"Why would I – Oh I see your cousin, the loss of the slave trade must have hurt your family's fortunes considerably. Believe me I settled all scores with him in Tortuga and have no feud with the rest of his family unless they threaten me or mine."

"I know you had something to do with it and I will prove it."

"Go ahead, I have nothing to hide, but I warn you do not make a move against me unless you are absolutely sure you are prepared to have all of your family's secrets exposed as well as exposing you as the lover."

"What do you mean?"

Marty noted he didn't deny being the lover.

"We didn't burn the plantation without taking his records. They show that all your family were complicit in transporting slaves after it was made illegal to do so. Something that is being prosecuted strongly by the government. So, you have a choice."

"That is blackmail."

"No, blackmail is demanding something, I demand nothing."

"Then you leave me no choice, I challenge you to a duel."

Marty looked at him in surprise then pulled the cord to summon a servant. Adam arrived so quickly he must have been waiting outside the door.

"Adam, would you please ask Mr Anderson from the house opposite us to attend me please. I need an independent witness."

He said nothing more, just waited until the door opened and Adam led in a studious-looking man in a brown suit who looked at the two of them curiously.

"Mr Anderson is a neighbour, we have no business dealings, nor do we interact socially. He can therefore act as an independent witness. Please repeat your challenge."

Graves, swallowed, he had paled, then said, "I accuse you of complicity in the death of my friend, Jonas Quin, and challenge you to a duel."

"I accept your challenge; my seconds will call on you tomorrow to make the arrangements. What are the terms of your challenge?"

"To the death."

Marty smiled chillingly, "then I choose sword and main gauche."

Graves recovered some of his colour he had been expecting Marty to choose pistols and while he was a fair shot, he was an accomplished fencer.

"A duel?" Caroline said in disbelief, "he must have a death wish."

"He is certainly much more passionate about the death of his friend than a normal friendship would suggest."

"You think the boys stumbled on a truth?"

"Maybe, this way he can attempt revenge without endangering his family's reputation."

"Who are your seconds?"

"Arthur Simmonds and Wilson Spears."

"They were your seconds when you fought a duel for me."

"Yes, they are both majors in the guards now and are in town, the war being over."

The place was agreed; a secluded corner of Richmond common, weapons were supplied. Marty had chosen short swords with cutting blades rather than Epée de combat which were only thrusting weapons. The main gauche had twelve-inch double-edged blades curved quillons and hilts wrapped in shagreen for grip.

The morning of the duel came, and Marty and his seconds arrived on time. As was traditional the duel was held at dawn and his seconds made sure that it would start with the combatants facing North and South to prevent the rising sun having an influence.

Marty adopted an attitude of calm indifference, he had after all, faced death many times and was confident in his own abilities. He said good morning to the attending doctor and master of ceremonies and took the time to do a few loosening exercises while his seconds talked with Graves' seconds.

"He won't withdraw or change to first blood," Arthur reported.

"Fair enough." Marty said and walked onto the field of honour whistling a popular tune.

The two men faced off, Graves in the classic fencing pose, right leg extended, left hand behind his back. Marty in contrast adopting a fighter's stance, feet shoulder width apart, weight over the balls of his feet, slightly leaning forward both weapons in front of him.

Graves sneered at what he saw, he thought it indicated a lack of skill, but all the same, he proceeded with caution.

"En Guarde!" the master of ceremonies said.

"Commence."

Marty circled to his right, his feet never really leaving the ground, maintaining his balance.

Graves bounced his weight back and forth between his feet keeping Marty in front of him, he launched a swift attack with just his sword. Marty parried with his.

He is fast and has excellent balance.

Marty waited, letting Graves have the initiative.

Graves' feet did a kind of shuffle and he launched a second attack at Marty's head forcing him into a high parry. Suddenly his left hand came from behind his back and thrust the main gauche forward at Marty's abdomen.

Marty parried that with his own blade with a sweep across his body. He barely stopped it and felt a sting as the tip nicked his stomach. He disengaged by stepping back a pair of paces. Now he had the measure of the man.

Marty spun his short sword in a circle from his wrist distracting Graves with the unexpected and unconventional move and as the blade started to came back to the front continued the swing in a slashing strike from high right to low left. As he expected, Graves parried with his main gauche as he stepped back. Marty stepped forward with him and swung his main gauche out pushing Graves short sword wide. He stepped in close and head butted him on the bridge of the nose.

Graves staggered back stunned and slashed with his sword to keep Marty at bay. He got lucky and cut him across the left shoulder.

Marty knew he had to finish it fast now and pressed his attack.

Step – high slash at Graves eyes' – follow with a step – main gauche thrust from close to his body in and up.

Graves eyes went wide and his mouth opened in an O. Marty felt his heart stop through the blade. Then he slowly folded to the ground.

Arthur and Wilson were with him in a second as he staggered back. There was a lot of blood coming from his shoulder and the doctor pressed a wad of linen to it to staunch the flow.

"Thought he had you there for a minute," Arthur said as he led him to his carriage where he sat him on the step so the doctor could work on him.

"He was better than I expected," Marty said.

"You are going to need stitches," the doctor said.

"Well get on with it man and use a new needle," Marty barked.

Eighteen neat stitches were required to close the cut which ran from his collar bone to his bicep. The nick on his stomach just needed binding. When he walked through his front door and Caroline saw him, she was as mad as hell which was worse.

"Why didn't you find out he was an expert swordsman?"

"I did."

"Too bloody late to find out when you're facing him."

Marty made to go upstairs.

"Where are you going?"

"To get a clean shirt and wash off the blood."

"Adam, help him. Sam you too."

Sam had wandered into the hall from the kitchen.

"You want me to carry him?"

"I am quite capable of walking!" Marty snapped.

The two men bracketed him as he climbed the stairs hands ready to steady him.

"You two," Caroline snapped at Arthur and Wilson, "I want the full story of what happened, now."

In his room Adam helped remove the blood-stained and ruined silk shirt. Sam sat him in a chair and Hanna arrived with a bowl of water, a decanter of brandy and a glass. She said nothing just poured him a glass and watched as her husband gently washed Marty down. When he had finished, he looked carefully at the wound.

"Go fetch Matai. Tell him to bring the ointment."

Marty rolled his eyes; at this rate all the Shadows would be crowded into his room. He was right because with Matai came the rest of the boys.

"Cor, that's a right nice un," John Smith said.

"Yep, straight as a die if me eyes don't deceive me," Wilson added.

"Very careless," Chin said

Matai examined the wound minutely, "It's only a scratch."

"Who's all that blood then?" Antton said from where he and Garai sat on the bed.

"It's his, he bleeds easy."

Matai opened a pot and dipped his fingers in the grey ointment. He gently applied it to the cut on the shoulder and the one on Marty's stomach.

The door opened and Hanna stepped in. "Lady Caroline said if you all have finished breakfast is served."

The reading of the lesson on Sunday was somewhat ironic, Marty was asked to read Jeremiah 22 which began:

Thus says the Lord: "Go down to the house of the king of Judah and speak there this word and say, 'Hear the word of the Lord, O king of Judah, who sits on the throne of David, you, and your servants, and your people who enter these gates. Thus says the Lord: Do justice and righteousness, and deliver from the hand of the oppressor him who has been robbed. And do no wrong or violence to the resident alien, the fatherless, and the widow, nor shed innocent blood in this place. For if you will indeed obey this word, then there shall enter the gates of this house kings who sit on the throne of David, riding in chariots and on horses, they and their servants and their people. But if you will not obey these words, I swear by myself, declares the Lord, that this house shall become a desolation."

Most of the congregation knew he had fought a duel the day before as it was all over the scandal sheets. He even had a constable call and ask about it but he had his independent witness to say he was called out and the authorities chose to ignore the matter.

They left for Dorset on Monday. Messages had been sent ahead to warn the house that they were coming, all twelve of them. The boys flatly refused to stay behind and rode as an armed escort around the carriage in which Marty was sat covered in blankets.

"I have had worse you know and sailed a ship through a storm with it," he grumbled.

"Not on my watch," Caroline said, and that was that. They started out slower than usual until Marty complained and told them to shake a leg. Then the coach moved along at the usual clip.

His wound itched more than hurt and he did his best to ignore it because if he made any move to scratch or rub it Caroline would tell him off.

"Daddy," Edwin said. "What is a duel?"

"Why do you ask that?"

"Because I heard Hanna tell Mary you had fighted one."

Caroline stepped in before Marty could answer,

"It's when two stupid men cannot come to an agreement to solve a dispute and end up fighting."

Edwin frowned as he thought that through,

"But Daddy isn't stupid and he won didn't he?"

Marty chuckled at that and Caroline sat back in exasperation.

To keep the children amused they played games. To help, the boys would ride with the twins in front of them which they loved. Beth was far too grown up for that and took Caroline's side whenever there was a disagreement.

It's all revenge for me taking her away from her boyfriend.
Marty sulked. Beth had written to her dashing ensign every day since
they came back and, to give the boy his due, he had written back. It
was Caroline's opinion that she would grow out of it or meet
someone else. Marty could only hope.

Church Knowle was just as they remembered it. There were more
climbing roses than before that were just coming into flower and the
gardens were well manicured. They were met by Arthur and his
wife. Marty had his arm in a sling which immediately begged the
question and he had to tolerate more sideways scolding from
Caroline.

Once they settled in, Marty went over the state of the estate with
Arthur and the manager.

"Wool is coming down in price now the war is over in
anticipation of the army needing less. Mutton and lamb still sell
well. We sell our beef through the local markets and most of it goes
to local butchers, so we won't be affected by the reduction in
demand from the navy if they scale down as they only buy the cheap
stuff anyway. Although we do expect the price will drop somewhat.
Corn and Barley are expected to stay strong as they cannot get
enough and are importing it from Canada," the manager, Mr Ridley
reported.

Marty was satisfied. They used the most modern techniques on
his estates and the tenants were encouraged to adopt them as well as
form cooperatives to maximise production.

"What is happening with Napoleon. We haven't had any of the pigeons come back yet," Arthur said.

"I'm waiting to see," Marty said, "but I expect him to try and take back the throne."

"So, we will be at war again."

"Yes, I don't think it will be truly over until Boney is dead or locked away on the other side of the earth."

The days passed and spring started to move into summer. Marty was delighted when Beth discovered horses again and developed an all-encompassing passion for riding. He got her a fine new forest mare who had spirit and enormous stamina. She rode like a man wearing the trousers she fenced in.

His letters from Napoleon increasingly complained about the lack of money coming from Paris. It appeared they weren't sending any and Marty wrote a warning letter to both Turner and Castlereagh. Then a pigeon arrived. Its message said:

Fleet now eleven ships, army is eleven thousand strong.

The sender was a member of the civil service. Marty sent another letter to Arthur Wellesley as well as Turner and Castlereagh. More pigeons arrived telling that Napoleon had bought cannons from Tuscany and was training a brigade of artillery. Then a final message:

Army embarking on ships, Napoleon moves on France.

Peace was at an end, Napoleon had been on Elba for one hundred days.

Epilogue

Admiral Turner, Castlereagh and Robert Jenkinson the Prime Minister sat with the rest of the cabinet at 10 Downing Street. They had in front of them copies of the intelligence reports from the Foreign Office and Naval Intelligence. Most attention was being paid to the Naval Intelligence report that contained copies of the letter from Napoleon to Viscount Purbeck and the messages from the informants in Elba's civil service and around the island.

"It is confirmed, Napoleon sailed for France at least a fortnight ago and has landed with around eleven thousand troops, many of which are members of his old guard. Since then, he was intercepted by Ney who was supposed to have arrested him. He, however, seems to have changed sides again and the rest of the army is flocking to Napoleon's banner," Castlereagh said.

"Gentlemen, if the French king is forced into exile again, we will have to declare war once more," Jenkins said.

He turned to Admiral Turner.

"Viscount Purbeck has performed a significant service to his country yet again, please pass on our thanks."

"Thank you, Prime Minister, I will when I see him next."

"Where is he by the way?"

"Last I heard he was on his way to meet Wellington via France."

Turner and Castlereagh sat in Castlereagh's office in the Palace of Westminster discussing the cabinet meeting. Then Castlereagh said, "How does he do it?"

"Who?"

"Purbeck, how does he do it?"

"He has always had courage, an enquiring mind and a total conviction that what he is doing is for the safety and security of his country and more importantly his family. He is a natural born leader and totally ruthless."

"You have known him for long?"

"I took him on as a cabin boy as a favour to my sister back in '92."

"Good grief, a cabin boy?"

"Yes, he saved my life, the purser from footpads and helped rescue the Comte de Marchets and his family all before he became a midshipman."

"An extraordinary man."

"Yes, he is and more important than that."

"What?"

"He is lucky."

The two men chuckled at that until Castlereagh said, "Is the sun over the yardarm as you sailors say?"

"Yes, I believe it is," Turner said.

"Fancy a brandy?"

Author's Notes

The war of 1812 between Britain and America went on to February 1815.

The British really did support Bolívar and the revolution in South America and later in the war a contingent of six thousand volunteers, mainly ex-soldiers from the Napoleonic war fought on his side

The short drop method of hanging was the standard method of execution until the long drop method was adopted in 1866. In Spain they used the garrotte and France the guillotine which put Britain at the less humane end of the execution spectrum. Victims took anything from ten to twenty minutes to die.

Spillikins was a game very much like pick-up sticks today, which goes to show there is nothing much new on earth.

It is estimated that over 800 American privateer ships were dispatched to the Caribbean. The royal navy caught a large number and made life difficult for the rest.

The treaty of Fontainebleau came about after the allies declared:

The allied powers having proclaimed that the Emperor Napoleon is the sole obstacle to the re-establishment of peace in Europe – the Emperor Napoleon, faithful to his oath, declares that he is ready to descend from the throne, to quit France, and even life itself, for the good of the country, which is inseparable from the rights of his son, of the regency of the Empress, and of the maintenance of the laws of the empire.

— *Napoleon: Fontainebleau, 4 April 1814*[5]

The British position was that the French nation was in a state of rebellion and that Napoleon was a usurper. Stewart explained that he would not sign on behalf of the king of the United Kingdom because to do so would recognise the legitimacy of Napoleon as emperor of the French and that to exile him to an island over which he had sovereignty, only a short distance from France and Italy, both of which had strong **Jacobin** factions, could easily lead to further conflict.[18]

How right he was.

An excerpt from - The Pharaohs Mask – A Charlamagne Griffon Chronical

Chapter 1: Trial By Class

"By the left, quick march!" Shouted the Sergeant and the platoon stepped forward in good order. "Left, right, left, right, watch your distance there private Higgins!"

Lieutenant Charlamagne Griffon paced the men as they ran through their evolutions on the quadrangle of the Grenadier Guards at Aldershot. They moved from column into line into square and back again, never missing a step. He was proud of his men in their red jackets and tall bearskins. They were marching out as infantry but were in fact a specialist sharpshooter unit and more used to skirmishing than marching with the main body of men.

They carried the pattern 1853 rifled musket as did all the men in the regiment, the difference being they carried the shorter barrelled cavalry version as it was easier to use when on the move. As skirmishers they wore a green uniform similar to the rifles regiments and a Kepi in combat to make them less obtrusive, which got them the nickname of Crap-hats from the rest of the regiment.

Charlie Griffon was the son of Doris and Raymond Griffon. Raymond was a professional gambler and Doris a music hall performer. They had both died when he was sixteen in an accident when a steam carriage boiler exploded. He had used his inheritance to buy a commission in the guards.

He was known as a fair officer by the men, he got the best out of them by pure leadership and not asking them to do anything he wouldn't do himself. Unfortunately, not all the officers in the guards were like him, which was a weakness of the system that allowed commissions to be bought. One in particular stood out to Charlie as a particular bad apple. Captain Stanford Barrington-Brown, son of General Archibald Barrington-Brown, had no leadership qualities, was afraid of his men and felt he had to lead by intimidation. Charlie despised him.

The drills finished Charlie dismissed his men and told them to be ready that afternoon at two o'clock to spend time on the ranges. Shooting practice was a core exercise in their training routine and Charlie not only wanted accuracy but speed as well.

He returned to the officer's mess and dressed for lunch helped but Etherton his batman. Meals were formal affairs run with strict protocol. Lunch during the week required a Number two dress uniform without stock. He dressed and made sure he was squeaky clean before descending the stairs to the dining room where he joined the other junior officers over a pre-lunch glass of sherry.

"Hello Charlie," Lieutenant Francis Leatherby called.

The two had been friends since they were ensigns which was surprising seeing they came from completely different backgrounds.

Francis was from a long line of military men and had soldiering in his veins. He commanded the third platoon.

Charlie joined him where he was stood with two other men.

Lieutenant Paul D'Eath, Fifth Platoon, and Ensign Graham Smith, also from the fifth were amiable companions at any time.

"Roast beef today," Smith squeaked, he had a particularly high voice even though he was shaving.

Charlie laughed, "It's Tuesday, it's always roast beef on Tuesday." He turned to the other two, "what have you planned for this afternoon?"

Paul grimaced,

"Route march, twelve miles full kit."

"Ouch, who did you upset?"

"BB decided we weren't working hard enough."

"Is he going?"

"Don't be silly."

"What about you Francis?"

"Shooting range for us and BB will be attending."

Charly felt sorry for them, having BB for a commanding officer of your Brigade couldn't be easy.

Charly's commanding officer was the amiable Captain Rodrigues Valencia-Smythe, mother Spanish, father English and a Wing Commander in the air core commanding armed dirigibles. As long as Charly's men were up to or exceeded his standards, he left him alone to run his platoon as he saw fit.

Lunch was splendid, substantial and took an hour and a half. Charlie had to hurry to get into his fighting greens and make it to the ranges in time to greet his men.

He had them form up in their fighting pairs. One would be shooter the other spotter then they would change over. The targets were set to four hundred yards, which was about the maximum accurate range for their weapon.

Three platoon were on the next, shorter, firing butts. Targets were set at one hundred yards and they fired in volley. Francis stood at the line shouting orders. Charlie grinned, his skirmishers never needed the timing called out they were the elite and they knew it.

Suddenly there was shouting from the other range and Charlie realised Barrington-Brown was throwing one of his infamous tantrums. He looked across and saw Francis stood in front of his Captain, rigidly at attention. He couldn't hear what was said but it was in front of his men and that was wrong as it was obviously a reprimand. Francis snapped a salute, spun on his heal and marched off.

Barrington-Brown went to a group of soldiers that must have been the cause of the spat and pointed down the range. Charlie couldn't believe his eyes, but the wind had changed and the order blew across, "Get down there and stand beside the targets!"

The men looked terrified but dare not refuse a direct order from the Captain. They put down their guns and marched the hundred yards to the targets and stood beside them.

The Captain then had the other half of the platoon take the firing position.

"Standing fire, three rounds, commence!"

Charlie set off across the range to the other butts and as the men raised their guns he shouted,

"Cease fire, stand down!"

Barrington-Brown spun on him and met him halfway,

"What do you mean, countering my orders to my men."

"Are you insane? You are putting your own men's lives at risk!"

"They will learn to shoot straight if it kills them! But that has nothing to do with you Lieutenant Craphat."

"The safety of the men in this regiment is every officer's first priority!" Charlie shouted angry to his core.

"How dare you!" Barrington-Brown shouted back and raised his swagger stick as if to strike him.

Charlie reacted without thinking.

Books by Christopher C Tubbs

The Dorset Boy Series.
A Talent for Trouble
The Special Operations Flotilla
Agent Provocateur
In Dangerous Company
The Tempest
Vendetta
The Trojan Horse
La Licorne
Raider
Silverthorn
Exile

The Scarlet Fox Series
Scarlett
A Kind of Freedom
Legacy

The Charlamagne Griffon Chronicles
Buddha's Fist

See them all at:

Website: www.thedorsetboy.com
Twitter: @ChristoherCTu3
Facebook: https://www.facebook.com/thedorsetboy/
YouTube: https://youtu.be/KCBR4ITqDi4

Published in E-Book, Paperback and Audio formats on Amazon, Audible and iTunes

Printed in Great Britain
by Amazon

61096369R00221